SNOWED IN

By Tricia Wentworth

SNOWED IN
By Tricia Wentworth

This book is a work of fiction. The names, characters, places, and incidents are products of the writer's imagination. Any resemblances to persons, living or dead, are entirely coincidental.

Published by Tricia Wentworth

Cover design by Parker Premades

To my Husker loving family that brainwashed me from a young age to love college football. Go Big Red.

Mom and Dad, this one is for you.

Table of Contents

Straight Up Terrible
CHAPTER 1

She was the biggest hypocrite in the history of hypocrites, and she knew it. Jordyn Mack hated everything about small towns. The gossip. The lack of anonymity. The way the people could turn against you. It was almost ironic she would work for a multimillion-dollar agricultural software corporation. But, here she was, working for a company that was helping the small-town farmer. The very type of people who had made her life hell.

She was good at what she did, and it paid well, so oh well. That was life. You had to do the best with what you'd been given. And sometimes life didn't give you lemons. Sometimes you had last week's Chinese leftovers, and if you were lucky, a half-eaten pint of ice cream in the back of the freezer. Life, she had learned, was about playing your current hand of cards like they were the ones you had wanted dealt to you all along. Even if they weren't.

She rolled her neck and twisted her long hair in a bun at the base of her neck. After completing the final touches on some new graphs for the app, she shut down her laptop, slipped her feet into the heels she'd ditched under desk, and mentally prepared herself for the drive home. If she hit traffic right, she just might be able to whip up a batch of her famous cookies and then binge-watch her favorite TV series. The stuff Friday nights were made of. Or her Friday nights anyway. And she preferred it that way. Her future was bright. A nice weekend of sweatpants, baking, and TV watching. A short week next week, and then the long Thanksgiving break. Yes, things were looking up.

"Jordyn, you got a minute??"

Her boss was at her door. His game face on.

Uh-oh. She'd be willing to wager money she'd now be working this weekend.

"Yeah, Walt. I was just leaving for the day. What can I do for you?" She hoped he knew she was trying to shrug him off. She'd been putting in some ridiculous hours on those graphs and needed a weekend off. They had big things in the mix for the next year, and she had been pulling some serious weight.

He scratched a spot on his bald head above where his glasses rested on his ear. Double uh-oh. His nervous tick. That usually meant he was about to deliver bad news.

He took a deep breath and blurted out, "I need you to head to Nebraska tomorrow morning."

"Ne—what? Excuse me?" Had he lost his dang mind? Gone senile? He wasn't even that old yet; they had just celebrated his sixtieth birthday this fall.

His shoulders slumped in apology before any words came out of his mouth. "Look. I know it's short notice and the weekend. I'll pay you overtime."

She suppressed the urge to roll her eyes. "Walt, I am not a field tech. Send someone else."

He winced. "I know, but I need you personally this time."

Realization hit her, and she softened a bit, the tension in her shoulders easing up. "Because next week is Thanksgiving and I'm your only employee without family stuff going on?"

His brow furrowed. "No actually, but that's another decent point."

"Why, then?"

More nervous itching. This time he ran a hand around the back of his head, rubbing where the hair was long gone. Boy, this was going to be good, whatever he was about to say.

"I need you on Beckett Harper's farm to run his quarterly soil checks."

"Walt, again, I am not a field tech. So why me?" And why was he being so weird about this? Yeah, he was her boss, but they were friends too. He'd always looked out for her after she moved to Houston.

"Well. As you already know, marketing has been trying to get him to do our Super Bowl commercial. He's not budging."

She again suppressed the urge to roll her eyes. Marketing had been acting like Beckett Harper was Moses delivering them to the promised land. She didn't get it. Or even care. The company should be strong enough by now to not need a famous face behind it. "So send one of the marketing guys. How is my taking his soil samples going to help?"

Walt sat down on the other side of her desk and she knew this was about to get real. As in real-ly bad.

"Jordyn. I'll be honest. You are one of maybe twenty women in this company. I need a nice face there in person to woo him over. I need to play on his reputation."

An eye-roll may have squeaked out. And a disgusted sigh. "So you need a woman?"

He nodded.

She groaned and fought off the urge to bang her head against her desk. Was this really happening?

Walt stood and bounced back on his heels. "You know what they call him. Heartbreak Harper."

If only he knew of her extreme distaste for football players. She couldn't help but roll her eyes again. A real, honest-to-goodness eye-roll to the heavens that she didn't even try to hide this time. "So you want me to suck up to an ex–pro football player to get him on our Super Bowl commercial because I'm a woman and he's known for being a lady's man? Since I'm unmarried, I seemed like the girl for the job. Does that about sum it up?"

He grimaced but nodded.

She counted to five slowly in her head. It didn't help. "You do realize this is by far the most sexist thing I've heard of since working here?"

He sighed again, defeated. "I know. But honestly . . . you know this company in and out, and so you'll be great at it. I do know how you feel about small towns . . . . " He shifted his weight back and forth uncomfortably. "But it would be good for you to get out of the office too. Go to Nebraska. Get out from behind your desk and graph designing and get some fresh air. Meet with Harper. If you somehow manage a miracle and convince him to do the commercial, I'll give you not only a raise, but two additional weeks of paid vacation next year." He paused to let that sink in. "You need a break right now just as bad as I need a pretty face. We both win here."

Now she sighed in defeat. This was not how she was planning to spend her Thanksgiving. Okay, she didn't exactly know how she was planning to spend her Thanksgiving, but this certainly wasn't it. Small towns gave her the heebie-jeebies.

"When does my flight leave?" she asked despite still feeling nauseous about what she was about to do.

He winced again and took off his glasses, probably to look more apologetic. "There's a winter storm rolling in and they're already cancelling flights. Since he lives in the middle of nowhere, we can't get you close enough without a bit of a drive anyway. I'm giving you one of the company trucks. I'd hate for you to get stuck at an airport overnight. If you leave early in the morning, you'll still beat the storm."

Don't roll your eyes, don't roll your eyes, she thought. "So I'm driving myself there too?"

He nodded. "Yep, but you aren't expected back until we have a Super Bowl commercial. He thinks you'll be shadowing him for greater understanding of improving our software. Stay for as long as you need. Take all of next week and have a nice holiday weekend in Nebraska."

That sounded straight up terrible, actually. "This is ridiculous, Walt. It's not going to work. My face, a woman's face, is not going to be enough to get Harper to change his mind here."

Walt shrugged, not to be deterred. "Well, you're my last shot, we are almost out of time. Either way, you get a break from the office. I want Harper on that commercial. If I have to do something ridiculous to get that, so be it."

She groaned, already thinking of the long hour she'd be stuck in traffic before having to pack up and go. She was contemplating leaving tonight to drive part of the way just to be sure to beat the storm. Good thing Walt entrusted her to keep a company card on her at all times.

"Jordyn?" Walt asked as he reached her door.

"Yeah?"

His shamed smile was wrapped around a wince. "Thank you. You're one of the best we have, and you and I both know it."

"I know, Walt. I know. If it were anyone but you asking, I'd have already told them to shove it."

He gave her a full grin at that. "That's my girl. Now go get me Harper."

****

"Hey, Harp! You hear what the weatherman's been sayin'?"

What a stupid question. Who hadn't? He slammed the tailgate of his pickup shut and turned to one of his neighbors. "Yep. Getting last-minute supplies and gearing up like everyone else. But knowing the weatherman, it'll probably be a dud like last year's supposed storm of the century."

"I hear ya. But we've always got to be prepared. Can't afford to lose any head in the off chance they're right."

He nodded. Couldn't argue there.

"You gunna be watchin' the big game Friday?"

Football. Of course. Beckett Harper both loved and hated the game. It had given him everything and then taken it all away in only a few seconds. He just so happened to own a farm in the one state in the entire country that lived for college football. In the one state that he would forever be remembered, a "hometown hero." The one state where no one would ever just leave him alone.

When he was their star receiver, there wasn't a better feeling. When he was washed up, out of the pros before he could finish his second season due to a career-ending injury, it sometimes annoyed him. Believe it or not, there was life outside of football. Only in Nebraska would he still be considered somewhat of a celebrity even though his football career had ended years ago.

"Of course. Go Big Red!" he yelled back with a polite wave as he got in the truck and started it up.

The rivalry game was always played the Friday after Thanksgiving. People got over-the-top amped up to beat the neighboring state at football. It was ridiculous really. The Corn Belt duking it out over a pig skin. You just had to love people from the Midwest. Even if they were a bit . . . obsessed? Maybe overzealous? Yep. Definitely overzealous.

When he played, he had lived for these types of games. Both sides determined to take the other out if for nothing more than bragging rights. Nowadays they just served as a reminder of better times. A career in the pros he dreamt of but would never get to have. A career that was over as fast as it all began. All his hard work over the years obliterated in one damn play.

But storm of the century or not, a storm was coming. As if the animals acting strange wasn't enough, you could feel it in the air. It took him a while to get last-minute blizzard necessities as the small town was full of people all thinking the same thing. It was Picketts, after all, and of course they had all heard the weather report. Hell, even his grocery-store run felt like a mini class reunion as he saw people he hadn't for ages. It had taken him forever just to get the things he needed and get out of there without chatting any longer than was necessary to not be rude.

It was much later in the afternoon than he wanted when he finally arrived back at the farm, three errands later. He immediately started up the tractor and got to haying the cattle. He was thinking of the list of everything he'd need to do in the morning with the storm when he noticed the AgGroSo pickup in the driveway.

Before the storm? Trip must already be here for the soil tests and trying to get out of town ahead of it. He got the AgGroSo email saying he would be staying a few extra days this time to shadow him to better understand what farmers were needing out of the software. He didn't mind. Trip was a decent guy, kept to himself, and didn't care about Beckett's semi-celebrity status. But he wasn't sure Trip would be much help if he got snowed in with him.

It seemed like odd timing, but then again, maybe the storm changed things. Maybe Trip just wanted to hurry up and get out of there before all hell broke loose to get back to his family before Thanksgiving. Maybe he'd want to shadow him a different time when a storm wasn't on the brew. His brow furrowed when he spotted some long dark-brown hair in one of his fields. Trip was looking awfully womanly these days.

The hell?

When she turned around, tapping on the soil vial and clearly knowing what she was doing, he couldn't help but be a little impressed. Then he saw her shoes. *Heels? Out here, woman?* Had she lost her mind? She was probably freezing. It was right at freezing temperature outside. In fact, his pickup had read thirty-two degrees exactly when he was on the way home from town.

He finished feeding, put his gloves in the pockets of his tan Carhartt coat, got out of the tractor, and quietly approached while watching this woman work for a while. She completely knew what she was doing, yet she was dressed like *that* in the middle of a farm in Picketts, Nebraska. Intelligence and cluelessness fought for control within her small frame. Well, small compared to him anyway. He was six feet, four inches tall. And she looked a solid foot shorter than he was, heels or not.

"You going to stand there all day watching or are you going to say hello?"

As a football star, the all-American boy, the small-town hero, he wasn't used to hostile-sounding greetings. He couldn't help but smirk. "Since you're on my land, I was thinking you should be the one to greet me."

She almost rolled her eyes, taking one long blink to reel it in, but he could tell she had wanted to.

"I'm with AgGroSo. Clearly." She stopped to gesture toward the pickup in his yard. "I tried your house. No one answered, so I figured you wouldn't mind if I got started."

"You mean Mable didn't let you in?" he asked.

"Um, no. No one named Mable."

She was saying all the right words, but still sounded pissed off. "They sent you from Houston? On a Saturday?" he questioned.

She turned to grab her kit and nodded. "I had to get here before the storm, of course. I'll just stay in a hotel until it passes. Then I'll be here for the first part of next week until I have adequate research. I'll just finish up my initial tests here and be out of your hair to go check into a hotel."

He laughed. She obviously hadn't done *adequate research* about Picketts. Her bright green eyes were sharp though; he knew she wasn't dumb.

"What?" she asked, looking him over with a puzzled expression.

He cocked his head to the side and couldn't help the smile slowly spreading across his face. "Welcome to the sticks, Houston. Picketts doesn't have a hotel. Closest one is seventeen miles north in Homesteel."

She groaned. "That didn't even cross my mind. I figured I'd be able to stay where Trip stayed. I was in a hurry to beat the storm and didn't even consider the distance or think to ask him where he usually stays. My bad."

Oh, this was going to be good. "He stays with me," he supplied honestly.

"Oh."

He grinned, enjoying her discomfort. It was just too darn easy to push this woman's buttons. After a moment he remembered his manners. "You're welcome to stay here until you figure out other arrangements." But he wasn't really sure he wanted this city woman anywhere near him or his farm. Still, it was the neighborly thing to offer. His mom raised him right, so he had to at least offer. Right? Especially since the clouds looked like they would be letting loose snow or rain or a combination of the two any second now.

She said it under her breath so quietly he almost didn't catch it. "Typical."

His eyebrows rose. "Where I'm from, this"—he stopped to point to her and back to him for emphasis—"is called being hospitable. Neighborly. Kind."

She squinted at him, sizing him up. "Oh, I'm sure you're *very*"—she pointed in the same way from him to her—"*hospitable.*"

"What the hell is your problem, Houston?" he asked bluntly.

She was so damn high-strung. Even when she was trying to be nice, she was still hostile toward him—from the way her green eyes seemed to scan him over to the way she stood as far away from him as possible. She was still close enough for him to catch a whiff of her perfume though, and it was nice smelling. Not as overpowering as the stuff the women he was used to wore.

"That's not my name, but small towns and football players are my problem. They're all one and the same," she fired back, clearly flustered. "Look. I'll do my job and be out of your hair as much as possible." Then she added under her breath, "This is never going to work."

She stormed off, back in the direction of her pickup. She took all of maybe ten steps when her heel caught on some gravel and she went down.

He was moving to help her before he thought twice about it. She looked okay at first, but as he got closer, he could see the tears glistening in her green eyes and her teeth clenching when she tried to move her foot. She'd probably really sprained her ankle. He knew from experience that could hurt like hell. He appreciated how she was trying to be tough through it. He had seen bigger wusses on the field.

He'd never seen a woman be so strong and such a mess at the same time. A chaotic heap of beauty and fire. He wasn't sure if he should be impressed or not, but he was at least entertained.

CHAPTER 2

Why. Why couldn't she have just made it back to the truck in one piece? WHY.

Pain shot up her entire leg. It hurt bad enough for her to look at her ankle to make sure it was attached at the proper angle. She was horrible with pain, a big baby. And she had to make a mess of herself in front of Beckett Harper. Go figure. She bit down on her bottom lip to avoid groaning or whining like a child.

Just who did he think he was in his boots and jeans? All dirty blond hair and facial hair and . . . *man.* He was a man. A man's man. What did that even mean? She didn't know other than he was obviously the kind of man women swoon over. Heartbreak Harper. She got it now, from the boots and jeans, to his one dimple, to his Adam's apple that kept trying to catch her attention. He was wearing a faded gray baseball cap that was doing nothing to hide his extremely blue eyes. She got it. Yes, indeed. He was a looker. Borderline model pretty, but his nose was a little too big and a little too crooked.

"Let me take a look."

She looked into those super-blue eyes and saw genuine concern. There was maybe some amusement there too, but she was choosing to ignore that for the time being. She wanted nothing more than to leave his farm and run away from this God-forsaken place, but the fact was that she wasn't sure she could even move, let alone walk or drive. Harper didn't even wait for her to say anything; he just knelt and gently picked up the twisted ankle to look it over.

She winced as she shifted to get all her weight as far away from the injury as she could, pursing her lips to suppress the pain. "I suppose you're an expert with ankle injuries—football star and all."

He smirked, but his heart didn't seem to be in it. "I've had a few. My sister is in PT school too, so I've picked up on a few things." He continued to gently check and feel along her ankle, making sure everything was in its proper place. "Lucky for you it's just a sprain and you don't need stitches. I had to stitch up a mama cow last winter because the vet was tied up. I'm not the best at those yet."

His words stopped her a minute. Was she being a jerk? Yes. But this situation was messed up. What she needed to do was regroup at the hotel and come back tomorrow. She wasn't usually this rude to people she didn't even know, but this was Heartbreak Harper here. He didn't get that sort of reputation without earning it. And then some.

And what was Walt thinking sending her here? That he'd just see her face and sign the contract? All, *"Hey, pretty thing, hand over the papers."* What was she? A girl scout selling cookies right now?

Yep. That was exactly what was happening. She was girl scouting. Even with strict no-soliciting policies, if cookies were to be had, girl scouts held special sorts of powers. *I'd kill for a thin mint right about now too.*

"Help me up so I can get to my truck?" she finally offered.

"Your pickup you mean?"

"Yeah, my truck."

He grinned, shook his head, and mumbled something about southerners. Before she knew what was happening, he had scooped her up, soil kit and all, and was carrying her like an overgrown child in his arms toward the farmhouse, which was a solid three hundred yards out.

"Put me down," she groaned. What on earth was he doing?! Heartbreak Harper sure didn't waste time.

He rolled his eyes. "Look. You're going to hurt it worse before you get all the way back to the house. Especially if you are stubborn and try to wear those stupid things." He nodded to her heels, one of which was now in her hand.

She only wore them because of the part she was supposed to be playing. Most guys liked a woman in heels, right? And she was here to woo him into doing the commercial after all. She was *trying* to play her part. Or at least look the part. She wanted no part in actually wooing this football player. *No way.*

He brought her in the front door of the farmhouse and sat her on a comfortable-looking gray sectional couch in the living room. She was impressed with how nice the place was on the inside, but she didn't say so. It looked like it had originally been a smaller farmhouse that had been redone and then built on. Judging by a quick side glance into the kitchen, the kitchen had been totally remodeled—HGTV swoonworthy. And it had a double oven! She had to be in some sort of paradoxical hell. A football player's home, but the most beautiful kitchen she had ever set her eyes on.

Without saying a word, while Jordyn kept taking in the farmhouse and tried not to drool over that kitchen, Harper got a blanket for across her lap and a bag of peas from the freezer. He placed it on her ankle. He then looked at her with a furrowed brow. "You bring a phone?"

She sighed. "It's in the truck."

The condescending smirk on his face reeked of annoyance. "I'll get it."

"Thank you," she begrudged as he opened the wooden door to go back outside.

When he returned after, having taken it upon himself to move the AgGroSo truck closer to the house, he gave her her purse and phone before he went into the kitchen and laundry area to take off his coat. When he returned, he was wearing his work jeans and an old faded-red college T-shirt.

She was texting on her phone, or pretending to be, but still noticed. Heartbreak Harper in all his glory. And those shoulders and neck, she noticed as he turned to get some warm coffee. It looked like even today he could be playing football! Even washed up he still looked great—hadn't let himself go at all. Maybe it was the high cheekbones and trimmed facial hair that gave him that "it" factor. Or the cerulean-blue eyes and boyish dirty-blond hair that was messy from his ballcap. Or maybe it was the "I don't give a damn" attitude he had going. She wasn't sure . . . . She just knew she needed to get out of here as fast as possible. She needed air that wasn't shared with this know-it-all football player. Air with significantly less Harper.

She finished her text and sighed before picking up the pea bag and standing to her feet, which hurt like the dickens. She tried not to wince, but she failed miserably. Still, she managed to get out a professional-sounding closing: "Well, thank you for the help, but I should probably be going now. I'll be back tomorrow to finish and interview you, and then I'll be on my way."

"I don't think so." That dang smirk was back again. And she wanted to smack it right off him.

"Excuse me?"

She was beginning to see that smart-ass smirk was a semipermanent feature to his face. "It's starting to snow. Even if your ankle didn't hurt and you could drive, there may be black ice by the time you get to Homesteel. It's half snowing and half raining out there now. You aren't going anywhere."

She groaned. "I'll drive slow—promise. If I can drive on I-10 or 45 in rush hour, I'll be fine."

He blinked hard twice. "Ice and traffic are two different beasts, *honey*."

The way he said "honey" was definitely mocking, and she clenched her jaw in distaste. She hobbled two steps toward the door. She really needed to get out of here. "I'm perfectly capable, I assure you."

He smiled and gave her a patronizing look. "I assure you walking out that door would be a waste of time, and on a hurt ankle too."

She rolled her eyes freely, super annoyed with this cocky man. "And why's that?"

"I took the keys to your *truck.*" Extra emphasis on the word "truck."

****

Lying in bed that night, Beckett couldn't help but think about the unexpected visitor now sleeping down the hall. There was something about this woman he just couldn't put his finger on. She was uptight, but it was so fun to throw her for a loop. He knew she was stubborn. Recognized it immediately. Maybe because he was too, so he knew what to look for.

He knew she'd try to leave, and when he went back outside and saw that it was half pouring rain and half snowing/sleeting out, he knew he couldn't let her. Add a bum ankle to the deal and he knew she couldn't go anywhere. If his mom were still alive, she'd be livid if he let her leave. That just wasn't the Nebraska way. We took care of our neighbors here.

But this woman. She wasn't a neighbor. Or friendly even. Even so, he was both dreading and looking forward to the snow and what the morning would bring. She wasn't half bad to look at and somehow her disdain for him was fun. He was used to being worshipped. He wasn't used to being . . . *disliked.*

CHAPTER 3

Jordyn woke up to light outside the window and a warm lump on her feet. She jolted awake before remembering where she was.

Beckett Harper.

She was at Heartbreak Harper's house. *The* Heartbreak Harper. And there was a flipping cat on the bed.

She moved her legs out from under the soft and warm ball of fuzz and threw them over the side of the bed. She stood up before remembering the whole ankle-and-heel fiasco from yesterday. Pain shot up her entire leg as she tried to hobble a few steps forward. To say it hurt would be an understatement. She could barely stand. Walking was definitely not desirable. And she could barely see because there were tears in her eyes from how bad the pain was.

She limped and hobbled, cursed under her breath, but eventually got to her suitcase and grabbed her bathroom bag. She decided a shower was in order. Maybe that would get her blood flowing enough to take away some of the stiffness in her ankle.

When she was through showering, it was light enough out for her to take her first look outside, which resulted in a double take. It looked *terrrrrible*. Apparently nature didn't care that this was Sunday, the day of rest, because snow was coming down every which way. *Alllll* the directions. She didn't know what was outside the guest bedroom window, but she couldn't even see a foot in front of her. And it was icing over around the outside frame of the window. It looked cold enough to frostbite a polar bear's bottom.

This was not snow in the beautiful sense of the word. This was a monster. A relentless and terrifying monster. For the first time since he said so yesterday, she realized that Harper had been right about her being in over her head driving in this stuff. Not that she was willingly going to admit that to him anytime soon.

She didn't even want to walk the short distance to her truck, let alone drive in this. Good thing Harper had retrieved her suitcase for her last night. She still didn't know where the keys to her truck were, but it was safe to say she was stuck here a while. Which is probably why Walt didn't hesitate to send her, storm considering. He was probably hoping for this to happen. *Jerk.*

After applying some light makeup and putting her hair back in a braid, she threw on jeans and a chunky sweater in addition to her furry slippers. Feeling refreshed, she made her way out to the kitchen to find the infuriating man she had found herself snowed in with.

But he was nowhere to be found.

She helped herself to some hot tea in the kitchen and found a granola bar for some breakfast. The thought of making herself something more than that felt a bit invasive; Harper wasn't there. This was his kitchen and his domain. It would be rude to take over. And probably send the wrong message. She didn't want to make herself at home here. Nope. Not even a little. Not even if his perfectly situated open kitchen with beautiful granite countertops and white cabinets was calling her name. *It was a thing of beauty really, but nope. That double oven though . . . but nope. Nooope.* Still, she couldn't help but run her fingertips across the island as she half walked and hobbled back to the couch, itching to bake something in this monstrosity of a kitchen.

She supposed the absence of Harper meant he was outside in this beast of a snowstorm tending to his livestock. The thought of someone having to be out in that mess made her cringe. Maybe she could have been a bit nicer to the man. Especially since it was up to her to get him to do the dang Super Bowl commercial—the reason she was even here in the first place!

Ugh. How desperate was Walt right now? For what felt like the hundredth time in the past forty-eight hours, she contemplated what on earth he was thinking for sending her to do this.

Never coming to a logical conclusion on that front, she looked around Harper's farmhouse again and took it all in from a cozy spot under a blanket on the couch. She was kind of impressed. The house was the perfect mixture of rustic and country charm. The rustic blended with the country to give off a manly vibe; it felt like a bachelor's house. The hardwood floors were the perfect shade of brownish gray. She loved the many windows that let in light and gave her an open view of the farm. As she looked at the decor and furniture choices, she wondered if he had decorated it himself. Then again, he probably had a girlfriend or two or three help him over the years. To this day, the tabloids still loved to point out the newest broken-hearted woman—usually a model or actress—who fell for Heartbreak Harper.

But, his place had a homey feel to it, she'd give him that. It wasn't outrageously huge, though she supposed there were two or three bedrooms upstairs in addition to the two on the main floor. His house didn't look that old, or that new, and it wasn't as extravagant as she was expecting.

Harper just wasn't what she'd expected him to be either. He was always smiling and seemed pretty intuitive too. He had been nice to her, though she had just been skeptical from the get-go. She supposed she could still be skeptical but try not to be so rude. Before she had time to make a game plan for being nicer to him, he came in through the garage into the laundry room off the side of the kitchen.

It seemed to take him forever to change out of the amount of clothes he was wearing. When he had, he entered the kitchen in sweats and a hoodie and headed straight for the pot of coffee, blowing on his hands to warm them. His cheeks were pink enough that if the storm wasn't indication enough, she knew it was dang cold outside.

"How's the ankle, Houston?" he hollered as he saw her sitting there in the living room.

She rolled her eyes. It really was going to be tough being polite to this brash man.

"Stiff and sore," she responded honestly from her spot on the couch.

She heard the freezer open and shut before he tossed the bag of peas at her, aiming for her head.

She easily caught it, glaring at his back. She somehow managed a civil "Thank you, Harper" as she put her foot up.

He surprised her by then bringing her two ibuprofen to take.

She gladly took them and looked at his broad retreating shoulders as he headed back into the kitchen. "What were you doing out in this mess?" *See? She could play nice.*

He shrugged. "Checking my cows. Making sure they made their way to the open-front shed to hunker down. Gave them some extra hay to lay in and made a wind break out of bales to help with the drifting now that I know which way the wind is out of. And made sure the water heaters were working."

Hmm. She worked for an agriculture company but forgot about how brutal farm life could be. It wasn't a full-time job; it was an all-the-time job. Sure, she'd grown up in a small town, just not right on the farm. But then again, she'd done everything in her power to make sure *that* small town was only seen in her rearview mirror.

"That sounds terrible," she thought out loud.

He laughed while still having his back to her, grabbing pans and starting something on the stove. "Imagine how my girls feel."

"Your girls?" she asked confused. *Dear Lord, was he admitting to having multiple girlfriends at a time?*

He turned around so she was sure to see his condescending look. "My cows."

"Oh."

Neither of them said anything more while he cooked himself breakfast. She drank her tea, sitting on the couch with the bag of peas on her ankle and a blanket across her lap while she took in the views of the snow outside. She was again surprised when he brought her a plate of eggs and bacon into the living room and sat on the opposite end of the massive sectional.

"Snow days call for bacon," he simply said.

She looked at the plate of food and realized both how hungry she was and how much of an inconvenience she must be. She hated feeling that way. She spent more than two years of her life feeling like a constant inconvenience. It gave her a bad taste in her mouth.

"I'm sorry I got stuck here," she said truthfully. "I didn't realize how bad this storm was going to be. I knew they said there was a storm coming; I just had no idea it would be like this." She again looked outside and suppressed the urge to shudder.

He shrugged. "It wasn't your fault. Most of the time when they forecast these things, they are half as bad as they think they'll be. You just caught the front end of a real-life midwestern blizzard." He eyeballed her slippers and broke into a grin. "Next time just bring better footwear, Houston."

He just couldn't resist taking a stab at her, could he? And why did his one dimple always bounce into action when he was trying to goad her? It gave off the impression he was trying to flirt with her. No wonder he had a reputation like he did. He was too charismatic for his own good.

She rolled her eyes. "You do realize Houston is where I live, not my name, right?"

He smiled again in response. That one dimple mocking her in all of its glory.

She took a deep breath, reminding herself to play nice. "Well. Let me know if there's anything I can help with. I hate being a burden, and it looks like you're stuck with me for a few days."

"Maybe all week," he said with a nod.

"What?!" He had to be joking her, right?

He nodded to the television above the wood fireplace and reached for the remote to turn on the local news. "They've been calling it the snowstorm of the century. It could break all sorts of Nebraska snowfall records. The snow is not to let up for three to four days. We are supposed to get dumped on with two feet of it. And not just snow, but wind too. The wind is always the kicker."

"Are you serious?"

He nodded.

Her brow furrowed. "I guess I thought only the mountains got storms like these. My boss told me there was a storm, but I didn't realize the extent of it or take the time to research it much. His decision to send me was kind of a last-minute thing." She also wondered again if Walt had really known how bad it would be and wanted her to get snowed in with this man. Boss or not, Walt was going to get a nasty email later. She was sure of it.

Harper grinned again, and she found herself both hating and loving the amount he smiled. "You've got a lot to learn, Houston."

She took two deep breaths so she wouldn't roll her eyes again. "My name is Jordyn. Jordyn Mack."

He just continued to smile. "I knew if I annoyed you long enough, you'd tell me."

She sighed. "This is going to be an eventful few days, isn't it?"

He nodded. "Indeed."

****

"I win again," he said, laying down his last *Uno* card.

They had the fireplace lit even though it wasn't even lunch because it seemed like the thing to do in a blizzard. They had the local television channel playing softly in the background so they would get the updates that popped in here and there about the storm. And they had decided to play some card games while they discussed storm preparations, because that also seemed like the thing to do. You could blame his grandfather for that one, avid card player that he was. But they had started it out slow; you couldn't find an easier game than *Uno*.

She wiped above her brow while sitting on the couch with her ankle up, clearly bothered by getting beat twice in a row. "So it would seem. Maybe we should try something with strategy rather than kid games that rely solely on luck."

He smirked. She was every bit as competitive as he was; she was just trying not to show it. "Sounds like a good suggestion coming from a loser."

She looked at him and squinted. He had to admit she was beautiful. And if she was this beautiful when she hated him, he couldn't imagine what she'd be like if she didn't. Not that he cared either way. He was done for a while with women. Especially city women.

That reminded him. "Why do you hate football players anyway?"

She sighed for a response. She did that a lot.

"Too personal?" he asked.

She took a deep breath and shrugged. "That's a bit personal, yes."

"So second-date material?" he asked. He was giving her crap, but he just wanted to see her smile more.

She grinned at that. "Maybe sixth or seventh."

He rose his eyebrows and let out a whistle. "Wow. That bad, huh? That dude must have done a number on you." And he couldn't help but think to himself, *What an idiot.* He didn't even know her, but he was usually a good judge of character. *Except for that one time . . . .*

She rubbed her left temple again, which he was learning meant that she was uncomfortable. "I guess so."

"So why the hatred for small towns, then?" he asked next.

She groaned. "Same thing. My hatred for both are related and intertwined. One and the same."

He shrugged. "Sorry, Houston, I was just trying to small-talk and get to know ya."

"I know," she paused, thinking. "Let's just say that rumors can spread like wildfire and small-town popular opinion is not easily swayed."

Hmm. He could relate to that.

"What about you?" she asked.

"What about me?"

"Why is Beckett Harper in small-town Picketts, Nebraska?"

He shrugged simply. "Well, I'm sure you heard that I had a career-ending injury."

"I knew that," she said quickly. "I mean, with your talent and skills, you probably could have done whatever you wanted. Coached. Been a sports analyst of some sort. Why'd you end up back here?"

He didn't respond right away. She was going right for the jugular, wasn't she? Then again, he had too, he supposed.

"Second-date material?" she asked with a soft smile as she expertly shuffled the cards.

"Since I saved you yesterday, all damsel-in-distress style, wouldn't that classify this as our second date?" Deflecting with a low-grade flirt. It had been so long since he'd been around a woman other than his sister, he was having to brush up on all his old skills.

She glared at him. "Absolutely not."

He chuckled. She was a challenge, this one—those green eyes filled to the brim with nothing but sass. She was not falling for his tricks either.

And he liked it. She might not care for him, but at least she was being real and upfront about it.

He took a deep breath and shrugged. "I'll give the answer to you anyway though. I inherited this place from my grandpa — well, my sister and I both did really — but she is going to be a physical therapist. My mom passed away from cancer not long after my pro career ended. I came back to be closer to her and take over the family farm. I never considered anything else. I never considered selling. This is home."

He could tell that wasn't what she thought he was going to say.

"And what about your dad?"

He tried not to clench his jaw. "Died when I was a sophomore in college."

She looked at him a moment, considering his words — as if doing the math to understand he'd lost both his parents in a span of less than five years. "I'm sorry."

"I'm not. He was a drunk and a mean one at that. It was a lot harder on my sister than it was on me, though she's less than a year younger than me." He wasn't sure why he was telling her all this. He usually liked to keep this stuff to himself. Granted, the fact that his father was a mean drunk was no secret in the small town of Picketts, but it felt weird having to tell a stranger. It was common knowledge around here; everyone just knew.

She didn't have anything to say to that.

"How about you? Family all live in Houston?" he asked.

She shook her head. "Nope. No family."

Now he was the one surprised. "What do you mean, no family?"

"I'm an only child, my dad was never in the picture, and though my mom is technically still alive, we aren't close. No grandparents alive either," she explained emotionlessly, like she was talking about the weather.

The hell? Well, that wasn't at all what he was expecting. But, he understood her better. He got her grit. He got her stubbornness. It came from being let down time and time again by the people that were supposed to love you the most. It cut you and gave you an edge, a chip on your shoulder that wasn't easily shaken. He and his dad hadn't seen eye to eye, but at least Beckett had one solid parent.

"What about a boyfriend?" he asked fearlessly, trying to find a brighter topic. He knew she didn't have a ring on her finger. He'd already checked. Both yesterday and this morning.

She shook her head. "No. No boyfriend. You?"

He gave an indifferent shrug. "No boyfriend."

She rolled her eyes. He guessed she probably knew all about the media's stupid nickname for him.

"No girlfriend either." He grinned.

She just stared at him like she was trying to decide if she believed him or not.

He couldn't blame her. He did have quite the reputation. He'd dated around a lot when his football career ended. He lost his dream and shortly after lost his mom. But the one thing he didn't lose was the attention from women. So for a while he'd gotten lost in that, the only thing he felt he had left. Hell, the only thing he could even feel. By the time he came up for air, he was sick and tired of the superficial relationships and all the stupid events and galas. Sick and tired of the jersey chasers. Sick and tired of women after his celebrity status or money. Sick of it all.

He hadn't been on a date in . . . six months? A year? He didn't even know. And now he was snowed in with this five-and-a-half-foot hostile woman. Heaven help him.

You Just Y'alled Me
CHAPTER 4

"I need to go back out and check the cows, but before I do, how about a quick lunch of some chicken-salad sandwiches?" he asked after winning yet another game of *Uno*.

She was just sure he was going to gloat, but he somehow managed to refrain. *Shocking really.* And here she was. Imposing again. "Uh, sure. I can cook something too, if you'd rather."

He shrugged. "It needs to be used up anyway."

"Well, I don't like feeling like a burden. I know my way around a kitchen. At least let me make them," she offered.

He smiled. "All right. I'll grab the bread; you run the mayo."

Sitting down with their sandwiches, they managed to carry on casual conversation. She didn't really want to get to know Harper, but she supposed it was the polite thing to do. It was hard not to get to know one another when they were stuck in this situation together.

She was slowly beginning to see the kind of person he was. And yeah, he could be smooth. She knew from past experiences that football players could be *too smooth.* But, because of little things—his care for the animals, and his positive demeanor despite all he'd lost—Harper just wasn't what she thought he'd be like. Not at all.

"So how long have you worked for AgGroSo?" he asked.

"Four years. Started right out of college. I met the CEO, Walt, at a job fair right before I graduated, and he wanted me to come work for them."

She smiled fondly thinking of it, even though right now she was a touch peeved with Walt.

His eyes pulled together, scrunching his forehead in confusion. "What was your major?"

"Statistics."

That made him look even more confused. "Why were you taking my soil samples, then?"

She felt her face falter for a split second. Should she just tell him the truth right here and now? Laying it all out there? "I don't typically, though I do know how. I work on graph making and data analysis for both the app and the software. Walt always makes us learn all aspects of the business. Says informed employees make the company better."

"Ohh. That makes sense." He nodded slightly, taking another bite of food.

She smiled. "Why? I don't look like a field tech?"

A slow smile hit his lips, and his sandwich halted before it got to his mouth. "Nope. You're much more . . . *analytical*."

The way he emphasized the last word made her think that wasn't what he was originally going to say. "What about you? What'd you major in? Other than the obvious," she said as he finally took a bite of sandwich.

"Other than the obvious?" he asked around a mouth full of food.

"You know, football and girls," she supplied with a sarcastic look and a shrug.

He cocked his head to the side as he considered that and finished chewing. "Wow. Your football-player prejudice just knows no bounds. Some guy really screwed you over, huh?"

She rolled her eyes. "Come on. You know what they call you."

He groaned and looked . . . embarrassed? "Don't even start, Houston."

"So what was your real major, then?" she asked, trying to appease him. "No wait. Let me guess . . . communications?"

Doing nothing to hide his disdain, he glared at her, zero appeased. "No. I have a finance degree."

Hmm. She was not expecting that. "How'd you find out about AgGroSo?"

"My grandpa and Walt went way back. But the software has been more than helpful and a time-saver, honestly. I don't have to take the time to do much book work at all anymore, whether it's tracking the lineage of my herd or deciding which crop to plant. The numbers are all already there, so I never have to guess. I know exactly where everything is at. And I like knowing and tracking the nutrient levels in the fields. That in and of itself is worth it to me."

She smiled. "That's good to hear. Sometimes when I'm designing all those charts and graphs behind my desk I wonder if anyone will ever really find them that useful."

His eyebrows rose. "Definitely. Last year I planted soybeans when everyone else was planting corn, and everyone thought I was nuts. My yields were crazy good because I was able to use the projection graph using the soil samples you guys had run. My neighbors think it's some sort of voodoo magic until I tell them about you guys. I think there's half a dozen of us just in Picketts now using your software."

So he thought of the company highly. Good to know. She'd have to tuck that away to use to her advantage later. "I'm glad we're helping y'all."

****

Did she really just *y'all* him? *The hell?* She was so hostile and sometimes downright rude, but that one real and genuine southern *y'all* was about to do him in.

"What?" she asked in his hesitation.

"You just 'y'alled' me, Houston." He grinned.

"Okay?"

"Just getting used to your southern charms is all," he offered sarcastically. "And trying to get used to you being nice. I thought you southern belles were supposed to be nice."

She snorted. "You must not have spent much time in the South, then. We southern belles will pour you a tea or punch you into next week. We come fully loaded." She paused to smile. "And are you always this belligerent?"

Fully loaded indeed. He couldn't help but answer honestly. "With you anyway."

She smiled that time. "Touché, Harper."

"I think at this point you can call me Beckett."

He hated it when people called him Harper all the time. Some did it out of respect for his football career. Some did it because of the media nickname, almost in a mocking type of way. In fact, he couldn't remember the last time anyone called him anything but Harper or Harp.

"First names, huh?" She was still smiling.

He scrunched up his nose. "Unless you prefer for me to keep calling you Houston."

She shook her head. "Beckett it is, then."

Why did it sound so good to hear his first name? It was only two syllables, but it sounded like a kind of music. "All right, Jordyn. I'm about to head out. You and Mable should be fine, but I'll leave my cell number on the fridge. If you need anything, just call or text."

"Mable is the cat?" she asked knowingly.

He nodded. Not that they'd see the dang creature for a while. She was full-on nocturnal. Slept the entire day away. For that matter, she also slept the night away. He'd never seen a cat sleep more than Mable. She'd go out about once a month and bring back a dead mouse she always left on the doormat. She liked to prove her worthiness as head couch queen every now and then, flipping her tail back and forth, as if super proud of her loot. So he put up with her and her moody ways.

"Yesterday you made it sound like she was a person," she accused.

Of course he had. He was trying to get under her skin. It had definitely worked too. "Well, don't tell her she's not. She'll be highly offended."

Jordyn laughed. A real laugh. Between the laugh and the *y'all*, he knew he was screwed. It needed to stop snowing so he could get this city woman out of his house before she did some serious damage on him.

****

By the time Beckett came back inside late that afternoon, it looked like he had icicles on his eyelashes, which looked longer than hers, she might add. The storm was not letting up at all though. Not even a little.

She handed him a warm cup of coffee that she poured while he undressed out of all his work clothes. She noticed he put two heaping spoonfuls of sugar and a little milk in his coffee, so she was sure to do that too.

He took a taste and looked to her with raised eyebrows and sharp, all-seeing eyes.

It wasn't that big of a deal; she just knew how to pay attention to the little things like that. She looked out one of the living room windows at the still raging snowstorm. "It looks terrible out there." She shuddered. "What I can see of it anyway."

He nodded. "I have to admit it is."

She wrapped her heavy cardigan around her tighter. "Is it always like this when it snows?"

His blue eyes met hers, a crease between his eyebrows. "What do you mean?"

"It's hateful, blowing snow and cold everywhere," she explained, gesturing for emphasis and looking back at the window in disbelief. "Like anarchy of the weather variety."

He shook his head, the corner of his mouth turning up and showing off his dimple as he clearly tried not to smirk at her. "No. Sometimes it's a quiet snow. No rain. No ice. Just fluffy flakes. It's serene and beautiful."

She sighed. That sounded nice. She'd like to see that.

"How many times have you seen snow?" he asked.

"Counting this time? Three." She stopped to smile. "Other than the occasional flurry, it snowed a few times in Houston. Didn't last long though, and we barely got a half an inch."

He considered that a moment, then asked, "How's the ankle?"

She winced. She was trying to hide how much it hurt while around him. "Still attached?"

He laughed, and she had to stop the warm fuzzy feeling she felt with his laughter. What the heck was wrong with her? This was Beckett Harper. Heartbreak Harper. Feeling fuzzy when he laughed and flashed her his one dimple was not allowed. Not even a little. She noticed he was still speaking to her, so she tried to pay attention . . . .

"Unfortunately, ankle sprains can take a while to start to feel better. But fortunately, I know from experience the first day is usually the worst. And we can call my sister if it doesn't get better or the swelling gets bad. She'll know what to do."

The first day? Thank goodness. It was still so stiff. She'd been babying it and icing regularly along with elevating it, but it still hurt. So much so she rarely wanted to be on it.

"What's that smell?" he asked, looking around.

Oh yeah. That. It wasn't possible for her to be cooped up all day and ignore the pull of that double oven and magnificent kitchen. She'd caved. And it was everything she'd thought it be and more. That kitchen was a thing of beauty. "I made a batch of cookies. I hope you don't mind? I also threw a few things together for a casserole for dinner."

He smiled. "Supper, you mean?"

She nodded. "Yeah, that's what I said. Dinner."

He laughed. She could tell he was enjoying their language differences too much. Next he'd be drilling her on pop versus soda. Then she'd be tempted to call him a Yankee.

While he grabbed a shower, she took the casserole out of the oven and set the table. She had already made up her mind while making dinner that she was just going to tell him the truth tonight. She was going to tell him why they sent her. He had been nothing but kind and upfront with her, so he deserved the same back. She didn't want to play games with him. She didn't want to have ulterior motives. If this was anyone but Heartbreak Harper, that's what she'd do. So she had to extend him the same courtesy, reputation be darned. Having been misled and burned in her own life, she refused to do that to someone else. Even Heartbreak Harper. Her insecurities with her past were not going to make her stoop to that level.

She was just biting into her first perfectly baked cookie for dessert when she noticed Beckett standing in the doorway with tousled wet hair. He was looking at her with his head cocked to the side, as if trying to figure out what was up. It disturbed her that he could read her so easily already. Then again, he was Heartbreak Harper, so he was probably used to picking up on when women were upset. He'd probably seen more than his fair share of *that*.

"What's on your mind, Jordyn?" He entered the kitchen and picked up a cookie before sitting across from her.

She sighed and mentally waved the white flag of surrender. "Look. I want to be honest with you. You've been nothing but kind since being stuck with me through this storm, and I feel like I've been a bit deceitful."

He kept chewing his cookie, waiting for what she was about to say, looking cool and calm. She felt a twinge of guilt that he was unaware of the blow she was about to deliver.

Oh boy. Here she went. It was now or never. If she was going to tell him, it should be now. If she waited until the snow stopped, he'd be mad. And she needed to cultivate this . . . friendship . . . snowship . . . whatever . . . if she was going to have a shot at convincing him to do the stupid commercial.

Before she chickened out, she blurted out, "The reason they sent me and not Trip wasn't to shadow you; it's because I'm here to try to get you to do the Super Bowl commercial."

He swallowed hard and moved to sit back against his chair while crossing his arms, which brought attention to how tense his neck was, a vein bulging on one side. *Uh-oh. He was mad.*

"I see."

She sighed again. "Look, I'm not going to force you to do anything you don't want to do. I just wanted you to know the real reason my boss sent me. I wanted to be completely truthful."

His demeanor was definitely cool. Though he was still looking at her in the eyes, he was now almost squinting at her in accusation, and his dimple was nowhere to be found. "And why exactly did he pick you? Why not just send Trip for the same reason? Someone I already know."

She looked into his blue eyes, caught red-handed. Dang it. She didn't want to get this deep into the truth with him. She wanted to tell him the real reason she was there, but not the real reason why Walt sent her specifically. But now they were there, so she might as well wade on out into the deep water. "Honestly? Because he knew I'm single and a woman and you're Heartbreak Harper."

Now he really was mad. He looked at her, and she could plainly see the anger he was trying to fight down and conceal. It was in his eyes, his tightened neck muscles, the way he held his jaw. Gone was the carefree man she had spent the last day with. He stood up and took a drink of his coffee. "So, tell me. How far were you willing to go to get the Super Bowl commercial? What exactly were you planning? And was your sob story all an act?"

"No! Beckett, no. I just wanted you to know," she offered firmly.

He turned to leave the room, shoulders tight. "Well, now I know."

Ugh. That could've gone better. She did the dishes and checked her email before retiring to bed early. It was still snowing and blowing so hard it was almost whining outside. With no escape, she guessed Beckett was going to have to get over this spat eventually.

****

Seriously?

He was ticked. He had to hand it to Walt; he must want him for the Super Bowl commercial pretty damn bad. They weren't taking no for an answer. They saw a weakness and attacked it, exploiting it fully. At least they were assertive.

He was still bothered though. He went downstairs in the basement to his gym and jogged a few miles, then did some weightlifting. Nothing too extreme, just trying to work off some steam. All things that were approved by his sister as workouts he could do with his back injury, which was good because he needed an outlet for his frustrations. If he didn't get this negative energy out somehow, he'd probably be up a while thinking about it. And he preferred not to.

Because more than he was ticked at Walt and Jordyn and how stupid it all was, he was trying hard to ignore the guilt he felt that he hadn't had to deal with for a while. If he didn't have such a negative reputation, maybe it wouldn't be so easy to manipulate him like that. So a huge part of this crapshow was on him.

Jordyn wasn't the first woman salesperson sent to his doorstep, and he highly doubted she'd be the last. Unfortunately, that was all his fault. For a time, he went through women like you go through clothes, a different one for each different event. At the time he had thought nothing of it. It's not like he was the only pro player that ever did it. It's funny how long a reputation like that followed you though.

He hadn't had a girlfriend in a long while, not that the media would ever admit that. Heartbreak Harper was probably going to be etched on his damn grave, so he may as well get used to it. He was *not* doing commercials either. He had dropped off the face of the earth on purpose. He could have done a bunch of endorsement deals before now, but he chose not to. And this offer wasn't going to be any different.

Except there was Jordyn. He was ticked that what had felt like the first honest and genuine connection he had had with a woman in a long time ended up being just someone else trying to manipulate him or use his name.

Women. They were all the same. He should've more than learned his freaking lesson by now.

How about That?
CHAPTER 5

She got up on Monday morning not long after he did and got to work in the kitchen. Since she loved baking, making them a batch of warm homemade cinnamon rolls seemed like the least she could do.

While the bread was rising, she threw a thawing chicken he had in the fridge in the oven for homemade chicken noodle soup. Then she sat down and sent a snippy email in which she told Walt she was coming back as soon as the snow stopped, Super Bowl commercial be damned. She even added a line about Walt being above this sort of tactic and that the company didn't need to stoop to this level.

Her ankle still really, really hurt, but she was trying to be as helpful as possible. For a few hours in the night last night, the wind stopped blowing and the snow slowed down. She thought maybe the storm was over and she would maybe even be able to leave this morning. Dawn found the storm back in all her hateful glory though, and the blizzard raged and blew as much as she ever had. Anarchy reestablished.

But, after Beckett had been nothing but kind to her — well, except for a little goading here and there — she felt she did the right thing in telling him the truth yesterday. And now that she told him the truth, they could have some honest conversations about why he was so against doing the Super Bowl commercial.

Truth be told, she couldn't care less about the commercial. AgGroSo was doing just fine without it. This was marketing's love child, not hers. She was more concerned with making sure the data analysis was spot on. Speaking of which, she had a few extra things she could go over today. That way she stayed out of Beckett's hair.

When he came inside, the cinnamon rolls were just getting out of the oven.

"What's this?" he snapped from the doorway.

Okay, so he was apparently still mad. She didn't figure him for someone that harbored animosity. He was so carefree and smiled so much. He was kind of acting like a brat about the whole thing.

She shrugged. "My version of a peace offering."

He blinked a few times, showing no emotion, looking at her with his sharp blue eyes. "Okay."

She smiled hesitantly. "Okay, like you're over it?"

He cocked his head to better glare at her. "Okay, like I'll eat a cinnamon roll."

"Harper, I'm sorry—" She didn't get to finish.

"Mack," he interrupted her, using her last name like she used his. He said it with deep sarcasm though. She didn't like it at all. "I don't want to hear it. What part is this in your ploy? Step one, you get snowed in with me. Step two, you cook for me. What's next? And how far exactly were you willing to go?"

With that, he stormed down the hallway and slammed the door to his room.

She bit down on her lip. He was more upset than she originally thought.

****

He didn't know why he was still so angry. The workout last night hadn't helped. Maybe it was because he thought he finally found someone who understood him, and it all turned out to be fake. That green-eyed, brown-haired beauty was having more of an effect on him than he'd like. And he was stuck with her. There was no escape.

And when it came down to it, she'd disappointed him. He thought she was different. He was used to the jersey chasers, the models, the actresses. With them they were obviously not discreet about wanting to use him for his name. He knew it going in. But with Jordyn, he was intrigued. Her story got to him. But she didn't want a thing to do with him, other than the commercial, of course. He had wanted to get to know her, to be friends in the very least, but she was apparently not interested in that at all. And he was disappointed in her for it—and disappointed in himself for even caring to begin with.

So he was hiding. Like they were in junior high, he was hiding and avoiding her. City women were all the same, he reminded himself. This right here was exactly why he took a hiatus from women.

He turned on the local TV channel in his master bedroom and lay down. He was not getting involved. He was not.

****

She had left the gooey cinnamon rolls on the counter and finished getting the soup ready to go. All it needed was to be heated up on the stove. Then she excused herself to her room so Beckett would quit hiding from her. It was his house after all. At least Mable seemed to like her. She didn't have any pets of her own, but she didn't mind holing up in the guest room with Mable.

She didn't know how to make things better with Harper. They barely knew one another; she didn't know why it was such a big deal. So she didn't show up here for what he thought. Knowing his reputation, she thought maybe he should have known better.

She'd been honest and that was that. Now she was waiting out both the wrath of the storm and the wrath of Beckett Harper. Which one was going to let up first, she had no idea.

****

He had successfully avoided her all day. He was acting like a brat, and he knew it. Fortunately for him, the storm still raging afforded him plenty to do outside. The snow had let up a bit, but the wind had not, and they were only about halfway through this damn storm. When he finally made it back inside after dark that night, he helped himself to more cinnamon rolls and soup.

Damn, the woman could cook though.

He noticed the light on in the guest room, where she had been hiding out. He supposed he should apologize for being so angry with her and get on with it, but he was still just pissed. With time to stew and think about it, he realized this wasn't *her* idea. Remembering her hostile tendencies when she arrived, he realized she was probably just as annoyed with this whole situation as he was. She probably even felt just as used as he did.

Still. As alluring as she was, he was *not* doing a Super Bowl commercial. Heartbreak Harper was not going to use his face to get more publicity. Even if for a good cause. He wanted out of the spotlight. Now and forever. It was hard enough living in a place where everyone worshipped him. He didn't need to add to that.

And now he was even referring to himself in the third person. *Great.*

So he decided to wait until morning. When he was good and over it. Hopefully.

****

On Tuesday morning, she had gotten up and made them some homemade banana muffins while he was out doing the morning chores. She was back in the guest room for the rest of the morning when she heard Beckett come back in the door, probably wanting a fresh muffin and the warm coffee she had been sure to start for him.

Was she sucking up? Yep. Was it working? Only time would tell.

And since when was she referring to him as Beckett in her head? She needed to get a grip. She had done nothing wrong and had been completely honest with him. Something she thought he'd appreciate, given their circumstances and the long hours they were forced to spend together while snowed in. Apparently not. Oh well, it would be a little awkward, but she could survive being locked up in the guest room with Mable. She'd try her best to stay out of the way.

She finished her email to Walt with another snide remark to him about the situation he had put her in. She had just finished her morning work and was about to start up a movie on her laptop when the lights in the bathroom blinked.

She found that odd, but it had to be the wind, right? The weather app on her phone had told her there was a real feel of negative twenty-seven degrees outside because of that dang wind. Even with the heater running, when you walked by the windows you could feel the cold trying to ensnare you. She was not acclimated to this kind of cold. Not even a little. This kind of cold was both brutal and shocking.

Mable got cozied up on her feet, as if sensing she was cold. Not even ten minutes into the movie, the lights went completely out.

Well . . . she guessed Beckett would be forced to talk to her now.

The movie kept playing on the charged battery, and she tried to take a few minutes to not panic as she considered how long it would take for the house to get colder without heat. *Losing electricity. That was bad . . . right??* She felt totally out of her element up here in Nebraska on the farm. She knew small-town life. She did not know this whole cold weather and harsh winter concept. It was new, and it was terrifying. Mother nature was a beast. A beast that got PMS sometimes even hourly. She wasn't sure she could ever live somewhere like this, where the winters were so evil. She whined enough when it dropped to the forties in Texas. This was on a whole other level. This was Nebraska, not Alaska. So what the hell was going on?

Not wanting to delay the inevitable and wanting to know how they'd handle the outage, she tiptoed out of the guest room and into the living room, where Beckett was starting a fire in the fireplace with huge wood chunks.

"I take it you noticed the power is out?" he said without turning.

"Sure did," she answered hesitantly. She tried to ignore the tightness across the shoulders of his long-sleeved T-shirt while he lugged some bigger logs into the fire. "Is there anything I can do?"

He didn't turn around, but she could have sworn she felt him smirking at her. "For starters, you and Mable can stop hiding in the guest room and make yourselves warmer out here in front of the fire."

She tilted her head to the side and resisted the urge to roll her eyes. "I meant cook something or help you do something with the electricity being out. And I wasn't hiding—I was trying to give you space until you were done being mad. You know, since you are stuck with me and all."

He spun around, still kneeling beside the now crackling fire, his blue eyes drilling into hers. "I'm not gonna lie. I'm still a little pissed, Jordyn." He sighed. "But, I also realize it isn't totally your fault."

Seriously? He was being a baby. She closed her eyes a moment to stop from rolling her eyes or losing her temper.

He must have caught on to her aggravation. "What is it, Houston? Don't hold back on me now."

She opened her eyes with an eye-roll, if that were even possible. "It only took you two days to get *halfway* over it?"

He shrugged. "I was hurt. And annoyed."

She tipped her head back to look at the ceiling. The way he always stared her in the eyes was unnerving. "Are you always this difficult?"

He shrugged for a response, but that darned smirk and dimple were back.

"Well, while we are on the topic, will you just tell me if you will or will not do the stupid commercial and why? I'll tell Walt, so we can never talk about it again. It was his idea to send me."

He stood, arms crossed. Not a good sign for her.

"I'm not doing it."

She wasn't surprised by that. Furthermore, she didn't care. He wasn't hurting *her* feelings any. He was so much taller than she was, yet she wasn't about to cower to this man. She looked him right in the eyes and asked, "Why?"

He clenched his jaw stubbornly and looked outside toward the barn a moment. "I won't have you use my face, and my stupid reputation, to further your company. I love what you guys do and offer, but I don't want to be the face behind it."

She thought about that for a moment. So he didn't want the attention? She figured it wasn't enough money they were offering him, but apparently that wasn't the case. Heartbreak Harper didn't want to use his reputation to make a few extra bucks? *Hmm. How about that?*

This man was nothing like she had assumed. He was also nothing like the nickname behind his name, but maybe that was because he didn't see her like that. It was easy for him to be nice to her because he wasn't looking for . . . *companionship* . . . with her. They were not romantically involved.

"I'll be sure to pass that message along and be out of your hair as soon as this hateful storm is over," she said with a smile.

****

Out of his hair and out of his life? Sounded good to him. *Or did it?*

He wasn't sure anymore. He barely knew this person. They had only known one another three whole days, but there was something about the way she carried herself. Something in the way they could banter.

Was he falling for her? Oh hell no. This was the farm, not some sappy romance movie. He wasn't falling for her at all, but he was getting used to her being around. A warm cup of coffee always waiting when he would come in from the chores. Someone there — conversations here and there . . . well, except for when he'd been mad at her. Plus, she was just nice to look at.

He needed to get off the farm, he decided. If three days stuck inside with a city woman were making him feel comfortable with having women around again, he definitely needed to go out. Not with women per se, but he needed to at least see his friends.

Lonely was not a term that "Heartbreak Harper" should ever be. And yet somehow, her mention of leaving made him feel lonely. Not at all what he was expecting.

How about that?

****

They had to camp out that night in the living room where the fire was keeping them warm. Beckett had told her he had a generator they could use, but since the oven was gas and the fireplace could provide heat, they would hold off on the generator until they absolutely had to. Save the fuel for if they truly needed it.

She had kept to herself and played games on her computer until almost exhausting the battery. Her phone was off to save for the next day in case she didn't get to charge it for a while. And when her laptop battery was starting to fail her, she resorted to reading a book on her Kindle. She didn't know what Beckett did, but he was on his tablet doing something.

The big argument was finally over. Beckett was talking to her again, yet it wasn't quite the same. He wasn't flipping her as much crap and felt a little withdrawn. But that was okay with her as long as he wasn't mad anymore.

It was hard enough being snowed in with a stranger. Being snowed in with a stranger who was ticked at her was just plain horrible. Good thing she had Mable, though all Mable did was sleep; this time, she curled up on the wooden rocking chair in the corner, close to the warmth of the fire.

Jordyn and Beckett had both fallen asleep that night on opposite ends of the huge, comfy couch. It was so soft she didn't mind. But she did notice he stayed as far away from her on the couch as he possibly could. It shouldn't bug her considering he now knew what she was there for.

Somehow early that next morning, Beckett had snuck out to do the chores before she woke. It was around 7:00 a.m. when she heard the door shut as he left. She noticed he had added his blanket to the stack of blankets over her when he snuck out.

That one little thing shouldn't have made her smile so much.

CHAPTER 6

Beckett had spent all of twenty minutes outside before he knew his Wednesday had gone to hell. The wind wasn't as bad as yesterday, but for some reason, the snow had picked up again. When it wasn't blowing, it was snowing. He guessed the weatherman had gotten the forecast right for once. And if the weatherman was right, then the snow and wind wouldn't let up until Thursday night—Thanksgiving. Jordyn was going to be stuck with him more than likely for the weekend before they could dig themselves out of this mess.

And oddly enough, he was okay with that.

The electricity was still out. That had meant the water heaters for his cattle had all stopped working and he had to chip the ice off the top of all the waterers. Then he did some extra haying and checking of his herd. He was about to go in for a break when he noticed one of his prized heifers was bleeding.

Crap.

There was no way he was getting the vet out here today. He was going to have to deal with this himself. It didn't look bad, but there was an exposed area of skin that could get irritated or infected if he didn't treat it; it'd at least need covered up. And knowing she would be hunkered down in the hay trying to keep warm would probably not help matters with all the particles that could get into the open wound.

Damn. How did this even happen? He supposed the wind had scared her and she got too close to the fence. That or some coyotes came wandering up for shelter and spooked her. Both were solid possibilities.

It took forever, and a lot of bribing her with corn feed, but he finally got the injured heifer over to the barn. Then he had to walk back and get the tractor. He had almost been done with the hay in the feeder, so he quickly finished up the morning feeding. Then he drove the tractor back over to the barn so he could work with the hurt heifer.

Fortunately, the last time this happened, the veterinarian stocked him with enough meds to help him sedate and clean any future wounds. He took a picture of the wound and texted it to his vet, Mason, who also happened to be one of his better friends.

As a retired pro baseball player from the neighboring town of Homesteel, Mason was one of the few people Beckett felt understood him. They both knew what it was like returning to their prospective hometowns after living out their professional athlete careers. And they were the only professional athletes in at least a fifty-mile radius. Mason was the only person who really understood the whole small-town celebrity thing.

After a long phone conversation with him about what needed done, Beckett realized this was going to take a while. He administered the sedative and got ready to clean the wound before he would have to roll up his sleeves and do some stitches.

****

Seriously, what on earth could be taking him so long? Was he all right? The wind didn't seem as bad today, but then again, maybe she was just used to it. Or maybe he was still just mad at her, trying to avoid the house.

Regardless, it was almost lunch. The morning chores never took this long. She was toying with the idea of starting up her truck and going to check on things when she realized that her phone was still mostly charged and Beckett hopefully had his too.

Though the electricity may still be out, this was the twenty-first century after all. *Smart phones. What in the world did people ever do without smart phones?* After searching beside her truck keys, which Beckett had hung on a magnetic hook on the fridge, she found the piece of paper he'd left with his cell number and sent him a text.

This is Jordyn. Are you still okay out there?

Having made breakfast hours ago, she kept reading on her Kindle, which was about to die, while waiting for his response. She tried not to check her phone every few minutes but failed. Where was he, and why wasn't he answering? Did he not have his phone?

Was he stuck out there in the cold? It was so cold out someone could get in trouble in a hurry if they were unconscious or something. And she didn't know her way around his farm. She wouldn't even know where to look for him. Twenty minutes passed, and she got nothing.

At the thirty-five-minute mark, she tried texting him again. *HARPER. Please answer me if you have your phone. I'm getting worried here.*

Exactly six minutes later, he did respond. *So it's back to Harper when you're angry, huh, Houston?*

Thank God. So he was okay. Whew. And his smart-ass tendencies hadn't froze off in the cold yet. Bummer.

At least I knew how to get you to respond, she texted back.

She could imagine him smirking at that, his one dimple doing its thing.

He responded not even a minute later. *Smart woman. One of my heifers has an open wound I'm tending to in the barn, but thanks for checking. It'll take me a while, but I'll be in in an hour or so probably.*

In the barn? She could see the barn out the big living room windows. And she knew for a fact that Harper hadn't had anything to eat or drink all day. He had snuck out in an effort not to wake her. Now it was almost noon.

She hit the remote start key for her truck and went to work. She searched around the cupboards until she found a coffee mug and set yesterday's coffee in a pot on the stove to warm. Then she put together a sandwich. She got out a plastic bag and threw in some cookies, a cinnamon roll, a muffin, and a bottle of water too.

When she was done, she figured the truck was probably warm enough, so she bundled up and headed for it. There was a small drift around the right front wheel, but she was hoping the four-wheel-drive truck was enough to take it.

It was terrifyingly cold out—so cold she sucked in that initial breath—but she tried to focus on the task at hand: getting Beckett some food. The icy wind stung her cheeks like she'd been slapped. What was this? The flipping Arctic? Satan had it all wrong. Fiery hell? Nope. He should just make people walk around in this crap eternally.

Finally in the warmth of the vehicle, she put the truck in gear and slowly headed for the barn. It was less than a quarter of a mile, but she wasn't going to walk if she didn't have to. Fortunately, once she got out of the driveway, she could just follow the path the tractor had made over the last few days. It was easier than she thought.

She pulled up by the barn. This barn was possibly her favorite part of the place. It looked just like you thought a barn should, from the red paint to the white trim. And it was big, its strong frame looming above her like a hundred-year-old redwood tree. It matched the house in that it exuded history from its weathered wood, but had also been well taken care of.

Being outside for the first time in days, she took a long look at all the snow that had drifted in white blankets across Beckett's farm. It was a beautiful place—she had to give him that.

She parked her truck at a safe distance where she was sure she wouldn't get stuck in the snow and walked the short distance to the barn. She slid open the door. There was Beckett on his hands and knees, humming away to music playing from his phone while working on a cow who was clearly hurt and bleeding.

Was he stitching – just like he had joked about days ago? What in the world?!

"Jordyn??" Squinting, he looked up at the door when the light spilled in with her entrance.

"I brought you coffee," she said, holding up the goods for him to see. "And food." She hurried to shove the heavy door shut, more than happy to stand in the warmer barn.

He smiled and looked at her appreciatively. "My hero. I wish you wouldn't have walked over here in this weather though. Especially on that bum ankle."

"I didn't. I brought my *pickup*." She overly emphasized "pickup" with a grin.

He chuckled. "You are quite resourceful."

She smiled at his compliment, sarcastic or not. That was two today if you counted him calling her smart earlier. It said a lot about the state of her current love life if she was counting and logging compliments from *this* man.

"Unless this is part of the ploy for the commercial?" he added, half teasing, half serious.

She shook her head. "No. Actually, this was just me trying to be thoughtful. A real southern belle."

He looked at her a moment, as if trying to decide if he believed her or not. "Well, thank you, then. But given what you've told me, I think southern belles wouldn't be out in this weather."

"That's definitely true." She laughed at that but added a "You're welcome."

"Let me finish up here cleaning this cut, and then I promise I will devour whatever you brought me before I go to work sewing her up."

"Anything I can do to help?" she asked. He looked like he had it under control, but he wasn't a veterinarian for Pete's sake. Should he really be doing this? Then again, with the weather as it was, did he really have any other option?

He smirked, as if he knew she was questioning his skills. "I've got it. But you can stick around and keep me company if you want."

What else was there to do? The house was empty and without electricity. Her Kindle was almost dead, and her current book made her angry with a stupid plot twist anyway. Mable was cute and all but kind of boring. Since this was the first time Beckett seemed fully back to normal, she didn't want to leave just yet. She didn't know why he was back to being this way, but she didn't want it to end.

****

After the sedating and cleaning, he had taken a break to get everything ready for the hard part. He took off his medical gloves and washed up in the sink in the barn. He had some coffee and ate the sandwich she brought, realizing how hungry he really was. Then he got right back to work. He was three stitches in when Jordyn went and blew his mind, not for the first time today.

He had been humming to one of his favorite country playlists on his phone while Jordyn looked around the barn. He would do a stitch and then pat the neck of his heifer. She was sedated, loopy, numbed, and not in any pain, but still sort of awake at times. He needed to keep her as still as possible, so he kept soothing her by murmuring to her and singing along with the music. Not that he had a good voice by any means, but animals in pain just needed to hear someone tell them it was okay; they needed to know the person working on them didn't mean them any harm.

And then here came Jordyn.

She plopped down cross-legged in the hay and rested the heifer's head right in her lap. Then she ran her hands along the heifer's neck, speaking gentle words to her so Beckett could keep working. If she was bothered by the hay, the smell of cow, or the bloody cut on the heifer, she was doing a fine job of hiding it. She took it all in stride.

Yep. Mind-blown.

He'd known a lot of city women. A lot. None of them would've ever been thoughtful enough to bring him food and warm coffee to his barn, and none of them would've been willing to sit in the smelly hay and pet a cow. Then again, he didn't let any of them near his farm. His farm was his place of solitude.

Or it was — until Jordyn got stuck with him here. And he couldn't help himself. He wanted to know her. He wanted to get to know her. Even though the storm meant more work for him in less than favorable conditions, he still felt okay with her being stuck with him for at least another day or two. She had texted him to check in with him. And in that moment, she was instantly forgiven for the real reason her boss sent her. She didn't have to check on him, but she did. That wasn't Jordyn working and trying to sell a commercial pitch; that was just Jordyn being Jordyn.

Maybe if she would just let him in a little, he could figure her out. That was one thing he hated about high society and all the fancy events he used to go to. Everyone was wearing a mask, putting on a show, trying to be their best, portraying something they weren't. One of the reasons he liked football so much was you couldn't fake it in football. If you went out there trying to do anything half-assed, you were going to get yours handed to you on a silver platter.

He wanted to know the woman behind this mask. He knew she had been burned. He knew she was analytical and logical in everything she did. But there was more — and he wanted to know it. All of it. All because she sent him a text and brought him some food. He was pathetic really.

And lonely. *There was that word again.*

He looked up at her. "This is going to take me another half an hour by the time I finish it and cover it, so why don't you tell me about why it is you hate football players so much? We've got time. And though this isn't our sixth or seventh date" — he paused to chuckle and look around the barn and at his furry patient — "it is something."

The Doozy

CHAPTER 7

She brushed the cow's neck again. Here they were, taking care of this gentle beast, and he wanted to talk about *that*??

"Why?"

He shrugged and looked her right in the eyes. "Because I want to get to know you."

The way he said it made her feel all warm. She couldn't tell him no. She didn't want to share this story though. Not here, not now, probably not ever. But if he wanted to know her, it was only fair. If he had even a spark of interest in her, even in just being her friend, it would vanish with the telling of this story. So really she'd be doing him a favor.

She sighed in defeat. "I don't hate *you*, Heartbreak Harper, if that's any consolation."

He looked at her and waited like he knew she was gathering both her thoughts and her courage — and the silence provided her a bridge to the past. A bridge she had wanted to burn a long time ago. And not just burn, but incinerate, pick up the ashes, back them over with her car, stomp on them, then reburn them in the flames.

"I guess I should start out the story with when I was sixteen," she began when he moved to get back to the stitching. She swallowed back the pain that still tried to overtake her when she thought of those years. "My mom and I were never close. She wasn't really much of a provider. Or much of a worker. She could never keep jobs, so she married as her form of working. When I was sixteen, she was about to marry the third guy, this time leaving town. She knew I loved my friends and where I was at, the small town we lived in. I was shy enough that she didn't want me to have to start over in a new town in the middle of high school. So she gave me the option to stay, which may have been the most motherly thing she ever did for me, honestly."

She paused. Beckett didn't even look up at her; he just kept working. So she kept talking while always petting the heifer with its head in her lap. The cow was sort of cute. Kind of smelly, but still cute, so she didn't mind.

"I had only a few close friends, but I didn't want to move in with them and be a burden to their families. So I asked the one person in the world I felt most comfortable with . . . my junior high English teacher. Her kids were all in college, and she and her husband were happy to take me in. She would end up being more of a mom to me than my mom ever was. And her husband was the only real dad I've had, though I don't call him Dad or anything."

Just when she thought maybe he wasn't even paying attention or listening, Beckett interrupted with "Do you still stay in touch with them?"

Before she replied, she swallowed down emotion again, feeling the grief lodged in her throat. "I did, but Andrea's cancer came back a year and a half ago. Unfortunately, it was a short fight. I still talk to her husband, Sam, weekly and see him on New Year's every year. I give him Christmas with his actual family, so New Year's is our thing."

He looked like he wanted to say more but simply stated, "Cancer freaking sucks."

She nodded and took a moment to stroke the cow's neck gently. After a minute, she continued quietly, as the cow was almost asleep. "So there I was. Sixteen and living with my teacher. I was kind of a bookworm. Well, I still am actually." She stopped to shrug and laugh guiltily. "But I studied my butt off because I always knew I was going to need scholarships if I wanted to go to college. It was a small town. Everyone knew everyone. And everyone knew I was *that* girl. That girl whose mom up and left her. That girl whose mom didn't take her with her. That girl that lived with a teacher. As far as small towns go, I was an outlier."

She looked at the cow. The heifer had fallen asleep and was completely still, but she kept petting her anyway. "Then out of the blue, junior year this boy in my class started paying attention to me. My mom was long gone, and I was finally adjusting, getting used to all the stares and whispers. And here he was actually talking to me. He was charming. *Very* charming. He had wanted help in trigonometry and asked me for help. We started studying together after hours and eventually hanging out. I couldn't believe it. He seemed so interested in me. And he was *that* boy. The quarterback. The hometown hero. The one that was going to play collegiate ball. Maybe even pros one day. He had everything going for him and ran with the popular crowd and I . . . *well* . . . I didn't."

Beckett gave her a look, one she couldn't quite decipher, so she just shrugged before continuing. "We had been dating or seeing each other for months before prom rolled around. My two best friends and I were so excited to go, and I figured it was only a matter of time before he asked. But then a month or so before prom, he told me he was going to go to some big football camp that weekend. There were going to be college scouts there, and though he wanted to take me to prom, he couldn't let that opportunity go by."

She took a deep breath for this next part. "And while my two best friends were at prom while I was at home alone, they saw him there with another girl. And not just any girl, but the cheerleader captain. It was so grossly cliché and typical. My friends came over after prom and broke the news to me."

She sighed. "Andrea had warned me about him and told me he could be manipulative. But I didn't see it. I just didn't *want* to see it. Andrea didn't ever know for sure what was going on because she taught in a different building than the high school, but she still had warned me on multiple occasions. There were times where he'd say he had football stuff on the weekends. I figured he was trying to avoid the parties and focus on his goals, so I was the supportive girlfriend and stayed home when he couldn't go, telling him it wouldn't be the same if he wasn't there with me. Same with prom. It turns out, he *was* there . . . all along . . . but with her."

She looked down at the cow, not wanting to see how Beckett was looking at her before she was done telling him everything. "So yeah. Then I found out not only was he dating this other chick, but he had been the entire time we were dating. I found out that I was the other woman. The side piece. And I had no flipping idea—I was completely blindsided. Sure, I was naïve and should've known better. Or someone should've told me. I was just too focused on pulling good grades so I could get a scholarship—too busy keeping my head in my books—that I ignored all the normal high school social stuff. I even spent lunch every day in the library. I just had no idea what was really going on."

She took a deep breath, moving to rub her temple. "Afterward, I went as far as talking to the other girl. To apologize. But the worst part . . . is that *she knew*. She knew the entire flipping time. So then I asked her why she didn't come to me and tell me. She told me that he was her meal ticket out of there, and if he needed to date a few nerds to get it out of his system, then so be it."

She had been talking for so long that when she looked toward Beckett, she noticed not only was he done with the handful of stitches, but the bandage was also almost done. "But in our small town, no one took my side over his. I was the other woman. I was the cheater. Like I forced him to date me at the same time. And the other chick just fed into those rumors even though she knew the truth. People scowled when they saw me, but they still loved and adored him. How messed up is that? And it wasn't as if I was new to town or something. We had all known one another and gone to school together for years. We had a graduating class size of fifty, for crying out loud. But I guess since they all knew how my mom was, it was just easier for everyone to lump me in the same category as her." She finished, and they both sat there in silence for a couple seconds, marinating in the heft of the doozy of a story of how she came to hate small towns and football players.

"And what did that *boy* have to say for himself?" Beckett asked, throwing down his gloves harder than necessary and moving to wash his hands.

She shrugged. "He told me it had been fun, but he was never really serious about dating me. He told me I was his escape from all the pressure. And he made up the lie about prom because he didn't want to hurt my feelings. He didn't want to hurt me or lose me. How ironic, huh?" She shrugged again, not even knowing what else to say. "So yeah. That's why I don't like football players."

"What's his name?" he asked as he dried his hands and gathered his supplies. "Did he end up playing college ball?"

She nodded. "It doesn't matter."

"It does." He said the words firmly, but then gently, ever so gently, reached to lift the still sleeping heifer's head out of her lap and helped her to her feet.

"No, it doesn't," she said matter-of-factly.

He pierced her with his gaze, and she had to note how close they were standing. "It does. Jordyn, what is his name?"

"Why?" she asked. "Why does it matter to you?"

He swallowed hard. "On the very small chance he went pro, I still have quite a few connections and friends. I can make his life hell." The blond stubble on his jaw bobbed as he clenched his jaw. His eyes barely contained the rage in them, the blue fury swirling within. Being this close in proximity, she could see it all, especially those enticing neck muscles all tense.

"Beckett."

He got even closer, their coats almost touching. "Jordyn."

"Beckett," she repeated, warning him in her tone. What were they even arguing about anyway? She couldn't even remember with him this close to her personal space.

And then he got so close she stopped breathing, the heavy coats on their chests finally brushing against one another. *"Jordyn."*

His need to defend her and that raw determination sent heat all over her body. She couldn't help but nervously smile as she took a small step back. "His name is Thomas George. He went on to play for Tech but played backup from what I understand. He never went pro."

Beckett snorted. He actually snorted. He never stopped looking her right in the eyes though. "Serves him right."

"Andrea and Sam told me he got in trouble while in college. Hit the drinking and partying too hard. Got in trouble for some marijuana use," she added.

Beckett nodded, his eyes still sharp with anger. "Sounds like he really shot his potential to hell."

"And he dumped the other girl as soon as we graduated."

He nodded again. "Mmm. Exceptional."

She smiled. "Why? What were you going to do? Kick his butt? Heartbreak Harper to the rescue?"

He cocked his head at the sound of his nickname, squinting at her. "Jordyn, football players are *not* all like that. Yeah, a lot are. In my short few years in the pros, I met some of the biggest, most egotistical pricks. But I also have met some of my best friends, people I consider brothers, playing the sport. We are not all like that. Please believe that."

She opened her mouth to reply, but he cut her off. "And please know, stupid nickname aside, I would never do that to a woman. I would never do that to you. Yeah, I slept around for a while, but all of those women knew that going in. They knew I wasn't interested in dating, and there was only ever one at a freaking time. I'm many things, but I'm not a liar, and I'm not a cheater."

She knew she should probably not believe him. With her past, she should probably run far, far away from him. She fell for a charming football player before. What was the difference?

Well, the difference was she fell for a boy. This football player before her . . . he was all man. He was not a boy at all. Not even a little.

She sighed, defeated, and after a long blink, looked him in the eyes. "I believe you." And then, because he had a weird look like he wanted to kiss her or some ridiculous thing like that, she whispered, "Can we go inside and get warm now?"

He grinned, that one dimple wreaking havoc on her poor heart. "Not used to the cold yet, Houston?" he whispered back.

She shook her head dramatically. "Never."

****

Yep. He was a goner. Done for.

Her story of why she hated football players. No wonder she didn't seem to trust him. She had every right to be hostile toward him. She had every right to be hostile for a lot of reasons. Her mom sounded like a real winner. Her dad nonexistent. And then the one good thing she thought happened to her turned out to be a lie.

No freaking wonder. This one story explained a lot about her.

He had finished stitching and bandaging that heifer. It was a good thing he had his hands busy and something to do while she was talking because by the time she was finished, feeling her pain and understanding her on a whole other level, he wanted nothing more than to make her forget Thomas George ever existed.

He still had some sources too. He wasn't lying about that. He'd see what that poor excuse of a man ever ended up doing with his life. His guess was a used car salesman.

He had been so close to kissing Jordyn. And he was pretty sure she knew it. She'd panicked. Which was probably for the better. It was probably poor timing. Chances were good he still had some dried blood on his forearms. The hay was everywhere, even in her hair. The smell of cow and hay was not exactly a turn-on. And she had just been talking about the situation that had destroyed her trust in men. Yep. Worst possible timing.

Still, he felt a strange connection to her.

They had left the barn and gone back to the house. They both needed showers and a hot meal. He had guzzled down the rest of the coffee and eaten the rest of the goodies on the way back to the house because he was starved. It had been a long day.

He was wearing sweatpants and an old college T-shirt, his usual evening attire. He was impressed when she came around the corner into the kitchen freshly showered and wearing some sort of legging pants and a hooded AgGroSo sweatshirt. Most women were always dressing up to impress him. He liked that she wasn't afraid to wear sweats and be normal. Her hair was in a braid, and she may have put on a little makeup, but not much. And she smelled amazing. Her perfume or lotion or whatever was one of the first things that attracted him to her. He couldn't wait to get closer.

They cooked together, oddly maneuvering the kitchen as a team quite well. He made chicken-fried steak, and she did some sort of chopping and spicing of some potatoes. It was 3:00 p.m., so it was hardly time for lunch, but they could eat this now and munch on leftovers whenever they felt like it.

He should probably mention that he could turn the generator on now and they would have enough fuel to survive until Monday. But for some odd reason—no actually, for a very good reason—he didn't want her out of his sight tonight. He didn't want her to be able to hide off in her room after her revealing story from earlier.

Things were just getting good.

CHAPTER 8

Later that night, after the evening chores chased the sun's disappearance, they sat together on the couch. They were no longer on opposite sides; they had naturally met somewhere in the middle without either one of them wanting to point it out or think of a reason why. She really hoped it wasn't just because he felt bad about her sob story. She didn't want him to feel sorry for her. It had all been a long time ago. And yeah, it had crushed her, but she was wiser for it.

After playing *Phase 10*—and Jordyn finally winning a match that may or may not have ended with her shouting "Boom!" in a very unsportsmanlike manner—they sat in shared silence, content with each other's company. Jordyn watched the orange glow of the fire as it wrapped and twisted itself around the logs Beckett had put in not that long ago. She liked the fireplace. She didn't have one in her townhome in Houston, where there really wasn't a need for one.

"Can I see your ankle?" Beckett asked randomly.

She nodded. "Sure. It's still bruised and swollen, but it's much better, I think."

He moved to sit on the pillowy footrest so he could see her ankle. When he took her foot, he had to remove her furry slipper—and not one but two pairs of fuzzy socks.

He raised his eyebrows in surprise, blue eyes twinkling in amusement.

"I was cold," she said, shrugging. "I hate being cold."

He smiled and shook his head. She supposed she should be embarrassed, but she wasn't. At least she had her toenails painted. Needing something to distract herself from his touch, she took out her braid so that her hair could fully dry. She hated wet hair. And the only thing worse than wet hair was *cold* wet hair.

He ran his hands across her ankle and gently pressed in spots. He expertly moved her foot at a few different angles to see if there was any change, rotating it around and around, asking her which spots it hurt in. She had to admit, just like with the heifer earlier today, he did seem to know what he was doing.

"So I'll live?" she asked softly when he finished.

He grinned. "I sure hope so."

There was that look again. What was he going to do? Kiss her? Why? They both knew what she was here for. And she wasn't going to get his cooperation for the commercial, so it would be back to Houston for her. And he knew her story, so he should understand she wasn't the type to have a fling, snowed in or otherwise.

So what was his endgame here anyway?

****

Hell, he wanted to kiss her. She looked freaked out again though; she wasn't ready. And that was fine. It had been a tough day for her. So he decided to return the favor and open up just a little to allow her to get to know him.

He moved to sit next to her. She had her arm propped up on one leg, and when he sat back down, he was sure to sit so that his shoulder was near her arm. Junior high move? Maybe. He didn't care. Desperate times called for desperate measures. Back to basics with this one.

"I'll share with you how I got my nickname," he began, looking toward the fire.

"Beckett, you don't have to if you don't want to," she said softly.

He turned toward her, getting even closer. "I do."

She nodded as he began. "Well, my best friend growing up was a quarterback, so I guess it was always in my nature to be catching things he was throwing at me. Even before that, my mom had always told me I had good hand-eye coordination—good and talented hands."

She interrupted to say, "You do. You proved that today."

He couldn't help but feel good hearing that. His ego was doing just fine, thank you, but she didn't seem to supply compliments that often. So when she did, he took them to heart. "When we were in high school, we made it to state. I loved football. I know you grew up in Texas so it was similar, but college football here is everything. After all, we don't have a pro team in anything—not baseball, basketball, hockey . . . I mean *nothing*. Like it's almost borderline obsessive how much the people here care about their team."

He shook his head, knowing she had no idea how obsessed some people could be. "So naturally, every Nebraska boy grows up with a football in his hands and hopes to make it to play for the university, become a Husker. Of course. We bleed red, as they say. And football was the one thing my dad and I did see eye to eye on. I didn't like how he worked the land or the cattle, and I especially didn't like his temper or the way he treated my mom. I mean, he didn't ever beat her or any of us, but he wasn't exactly a doting husband either. But when it came to football, we could talk for hours and hours. Plays, defensive schemes—it didn't matter. Football was really the only glue keeping us together. Maybe the only thing we ever had in common was the love for the game."

He paused, noticing she was so intently listening she had stopped playing with her hair. Hair he'd love to sink his fingers into. *Where the hell did that thought come from?* He shook his head and continued on. "I made a name for myself my sophomore year of high school. I was growing like a weed, spending a ton of time in the weight room, and could catch anything. I played cornerback too because our high school was so small we had to double up and play both sides of the ball. Offense or defense, didn't matter—I was catching it all."

She interrupted to ask, "Why didn't you want to play quarterback? It seems like you'd be the type."

He tried not to take that personally. Her ex who played quarterback sounded like a prick, and Beckett didn't want to be associated with the likes of him at all. "My best friend was QB. I loved knowing the routes and the plays, but I always enjoyed the fight in the air—jumping up and having a mini wrestling match for the ball. Sure, I knew how to throw the ball and what the plays were too, but I wanted to be the playmaker, not the one calling the shots. I wanted in that endzone, and I knew I'd do more of it as a receiver than as QB." He smiled. "Plus I got tackled way less that way."

She nodded and laughed. "Interesting. Sorry, go on."

"So colleges started showing interest when I was a junior. We made it to state but got beat out a few rounds in. I got named to some watch lists. And then, after my best high school game ever where I caught this ridiculous ball one-handed, I got the first call from the university. From that point on, it didn't matter to me who came calling. That was where I was going. I didn't care if I had to be a walk-on, though I really hoped for a scholarship. It didn't matter . . . . I was going to play for Nebraska."

He smiled as he remembered what it felt like to work your guts out for something that seemed so unattainable, but that you wanted more than anything. Then, one day, all those early summer-morning workouts finally paid off. He didn't just chase down his dream; he quite literally snagged his dream out of the sky and ran off with it. The highlight reel of his remarkable catch was played on all the local television channels the following weekend and got the attention of recruiters. The rest was history.

"My senior year of high school we won state, and it was . . . surreal. Just completely unbelievable. Then that spring, I committed to the university. It was pretty crazy. I wasn't the only one from Picketts that was going to play college ball; there were quite a few of us actually. We had a good team, and the scouts came watching. I was just the only one of us going to NU. The rest were going to other smaller in-state colleges."

He sighed. He loved talking about football, but the rest of the crap surrounding his reputation was stupid. "But from probably the summer of my junior year on, I became somewhat of a celebrity here. And I loved it at first. It really fed my seventeen-year-old ego. But then, somewhere along the way, it became a bit much. And I didn't realize it until it was all over.

"Even while still in high school, girls would date me because I was *that* guy. The guy going to play for the Huskers. I learned very early on that relationships weren't going to go far with that sort of thing. Sure, I had one serious—I guess—type of relationship, but I just knew that it wasn't going to go that far. I had realistic expectations and so did she. We both wanted different things out of our lives, and we were good with it.

"So then I got to college. I didn't even party much or date at all my freshman year. I was back to being the underclassman and had to work my ass off to snag a starting position. Which I did—halfway through my sophomore year. My dad had never been prouder of me. We had never gotten along better. The distance was good for us too."

He paused, gathering his thoughts. It'd been years, but his feelings were still so jumbled about this. "But then he passed away that winter, a few weeks after the bowl game. When I got that call, it scared the hell out of me. If he could die out of the blue like that, none of us were safe. Granted, he shouldn't have been drinking before he drove himself home that night, but at least it was just a telephone pole that took him out—and not another car he ran into." He stopped to take a deep breath. "My mom and sister really struggled. He was always a bit more loving towards them, so they took it harder—felt like they should have done more to stop his drinking habits. I knew there was nothing we could have done. He was an alcoholic, an addict. He had zero interest in changing his ways no matter how hard any of us tried. Since he had no desire to fight it off, his disease eventually killed him."

She moved to rest the hand that was across her leg onto his shoulder as he continued on. "So that summer, in the off-season, I started partying. Which in retrospect was the stupidest thing I could have done. I lost my dad to his alcohol addiction, so what did I do? I started partying myself. I think I was trying to prove to myself that alcohol held no power over me. I wanted to prove that I was better than he was. I wanted to prove that I could drink to be social and not get carried away, that I wouldn't turn into a monster.

"So party it was. And along with the parties came the girls. I should point out here that I was blatant in telling every single one of them I didn't want a serious relationship. I just didn't have the time for it. I couldn't give a girl one hundred percent of my time and effort because I was reserving it all for football, every spare second. I wanted zero distractions, and being a collegiate athlete, my schedule was already full."

He paused to look her in the eyes to show he was telling the truth, though the truth made him look like a gigantic jerkwad. "I just wanted fun. And sadly, partly because this state worships football and partly because it was college, I had girls lining up every night. I never even drank that much, but I always went to the parties. A few times I got a little too drunk, but after the first time that happened, I made sure I never let it happen again and dialed it back. I was not going to get blackout drunk like my dad. Ever.

"It was weird, but the girls kind of made me feel good about myself too, so I went along with it . . . ." He gave her an embarrassed shrug. "When my mom was diagnosed with cancer during my senior year, I clung to it. The parties and the girls were the only thing that allowed me to feel free. Football too, but there was a lot of pressure there. A lot of practices. My whole life revolved around football and the pressure to go pro. Everyone knew I would end up going pro, but would I be successful? Which team would want me? I was drowning in stress, and sadly, that's what I used."

He sighed, turning his attention to the fire. "But I guess I didn't officially get pegged Heartbreak Harper to the extent as you know it until after Mom died. I ended up getting drafted, and I think during the draft was the first time the media called me that, but it didn't stick. Some announcer made some comment about me looking like a real heartbreaker, and the nickname was born.

"Being drafted to the pros was weird too, even more so being a top-five pick and being followed around with cameras. I remember at the Scouting Combine being afraid to even pick my nose because there were cameras all up in my business. And here in Nebraska? A hometown Nebraska boy that played for the university and went pro? The state loved me. I was their boy. I couldn't even go to the grocery store without signing autographs or getting questioned. Two others from NU drafted that year too. We always compared the number of women that would proposition us on social media. Personal messages of offer after offer."

He didn't want to look at her and find what he was sure would be disgust all over her face, so he maintained looking toward the fire. "So I ended up going to Denver. Lucky for me it was as close to home as I could get, and I was relatively close to my mom should she need me. It took about two games into my rookie season, and I had to work my butt off, but I got a starting position. I had done it. It was a crazy time in my life. I was always at the gym, at practice, watching film, or on the phone with Mom and my sister and the doctors. I didn't even have time for parties or women. And I was good too. 'Rookie of the year' was being thrown around in association with my name. They called me Heartbreak Harper every once in a while because I broke down even the best defense's secondary. It had nothing to do with women. Denver was on the rise that year and had just spruced up their offense with drafting a young QB and some young legs — me — for him to throw it to. After we got in sync with one another, we had a good thing going."

He stopped for a moment, and the fire crackled as if right on cue. He wanted to hurry up and get through this last bit. "I finished my first year and turned the 'Rookie of the Year' hype into a reality. Then the next year began and things were getting out of control. I had never played better, was at the top of my game, Denver was looking good and favorited to win the Super Bowl, but Mom was getting weaker. And then one game early

November I was in the endzone, going up for a ball, got tangled up with a guy, blew out my knee, and messed up my back on the way down. It was bad enough that by the time the cart made it onto the field, we all knew my career in the pros was done. Not willing to admit my football days were finished, I went back home to be with my mom. When I got there, and actually saw her with my own two eyes for the first time in a month or more, I saw how fast she was deteriorating. It wasn't going to be long."

"Cancer freaking sucks," Jordyn said softly, repeating his words from earlier and swallowing hard.

He stopped to gather his thoughts again, and she squeezed the shoulder her hand was still resting on. He moved his other hand across his body to his shoulder, placing his hand over hers. "But I honestly feel grateful for those few months. Had I played that whole season, I would've missed time with her—time she was desperately running out of. I don't resent that at all; I just wish that my injuries could have been ones I would've bounced back from. The knee was one thing. The back another. The two combined were just too much. Back injuries in the NFL are known to be dream killers. And to add insult to injury, Denver got beat in the second round of playoffs that year. When they needed me the most, I just couldn't be there for them."

He paused to take a deep breath. "So after Mom died and my little sister went to college, I went back to Denver."

"Are you still close with your sister?" she interrupted.

He nodded.

She added, "I didn't even know you had a sister."

He felt a smile creep across his face. "I like to keep it that way and so does she. She was also somewhat of a celebrity herself for being the sister of Beckett Harper. She graduates this spring from PT school. She was worried about the storm causing her to miss her clinicals and having extra time to study for finals—otherwise she'd have been here for Thanksgiving." He moved his thumb back and forth across the skin of her hand, half expecting her to jerk it away.

She didn't.

She simply nodded while he continued on. "So I still had my house in Denver. I wasn't officially cut from the team until after my surgery. And that's when the dating around, if that's what you call it, got out of control. My whole life was out of control, and here I had random strangers, models, actresses all interested in me—or interested in being seen with me on social media. Some were friends of the girls my teammates were dating; others were people that randomly sought me out. It was bizarre, but it was the only thing in my life that I could cling to. Dating around became my new game after I lost the game of football. Sadly. I still mattered to those women—all of those women. And I felt like I needed to matter."

He paused this time to shake his head, giving her hand a squeeze. "I'm not proud of it. Though I didn't have sex with every single one, I did honestly sleep around a lot. And there were some girls that, though I was completely honest with them, thought they'd tame me or make me settle down or something. Then, when I wasn't different, they were upset, going to whatever news station would take their story. So that definitely didn't help matters. And it was about the time that started happening that I was so fed up and sick of it all. It was flattering at first, but after so long, it was just . . . unfulfilling.

"Then there was one girl, a city woman, a model . . . all about her status and her beauty. I actually broke my no-more-than-once rule and went on a few dates with her—thought I'd give the whole dating thing a go. We were getting along great, and everything seemed fine until this big charity event came up. I asked her if she needed me to go with her, and she point-blank told me I was a nobody now, that my career was over, and that I would never be able to provide for her long term. She had a different high-profile date lined up for that event and had just chose not to tell me about it until the last minute. It was such a waste of time, and she ended up being nothing like I thought she was.

"Finally, I saw the truth behind the type of woman I'd been attracting. Woman after woman after woman—they were all chasing my status, fame, or money. I was sick of it. To say it was surface level is the understatement of the decade. I sold my home in Denver, moved back here, and never looked back."

Just as she was about to say something, he butted back in. "Do not get me wrong. I am not the victim here. Not even a little bit. No one forced me to date around like that. That's all on me. But at the end of it, I was left jaded and empty. It got me nowhere. It left me cynical towards women, feeling the weight of a thousand pounds of regret."

He sighed and again looked at the fire to avoid looking at her. "But this place. My grandfather's farm . . . it got me back on my feet. It reminded me there was more to life than football or meaningless hookups. And I've always been more comfortable around animals than people anyway." He played with the skin of her hand again, not wanting to look at her, and not wanting her to pull away.

"Why don't you have a dog?" she asked softly.

He snapped his head to the side to look at her in surprise. After all that . . . *that* was her question? "I did. He died about six months back. A yellow lab I had with me everywhere I went. He was twelve."

"Oh." She frowned.

He smirked, looking her in the eyes and shaking his head.

"What?" she asked, searching his face.

"I just bared my soul to you, and your number one question was why I don't have a dog?" He shook his head again. This woman was something else. Other women would have a ton of other questions.

"Well, I have one more question too, if that's okay," she offered They were still sitting close, his hand covering hers, and her palm warming his shoulder.

"Shoot, Houston." He smiled.

She hesitated like she didn't want to ask it but went for it anyway. "On the play when you blew out your knee and hurt your back, did you make the catch?"

This time his grin was immediate. She was definitely unlike any woman he had ever met. She was a glass of sweet iced tea in a long line of lemonades. "You're damn right I did, honey."

Honey.

He'd called her that before, but it had been used in sarcasm and made her nerves grind. The way he said it this time . . . oh wow. Honey indeed. Honey to her ears. Honey to her insides. *Honaaay.*

Why was he telling her all this anyway? They both knew she was only here until the storm let up. She'd report to Walt it was a lost cause, and then she'd be on her way. It felt nice to know the real story behind the reputation he held though.

And again, she felt a bit wary. She had fallen for the charming football player before. She had believed he was different. She hadn't listened to the rumors. And where did that get her last time?

Heartbrokenville, USA. That's where.

But, Beckett and Thomas were two completely different people. They were nothing alike. Not that she was going to fall madly in love or anything. She just didn't want to punish Beckett for the way things turned out with Thomas.

They ended up staying up talking. Just talking. She told him about what the rest of high school was like, and he told her some stories from college. They just got to know one another and bantered back and forth like what was becoming normal. He didn't try to kiss her again, and she was relieved. Not that she didn't want to—she just wasn't going to be another one of his conquests.

She didn't even remember falling asleep, or if he had been talking or she had, but she did briefly wake back up when he placed a kiss on her forehead and said, "I would've never done that to you. He's an idiot."

Afraid to move, she swallowed down her emotions and kept her eyes shut. She wasn't sure what was going on between them, but it was safe to say there was something there. And she was pretty sure he knew she wasn't going to be okay with any sort of short fling.

And then in the morning, much to her surprise, she woke up warm. It took her a minute to assess why. She wondered if the power was back on—but then felt the arm on her waist move.

Oh no. She fell asleep on him?! Talk about sending mixed signals! When did that happen? How did that happen? And what did that mean? This was like the one day ever he wasn't doing chores already.

What did *that* mean?

****

She'd fallen asleep on him and he didn't want to move, so he hadn't. By morning she was curled into him with her head on his shoulder, facing toward the fire. He was behind her with his arm around her. They were spooning. Appropriately spooning, but totally spooning. And when she realized it, she panicked. He could see it written all over her pretty face and feel it in the way she immediately tensed up.

He loved when she got unnerved, and this was definitely one of those times. Before she got mad or freaked out too much and tried to leave, he kissed her on her temple. "Don't."

"Don't what?" she asked, looking like she was ready to sprint to the guest room and slam the door.

"Don't overthink it," he said.

She sat up and looked at him but didn't move away from him. "I don't know how to not overthink it."

He laughed at that. At least she was honest. "That's valid."

Her level of panic seemed to increase before his eyes, and suddenly she blurted out, "Beckett, I'm not going to be another one of your one-night stands."

He grabbed her hand and squeezed it. "I never asked you to be, Jordyn. And I would never ask you to be."

"I'm just not that type of woman," she said firmly, like she was trying to make sure he knew that. Hell, she didn't have to say a thing and he heard her loud and clear.

"Jordyn, I am well aware you aren't the type to sleep around, and I'm still interested. So how about we just see where things go instead of overthinking? Instead, how about you make us some breakfast while I do the chores, and then we can make a good ol'-fashioned Thanksgiving feast together."

She looked pleased with that idea. "You have a turkey thawed?"

"Sure do. Fridge in the garage."

Then her brow furrowed. "You don't have anyone else you'd be having Thanksgiving with?"

He shook his head. "The little ol' lady that runs the café in town would have had to-go dinners or dinner for whoever wanted to come. She's my great aunt. So I could have gone there, but it's not like I can now. Took the turkey out when I first heard the forecast. You can't be without a bird on Thanksgiving."

She nodded. "Fair point."

"I'll even fire up the generator, and we can watch some football . . . or whatever you'd like."

She grinned, like she knew some big secret. "Football is fine."

He was a little surprised. Most women jumped at the chance to avoid sports on television. "But you don't like football, honey."

She laughed and gave him a playful look. "No, I never said I didn't like the game of football. I said I didn't like football *players.*"

And while he was picking his jaw up off the floor, she was on her way to the kitchen to make breakfast. *This woman . . .*

****

It was almost two in the afternoon by the time they had finished creating their feast. It seemed absolutely ridiculous and a bit wasteful to have so much food for two people, but what was Thanksgiving for? They had turkey, mashed potatoes with gravy, a corn casserole, as well as the homemade dinner rolls and pumpkin pie she'd made to round it all out. He had even had a tub of whipped topping in the freezer. *What could get better than an impromptu lavish Thanksgiving feast?*

She put that double oven through the ringer too. It didn't disappoint.

Then there was the issue of what she woke up to this morning and was trying her hardest to forget. Yes, she had flipped out, and he had known it. He seemed oddly chill about the whole thing. But wasn't that what he did? Not putting a name to a relationship? He said he knew she wasn't the sleeping-around type of woman and that he was still interested in her. What did that even mean? Did *he* even know what that meant? She highly doubted it. They were both swimming in uncharted waters here.

Maybe he just thought she was going to be fun to be with while they were snowed in and then they would be over as soon as the snow stopped and she left? Like one super long date? That would be the most logical explanation for this turn of events. Wasn't it just a day ago he was still mad at her? How did they even get to this point anyway?

And speaking of the snow, the wind had finally stopped, but the snow had picked up again. Unlike before, when it was a violent fury of cold, ice, and wind, this time it was a more peaceful snow. The weather report on the local channel had told them they were to get a maximum of four more inches, and then the storm would finally be done.

She wasn't sure how she felt about that. That meant she was leaving soon. Which was what she had wanted . . . right?

Now that she was finally sitting down, she was struggling to even enjoy her pie, which was a flipping tragedy in and of itself. While they were cooking, it was fun and lighthearted. She felt she didn't need to name what was going on between them; she could just let whatever happened happen. But with his past, and hers, she just couldn't let him think she was interested in anything casual. She didn't do casual. Actually, she didn't do much dating. Sure, here and there a little. One steady boyfriend in college. But that was about it.

"What's on your mind, Houston?" he asked, never missing a thing. Her nickname had stuck, and though it was annoying at times, it just made her appreciate when he did actually say her real name.

She was pretty sure her honest answer would ruin their pie in five minutes or less.

****

She was on her second piece of pie. He didn't know why he found that so endearing, but he did. He guessed it was because a lot of the women he had dated spent every second calorie counting or caring about their looks. Not that Jordyn was lacking at all in that department. Sure, he supposed he had dated prettier girls or skinnier girls. But Jordyn's beauty was a different kind. It was less of an overpowering beauty and more of a subtle, calming one. And those curves were in all the right places too. He'd have to have been blind not to notice. She didn't need to dress her beauty up and throw it in his face either. It was just there. Without being loud about it.

And with those thoughts, he was just sure he was turning into a sap.

But he knew she was still bothered by this morning. She had no idea what was going on and probably didn't know what do with her feelings. Hell, he had no idea what was going on either, but that didn't mean she needed to get all bent out of shape about it. If there was anything football had taught him, it was that you couldn't control it all. The only thing you could control was the next play and what you did with it. So that's what he planned on doing.

"Honestly, I was thinking about my ex-boyfriends," she said, her voice wavering.

He almost choked on his pie. His eyebrows rose in surprise, and he tried to rein in the weird feeling in the pit of his stomach. Irrational anger? Jealousy? *Nah. Couldn't be.* "Were there a lot of them?"

She laughed. "Gosh no. Definitely not."

He couldn't help but ask the next thought on his mind. "Any recent ones?"

She shook her head no. "Maybe a year ago? I had a Valentine's date with a friend of a friend. She knew he was my type, but we didn't really hit it off."

She had a type? "And what exactly is your type?"

"Not you," she said quietly and honestly. She looked to him, and he saw her vulnerability swimming in her eyes. She was trying not to let it drown her. He knew she had feelings for him, and she was constantly trying to categorize them and figure them out, which was very much her analytical way.

"What is this?" she finally asked as she pointed to him and then back to her, not surprising him at all.

He couldn't help but smirk. "I believe they call it dating. Ours is just a little untraditional since you're living with me, compliments of the blizzard. But I mean, it has been a while though, so maybe I'm not the expert here."

She snorted. "But you don't date."

He grinned that cocky grin he knew he had. And it worked for him. Usually. Well, 90 percent of the time. The other 10 percent ended in slaps, mostly from his sister. He guessed he'd try his luck. "I do now."

She rolled her eyes.

Dang it. Not impressed with the dimpler. Yes, he had a nickname for his own single dimple. He had named it in high school and was proud of that thing. That served a reminder that he was an egotistical man after all. Good. He had thought he was going full sissy there for a minute.

"When this snowstorm is over, I'm leaving. You know it and I know it. It's not like I live here so we can see each other all the time," she explained, not looking up as she moved the whipped cream around her plate with her fork. "So it seems unlikely that someone who doesn't really date would want to jump right into a long-distance relationship."

That type of talk needed to stop right this damned minute. "Jordyn."

"*Beckett,*" she hissed as she forcefully stabbed another bite of her pie. Though she was upset, her southern drawl, ever so slight as it was, flared up when she was mad. And he vowed to tick her off at least a dozen more times just so he could hear her say his first name with that drawl. He didn't want her mad at him, but it was such a turn-on.

He stood and walked over to her. He scooted her chair out so they could face one another, placed his hands on both arms of the chair, and then crouched down so they were eye level. "I said no overthinking. I don't typically date, but I want to date you. I'm not an idiot and I know you where you live, honey. We will take it one day at a time, okay? I'm interested in you. Are you going to try to tell me you aren't interested in me?"

"No."

He looked at her with one eyebrow raised in confusion to clarify what the "no" meant.

"No, I am not going to tell you I am not interested in you," she said, then added at a whisper, "I don't want to be, yet here I am."

He was smiling. This was going just fine. If only the snow could keep coming for a couple of weeks, this could get mighty freaking interesting. "Also. There's just one more thing."

She looked at him, green eyes skeptical. "What's that?"

He leaned in super close and whispered, "You have a little whipped cream on your face." And then, before she could even react, he kissed the corner of her mouth where it was. A peck, not even on her mouth, just the corner of her mouth. He didn't trust himself to not kiss the hell out of her, so just a little something to show her he cared would do.

She was grinning like he imagined he was too. "Real smooth, Harper. Way to use that to your advantage."

He laughed. "You will find I am quite the resourceful man."

She shook her head with an eye-roll, then mocked his words from their first meeting: *"Indeed."*

****

Seriously. One kiss on the side of her mouth and she was ready to say goodbye to her vow to never date football players ever again. That was all it took. She was weak. She needed chocolate. And a hormone suppressant. But how could you be in the presence of this man and not fall for him just a little?

Make that a double shot of chocolate.

This was a man who had lost everything, *everything,* that mattered to him, in a year's time but had dusted himself off and made something of himself. This was a man she found bloodied in a barn because he couldn't bear the thought of one of his heifers getting an infection or being hurt out in the cold. He was smooth, he was confident and cocky, and then at the same time he was down to earth, gentle, and simple. Simple in his morals anyway. Definitely not simple in the looks department.

She usually didn't like men with facial hair, but Beckett's stubble was really starting to grow on her. Everything about him was. And she had a feeling that the super serious conversation they had last night about his football career and how he got his nickname was a conversation he didn't have often.

So there was that. That had to count for something, right?

They had made everything in disposable casserole dishes that Beckett kept a stock of, so the dishes didn't take too long. He grabbed a beer and she made an iced tea, and they got settled in the living room for some football. There were mostly pro games on, but they didn't mind. It felt nice to be back with the living and live television. And the ability of charging their electronics.

She noticed he purposefully sat close to her on the couch. That first night they slept in here, it was like the middle of the couch was their dividing line. And now it was like this couch was so small they needed to crowd. Funny how things turn around in just a few days.

And she tried to rein in her cheering — she really did. But with her favorite pro team playing, she knew that Beckett was quickly going to learn that she actually did like football quite a bit.

****

"Come onnn." Jordyn gripped the side of her tea glass harder and leaned in.

He rubbed his fingers across his dry lips to hide his grin. "So Houston is your team, huh?"

She rolled her eyes. "As you so often like to remind me with my nickname, I do live there."

"Who's your favorite player?"

She named the number and first and last name for him without hesitating.

"And this coming from someone who hates football."

"Again, I hate football players, not football itself. Also, mostly because of Thomas, I like to think of myself as more of a defensive fan than an offensive one," she explained without looking at him, zeroed in on the game. "Defense wins games."

"You don't say." He had never been more entertained by a football game. And he wasn't even watching the game; he was watching her. Never in a million years did he think she would be the type of woman to love football. She couldn't sit still she was so into it.

"Why do you even watch football?" he asked. "How did this love of football come about? When you got to Houston?"

She shook her head. "Sam and Andrea were big sports fans. I started watching with them and became a fan before I even dated Thomas. Not that I ever admitted to Thomas that I knew anything about the game."

Interesting.

"Come *onnn*!" she said a little louder.

He couldn't stop grinning. The only thing better than what he was witnessing would have been if she was cheering for him. That thought was a little more than he could handle.

"What?" she said and looked to him for the first time in a while.

"You're just so animated right now," he admitted. "And much more attractive than who I normally watch the games with."

"I take it you are talking about your friends and not insulting Mable?" she joked.

He nodded, put his hand to his heart dramatically, and whispered, "I would never insult her." He looked to where the cat was curled into a ball on the old rocking chair beside the fire, her favorite spot to be in the winter.

"Oh my word!" Jordyn exclaimed, almost jumping to her feet.

It was a close game—he'd give her that. Her team was playing very well against a much better team. But every time Houston was on offense, she got angry.

"What's the problem?" he asked.

At that point she stood up in frustration again. It was cute how she was trying to be calm, but just couldn't help herself. "The problem? The problem is this play calling. I mean, come on!"

Play calling? She was mad about the play calling? "You don't like run plays?"

She shook her head strongly and glanced at him before looking back to the TV. "No. I like them just fine. I just don't like them on second and long. I mean, come on. Get the ball down the field!"

Holy crap. Did she really know her stuff? He couldn't count the number of women who spouted off that they were big fans because they wanted to get into his good graces but then really knew nothing about the sport. His personal favorite was the model who asked him why they didn't "kick some points" to tie up the game. It was called a field goal for God's sake.

"So what would you have run, then?" he asked, secretly testing her.

She watched the end of the play intensely before responding with a shrug. "I don't know. A slant route to the running back would be a better option—or maybe a pass play to their star receiver off on the right side because their corner on that side gets burned every single time."

Holy crap. She had him at *slant route*.

It was official. He was going to marry this girl.

CHAPTER 10

Jordyn woke up and realized she was on the couch again. And just like last night, the first thing she saw was Mable curled up in front of the fireplace on the rocking chair. Jordyn only woke because her face felt warm . . . more like on fire. And now she knew why; her cheek was located on a very large pectoral muscle belonging to Beckett.

They had stayed up watching football and talking again. And though they had stayed up later than usual and were closer than usual, she didn't remember being quite so cozy with him before she had fallen asleep. She was literally in his arms on the couch, using his upper body as her own personal pillow . . . the best kind of pillow. She had her arm thrown across some abdominal muscles that felt pretty in shape for him not playing anymore. And she wasn't mad about it. No, sirree.

"Good morning," he offered with a sleepy smile.

She had never seen him like this, and she had to admit she liked it. She wanted to be mad about last night. There was no valid reason they needed to sleep on the couch. She could have slept in the guest bedroom. But for whatever reason, with whatever was going on with the two of them, she didn't regret it. Getting to know Beckett was a surprise she was not expecting. It wasn't something she thought she'd ever regret.

"Good morning." She sat up with a slight smile, trying not to blush. "Think today is the day the snow stops?"

"I freaking hope not," he huffed, weirdly serious. "I would actually prefer for the power to go back out if we get to cozy up like this every night."

She grinned. "Greedy."

He sat up and kissed her on the temple. "With you I am."

Her breath caught in her chest. How was she ever going to leave, go back to Houston, and act like this man didn't exist? She had known him a terrifyingly short amount of time for as terrifyingly strong as she was starting to feel toward him. She was supposed to hate football players, have her guard up. What was wrong with her? Had the cold done something to her brain cells? She was usually more levelheaded than this.

"Hey." He interrupted her thinking by brushing his thumb across the crease she was sure lined her forehead. "Stop overthinking, remember?"

"Trying here. I'm trying," she insisted.

He smirked. "With you I have a feeling that's like asking a fish not to swim."

She nodded exaggeratedly. *"Exactly."*

"Well, my little overthinking beauty, what do you say after chores we decorate the Christmas tree?" he asked.

"You? You decorate for Christmas?" She was *not* expecting that. She was really not expecting him to offer that.

He nodded. "Every Friday after Thanksgiving. Black Friday shopping? No thanks. I put up my tree, and if I feel extra frisky, maybe the outdoor lights too."

"Wow."

"Wow, what?" he asked.

"There's just so much about you that surprises me," she said honestly as she folded one of the blankets they slept in and put it over the back of the couch.

He was almost to the kitchen, going to get ready for chores, but he turned back around and lazily leaned against the doorframe. "Right back at you, Jordyn. Right back at you."

They just looked at each other for a long moment, probably both wondering what the heck they were doing. Probably both wondering how they ever got to this point. Probably both not wanting to consider that her time here was almost done. This, whatever *this* was, was on a timer that would eventually go off.

****

"What, no axe?"

He tried not to roll his eyes at her as he heaved the large tree bag into the living room after manhandling it up the stairs from the basement. They had cleared the rocking-chair area where Mable usually slept and were ready for the tree. The power was back on, more than likely for good, so they didn't need to rely on the fire as much as they had. But knowing how much she hated being cold, he still always made sure to have one going for her.

"Seriously. You've got the rest of the lumberjack look going for ya," she teased.

He felt his eyebrows go up and tried not to smile with her. "Which is what exactly?"

"You know . . . . Muscles? Flannel shirts? Facial hair? Can chop wood or take down a tree? Easy on the eyes but hard on the hormones?" she asked with a blush.

"I suppose so, then," he said with an amused eye-roll. "But, lumberjack or not, I do not cut down any of my trees for my Christmas tree. I need that tree belt on the north side of the farm as a shelter for storms like these, so unless it's a small one that isn't going to survive anyway, I try to leave those trees to grow as big and healthy as they please."

"Huh," she said thoughtfully. "Makes sense. A little hippie but makes sense."

He snorted at that.

The banter continued as they got the tree standing. It only needed to be put together in three parts, and he didn't even need a ladder for the nine-foot tree because his six-foot-four frame could reach it. Even the star he carefully placed on top.

They plugged in the lights, added a few extra strands, and got to work on the decorating. She hooked and handed him the balls and other ornaments, and he placed them around the top since he could reach it — and she clearly could not. He made sure to accidentally brush her hand as many times as possible, just wanting to be near her. And he thought it was cute as hell the way she handed the ornaments to him in a pattern, to be sure that the red balls weren't all in one place.

While they worked, she asked about the farm, and he asked her about her job and why she liked working for AgGroSo. She explained to him the parts she liked, mainly working for Walt and access to steady income, something her mother never had. It was an easy conversation, but a tough one when it kept reminding him that she was going to have to leave eventually.

"So if they are doing so well and have doubled in size already, why do they think they have to have me for the stupid commercial anyway?" he asked. "I'll give it to Walt — he's relentless. But I thought the company was doing just fine on their own?"

"They are." She nodded aggressively. "It was marketing's idea from the moment they found out you were a customer, and they can't seem to let it go. We spent a pretty penny on our time slot, and we need for that commercial to be as powerful as possible. Having a big name — having a household football name attached to our brand during the biggest football game of the year — would make our commercial more efficient." She stopped to sigh. "And it's not like we're just paying you to be the face of the company like actors and actresses do all the time with zero interest in using the actual products. You do actually use our stuff. It's more authentic that way."

He nodded, understanding now why they wanted him specifically. He was probably their only famous customer. Not many retired athletes became farmers. "Makes sense."

She smiled tentatively. "Why? Having second thoughts, Harper?"

He fired right back, "Are you working right now or just asking as a friend, Houston?"

She shrugged innocently. "Yes? To both?"

He laughed and elbowed her softly. "I still really don't want to be in the commercial. If you got to stick around for longer, it doesn't seem so bad though. I just don't want my face plastered on anything, if that makes sense. Some guys totally overdo it with the endorsements. The sports drinks, shoe deals, cereal boxes even . . . it just seems so . . . *fake.* I don't like the concept of using my face to sell a product. Not just because I'm retired and washed up, or even because of the stupid nickname . . . I just never did."

She turned to him with her eyes bright, with an idea so good it looked like it was ready to jump out of her short frame. She reached for his forearm, but when she did, she dropped the sparkly gold ball in her hand.

She went to catch it before it shattered all over the hardwood floor, but he beat her to it. And he caught it before it broke, of course.

Ha. He still had it after all these years.

"Nice catch," she said breathlessly, now in his arms and way too close to not do something about it.

He had caught the ball and managed to get her into his arms. A damn nice catch. As he leaned in for the kill, he whispered, "Don't look now but there's mistletoe."

"No there's not," she whispered playfully but didn't panic. She didn't pull away this time. She let him pull her in until their lips crashed into one another.

****

One kiss. How could one kiss be so . . . *good?* Granted, she was nervous, but she had been kissed before, so it's not like it was that big of a deal. And she had had plenty of first kisses . . . . Well, okay, maybe just six or seven if she was being honest. Some were short and sweet. Some were slobbery and disastrous. But *that* kiss. That kiss single-handedly proved to her why he was called Heartbreak Harper. One of those kisses and she was just sure she would like to do nothing more than repeat the experience. Over and over and over again.

She was pretty sure he had enjoyed it too. At one point he chucked the ball — the one he had freakishly caught in his hands — onto the couch, so both of his hands were free to wrap around her and bring her in closer.

By the end of it, he mumbled something about being a gentleman and removed his hand from her hair and the other from around her body and took a huge step back. She had to physically pry her fingers off his T-shirt.

Both taking heavy breaths, now a few feet apart, she busted out laughing.

"This is funny? *That* made you feel like laughing? I feel many, many things right now, but laughing is not one of them."

She laughed even harder at the look on his face. "No. It's just . . . I mean . . ." She paused, the laughter consuming her. "Okay, first it was the whipped cream that may or may not have been there, now fake mistletoe." She was laughing so hard again she had to stop to breathe. "You are, in fact, the most resourceful man I have ever met."

He walked back over to the couch to pick up the ball he had thrown and gave her a cocky smile. "Damn right, sweetheart."

She got back to work on the tree, though neither of them seemed as into the decorating as before the kissing. They were both distracted. By each other.

"And what were you going to say anyway, before you attacked me like a teenager? It looked important." He grinned as he took another ornament from her.

"Oh, so *I* am the teenager here?"

He nodded dramatically.

She rolled her eyes and thought a moment. "Oh . . . *OHH!*"

He cocked his head to the side, waiting for her explanation.

She tried not to be overly excited, but she couldn't stop from blabbing out, "What if AgGroSo didn't have to use your face? What if we just used your farm and your name? You said you didn't want your face plastered on anything . . . . What if we used your farm—and maybe your voice—but not you, yourself? What if there wasn't even a single shot with you in the picture—just your voice reading over the information and shots of beautiful outdoor scenery taken here? As a way to honor the American farmer?"

He thought on that a moment and put another ornament on the tree. "I think it's pretty here and all, but do you really think it's beautiful enough for a commercial?"

She looked at him seriously. "Yes. Beckett, definitely. This place is amazing. And I'm not saying that as someone who is into you. I'm not saying that as an AgGroSo employee that wants you to do the commercial. I'm saying that as your everyday, average American. This place is *gorgeous.*"

"Nothing about you is average," he responded and seared her with his blue eyes.

She smiled and felt the blush in her cheeks. "You know what I meant."

He smiled slowly and thought about it for a moment. He turned and walked over to the windows in the living room and looked out, as if thinking about this version of a commercial. She stayed quiet and let him think for a few minutes, until she couldn't take the silence any more.

"Beckett . . . it could be a way for you to do something as Beckett Harper, not Heartbreak Harper," she offered. "It would get your name out there in a good way. I know you don't like the spotlight or the celebrity of who you are, but this could be good. Yes, you would help out AgGroSo, but you would also show all of America the power and beauty of the heartbeat of our country. You would show them why agriculture matters."

He turned back around, looking a little sad, and she thought for sure he was going to say no.

"Just think about it?" she asked.

He sighed his agreement. "I'm assuming this will need to be done right away? The Super Bowl isn't until February, but I assume the commercial would need to be shot shortly?"

She nodded. "I was Walt's last-ditch effort to try to get you to do it. Otherwise, their plan B was going to be shot the week after next."

If only Beckett would go for the idea . . .

****

He had to admit this sounded much better than the original offer. He cocked his head to the side, a plan forming. "So a week? That's really going to put me in a bind. I'm behind on other things with this storm showing up, and now, if I were to have this on my plate too . . . *hmm*."

"Walt would hire someone to help you get it all done as long as you agree—I'm sure of it," she assured him. "Don't worry about it. We wouldn't expect you to throw away your responsibilities here."

"In that case, I need *you*." He smiled, his plan sounding better and better the more he thought about it.

"What?" she asked, her confident look faltering.

"I'm going to need *your* help this next week if I am going to be doing the commercial the following week. You just told me not even an hour ago that a lot of what you have to do on a daily basis can be done from your computer. Stay here. Then stay here for the commercial. The only way I'll agree to it is if you are in charge." As soon as he said it, he knew it was true. And not just because she was pretty. It had everything to do with trust. "You're the only one I trust to make it like you described and less like an endorsement with my face plastered on everything."

She smiled and looked a little like she was on the verge of tears or something. "You know I won't be much help around the farm to you."

He shook his head. "I disagree. You helped with my heifer just fine. You can help with the meals, and you can help me do a little picking up around the farm so everything is all cleaned up for the commercial. I'll let you help as much as you want."

She swallowed hard and stepped closer to him. "Tell me you aren't just agreeing to this to keep me here longer. Tell me you actually want to do this, and this doesn't have to do with whatever is going on between us."

He stepped forward until he was right in front of her and took her face in his hands, refusing to lie to her. "I can't tell you those things. I will tell you that I am interested in doing the commercial if it will be how you described. And as for this thing between us, I'd do pretty much anything to keep you around a little longer."

She sighed. "Beckett. That's what I was afraid of. Don't do this for me. Do it for you."

He grinned in that cocky sort of way, his dimpler springing to action to aid him in his cause. "Oh, I'm doing it. For the both of us. It gets me an extra paycheck, and it gets us more time to figure this out. It's a win-win."

She smiled but still looked like she was battling tears. "You do know that eventually I am going to have to go back to Houston, right?"

He nodded. "And we will figure it out, okay? I'm just buying us a little more time."

She nodded with him and said softly, "Okay."

Did she believe him? Probably not, but he'd show her he meant it. He was a man of his word.

He kissed her just once, soft and slow. "Now let's finish this tree, and then later you can talk to your boss and get us a timeframe and game plan for what we need to do next week."

"Deal," she said with a smile.

CHAPTER 11

That one gentle kiss may have done her in more than the first one. The first one proved they had chemistry. The second one promised he cared. Both had their pulls, but the second one about took her knees out from under her.

What were they doing? What was *she* doing?! She was falling for this man. After another week with him, she was just sure she would be completely head over heels. And that was only going to make her departure for Houston even harder.

Still though. She had another week, maybe two, depending on how long the commercial took. She could spend it moping around or she could spend it getting to know Beckett better. She had to make sure this felt as real to him as it did to her. And maybe, just maybe, after another week of her baking and cooking, she'd make it that much harder for him to forget about her. *Ha.*

After they finished the tree, his alma mater was playing their designated Black Friday rival college football game, so they cozied up and watched that. It was fun to listen to Becket explain his former school, including its rich traditions. He even showed her how to properly wave her hands in the air back and forth after a touchdown, Husker style.

Unfortunately, his team ended up losing because they were in some rebuilding years after hiring a new coach — but the loss allowed her to see how truly fired up Beckett could get over the game. As she watched his intense gaze on the screen, the tightness of his jaw, she *knew* how much he still loved football — how loyal he was to this very day. His input on how they should use the talent they had instead of straining to reach talent levels not yet achieved was spot-on. And his ideas about which plays they should be running were brilliant.

She couldn't fathom how he could just give it all up cold turkey. He could have been an analyst. He could have gotten into coaching. Instead, he came back here to live a quiet life. He loved the game but loved it from afar. Maybe someday he'd go back to it. Maybe not.

The fact that he could give up his love for the sport and still be himself showed her that he cared more about this farm than he let on. His love for football and his love for the farm had always been fighting for which came first. And at this phase in his life, the farm was coming in first place. It had to because he couldn't play. And she supposed he probably didn't want to coach or be an analyst until the pain over not being able to play subsided.

Since the snow had stopped that afternoon during the game, Beckett had decided afterward to put the outdoor lights up. Just around the roof of his house. Nothing too extravagant. Which was good.

People in Jordyn's neighborhood went all out over Christmas décor, piling inflatables on one another and installing flashing lights that didn't match at all with the rest of the house. She loved Christmas decorations as much as the next girl — she really did — but she just believed there was such a thing as overdoing it. There was a place an hour from where she lived that had a huge display of Christmas lights. And you could take a horse drawn carriage through them. Last year she went with Sam and his three kids, two of whom had kids already. It was one of her favorite Christmas memories. She'd like to take Beckett there sometime.

But she needed to stop thoughts like those. That sounded like a date. And would she ever get to take him there? She wasn't exactly his girlfriend now, was she? He said they were dating, but there was a difference between having a girlfriend and casual dating. One promised commitment while the other just promised the opportunity for another date.

This was definitely not your normal relationship. Would they even see each other once she left? He had said they'd figure it out, but what exactly did that mean? They'd figure out how to be without one another, *orrr* they'd figure out how to still see one another?

Setting those thoughts aside, she decided to call Walt and let him know the good news. He answered immediately.

"You on your way back?" he asked after greeting her hello.

"Not exactly. I think I've figured out a way to get Beckett to do the commercial." She winced when she realized she had called him Beckett, but her news was so exciting to Walt that he either didn't notice or didn't care.

"Hot dang! Tell me more."

By the time she was done explaining her idea, Walt was practically bouncing with excitement on the other end of the line, his voice getting louder and louder the longer the conversation went. A few times she even had to hold the phone away from her face.

"Jordyn, you're a genius!" he hollered. "That sounds better than the theme marketing had decided on. I'll make sure they change gears, but I'm going to need you to lead this. It's your vision, and I want you to make sure they get it done right. I don't want to mess this up now that we finally have a fighting chance with Harper."

She sighed. "I know. Beckett insisted upon my being in charge too."

"You sure he's not just trying to get you to stick around longer?" Walt asked with a laugh.

"Actually, I'm quite sure that has a lot to do with it. He's demanded I stay through the filming, partly because he trusts me to be in charge and partly because he wants me around," she explained seriously. No sense in lying to her boss about what was going on when he was a huge part of the reason for it. This mess was *all* his fault.

It took a good long minute before she could say anything more over the robust sound of his laughing.

"Are you done laughing now?" she asked, trying not to smile.

Walt chuckled again. "Jordyn, I'm not laughing at you. I just—I should have known. You're a force of nature, girl. You get stuff done. The poor man never had a chance."

She rolled her eyes and sighed. "At first I didn't want him to do the commercial if I was part of the reason he was agreeing. But now I think his reputation could use us. He needs to do something as Beckett Harper and not Heartbreak Harper, you know?"

Walt was thoughtful a minute, back to being serious. "Interesting. But if he ends up breaking your heart, he and I will have words."

"Says the man that sent me here because he needed a cute face," Jordyn reminded him, annoyed.

"Fair point, Jordyn. Fair point. But I knew you were just the woman for the job. And look? You got it done. I'll make sure you get your raise and your extra vacation as promised. I'll have to speak with Harper and send him the contract soon."

She nodded, though he couldn't see her. "I figured as much."

"Good work, Jordyn. I swear there isn't a department in this company you couldn't lead. You aren't after my job, are you?"

She laughed at that. "No, and no thank you!"

Having gotten things in motion for next week while Beckett finished up the lights and the chores, she decided she had to live it up and do something she couldn't ever do in Texas—build a snowman!

****

He had finished the chores and headed inside as the sun was setting. It was early, around 5:00 p.m., and he couldn't wait to talk to Jordyn. She would have called work by now and officially bought them some more time together. He didn't know how much time; he just knew he had to keep her around longer. He was insane doing this commercial just to have more time with her, but her idea really was a good one. Honoring the American farmer was the only way he'd do it. Bonus points for it allowing Jordyn to stick around. And now that the decision was made, he felt good with it; it felt right.

He walked in the house, and for once a meal or some sort of goodie wasn't ready. The oven wasn't even on. Not that he cared at all, but it just wasn't like Jordyn to not be baking or cooking something. He wasn't sure which she liked more, him or his kitchen. Probably the kitchen, honestly.

The house was oddly quiet. He was starting to get concerned when he spotted some movement through the living room window. He squinted. It was Jordyn making a snowman in the yard.

Or trying to.

He chuckled. She was such a weird combination: a bookworm and kitchen dynamo, yet competitive and adventurous. She was predictable in some ways, but then totally unpredictable in others. He'd been putting women in categories all his life, and she was just not categorizable. She could have done anything she wanted while he was doing chores, and she chose to make a snowman.

And he loved it.

"Hey," he called as he grabbed his boots and jacket and headed out the patio door.

"Hey," she said, stopping only to give him a quick smile.

Her snowman was significantly leaning. As he walked closer, he noticed she had to get creative with her buttons on the snowman because they were rocks, not buttons. And though her snowman did in fact have a carrot nose, it was a baby carrot and looked ridiculous in size proportion. The sticks for arms were at least decent shaped; they just weren't even in either length or position. And for the hat, she'd stolen one of his, but it was too small for the snowman's head, so it looked like a bad attempt at one of those things Jewish men wore.

Ridiculous. It looked ridiculous.

"I know. You can say it." She wrinkled her nose and threw a sideways glance toward the snow creature.

"Say what, sweetheart?" he asked, hands in his pockets, trying his best not to laugh at her work.

"My first ever snowman is . . . well . . . he sucks." She busted out laughing as she admitted it. "I don't even care. I'm still proud of it. My first ever snowman. My sucky snowman." As she finished explaining, she took off her own scarf and added it to her odd snowman. "It was more work than I thought it'd be."

"You could have told me what you were up to—I would've helped."

She shook her head. "Nope. I think this was something I needed to do for myself."

"I can't believe you haven't ever made a snowman before." He shook his head with her.

"We get maybe an inch of snow maybe every two or three years in Houston. Of course I hadn't." She shrugged.

He looked at her mischievously. If she hadn't ever made a snowman, chances were good she hadn't ever done a snow angel, right?

"Whatever you're thinking right now, Beckett Harper, the answer is no way," she said, eyeing him suspiciously.

"Come on, Houston. Time to make a snow angel. I'm assuming you haven't done one of those either?"

She sucked in a breath of air. "And lie down in the snow? Brrrr! No, and no thank you."

He laughed. "Scared?"

She nodded aggressively. "Yes. It was cold enough touching the snow through waterproof gloves."

She was in his sister's overalls. Granted, they were a little big, but she'd be fine.

"*Beckett,*" she warned.

And then he took off after her. She got all of three feet before he caught her and gently tackled her to the ground. They were rolling and laughing in the snow before she suddenly got serious on him. He propped himself up on an elbow in order to look at her.

"Okay, since I'm already in the snow, teach me your ways," she said.

Unable to help himself, he rose his eyebrows, flirty-like. "*Alllll* my ways, Houston?"

She blushed and reached out to punch his arm. "What's your middle name?"

What? Where did that come from? "William."

She punched him again. "No, Beckett William Harper. Not the ways you are thinking of right now. I mean angelic ways, of the snow variety."

He laughed, actually liking her using his full name on him. He wasn't sure he'd heard his middle name since his mom passed away. "I knew what you meant — I just like to see you squirm."

"Rude," she pointed out as he began showing her what to do.

Snow angels soon freshly made, they lay there a moment.

"Will you help me up?" she asked. "I don't want to ruin my masterpiece before I can see what it looks like."

A chance to get closer? She didn't have to ask him twice. He got to his feet and took it upon himself to lift her into his arms and move her back so she could see her finished product without footprints messing it up.

"Well played, Beckett." She was smiling as he put her down to stand side by side and look at their snow angels. "Mine is better than yours though."

He nodded his agreement and put an arm around her, noting how red from the cold her face and nose were. "Let's go inside now, Houston. Get you warmed up by the fire before you freeze."

She bent down to fix her boots, which were again his sister's pair and way too big for her. Chances were good there was snow in them and her feet were freezing by now. "One more thing," she said softly. "Come here."

Well, that sounded more like it. Things were looking up. Maybe a little make-out frolic in the snow wasn't off limits after all. Sometimes the best part of playing in the snow was getting to warm up . . . right?

He closed the distance between them in a hot second and was all up in her wheelhouse, pulling her into him. "This what you had in mind, honey?"

She leaned in, gave him a kiss on the cheek, and then stopped a moment to whisper in his ear, "No, but this was."

And then, as snow came crashing down on his forehead, she was out of reach and running for the house.

****

So after a little impromptu snowball fight — or were snowball fights always impromptu? — Beckett again tackled her into the snow, this time getting what he was bargaining for in kissing her again. It was cold and fast, but it made her heart ache that he wanted to do fun things like that with her. They were so playful with one another, from their banter to the stupid excuses they created to be close to one another. It was good to feel so carefree with him. She wasn't sure she had felt carefree since her mom left town at sixteen.

Actually, she hadn't felt carefree since she was old enough to know her mom wasn't being much of one. She had had to grow up fast. She had a few good memories, and she tried to hold on to those ones. Thinking of all the hard times did nothing but frustrate the heck out of her. She didn't have kids, but if she did someday, she vowed she'd be *nothing* like her own mother.

She had totally forgotten about making supper in her snowman-making concentration, so they decided to make breakfast for supper together. They laughed and laughed about her snowman and how preposterous he looked. She had to go back out to take some pictures of both her snowman and her snow angel for future use. Then Beckett shared some snow-related stories from his childhood: sledding behind four-wheelers, making huge snow forts with tunnels — stuff like that.

Afterward they settled in for popcorn and a movie on the couch. Apparently the day's events had worn her out, for it wasn't long into the movie, snuggled into Beckett's warmth, that she nodded off and fell asleep.

****

He finished the movie, and though he wanted to do nothing more than be selfish and stay on the couch again with her, he also wanted to show her how much he respected her. So he did the opposite of what he wanted to do and picked her up and tucked her into the guest bedroom. Mable followed him in and curled up at the foot of her bed.

"Traitor," he whispered at the cat, who just curled tighter into a ball as if to tell him to shut up.

He kissed Jordyn on the forehead and left like a freaking gentleman. It felt weird, but he wanted to impress her, and he wanted to do this right. He had no idea what the hell that even meant for the big picture.

He lay in bed for a long time after that, wondering about what to do with Jordyn and this new relationship. He liked her. Hell, he more than liked her if he was being honest with himself. And yeah, he had bought them some extra time—but what was he going to do when she finally did run out of time?

He couldn't keep her on the farm forever. And he couldn't ask her to quit her job and move here. Yeah, it sounded both ridiculous and awesome. But if he could actually convince her to move, between the small town talking about them and the resentment she would eventually feel for her having to give up her job that she was good at and liked, they'd be over before they ever really began. And that was the last thing he wanted.

So what could they do? The long-distance thing?

He didn't like it. Actually, he hated it. He was so used to her being with him every day that he didn't like the idea of it at all, but if it was what he had to do to prove to her that he was willing to date her seriously, he'd do it.

Tomorrow was a week. One week with this city woman and he was not only ready to try dating, actual dating, but he was thinking of long-distance dating?

She had some sort of womanly superpower. He was just sure of it.

He had been doing just fine. Life was good; the farm was great. He didn't feel lacking in anything. Then she sprained her ankle and got stuck with him, and he was afraid that life was never going to be the same.

Jealous of the Pie
CHAPTER 12

"Good morning," he said with a kiss to her forehead as he grabbed his coffee and headed for the laundry room to dress for chores.

When did they become this close? She knew how he liked his coffee, and he gave her a kiss on the forehead before he went out to do chores? She almost felt like she was playing house with him. It was fun. Okay, fantastic really—but the truth was that this wasn't her house. His house and this farm were quickly coming to feel like more of a home than she had ever had before. And it scared the heck out of her. How could she ever leave this? And not just leave, but go back to her life, which was nine hundred miles south of here. She wouldn't be an hour or two away; she'd be sixteen hours away.

"Good morning," she said, trying to shake her bad feeling. Waking up this morning in the guest room—knowing that Beckett had the decency to tuck her in and sleep in his own room—messed with her emotions. Is that something "Heartbreak Harper" would've done? No. That was something Beckett Harper would do.

"I'm going to do a quick job of the chores, and then I'm going to try to scoop out the drive. If I can get it accomplished and the highway is clear, we may have to head in to town for a late lunch at my aunt's café. What do you say to that?" he asked, dimple popping.

"That sounds amazing." She nodded. Maybe that was what she needed. Fresh air. Perspective. A reminder of who Beckett Harper was and who she was. And she wondered if he would still dote on her in public. This could be good in more than one way. It would get them out of this little idealized bubble they were currently living in. Blizzard conditions weren't real everyday-life conditions.

"It'll probably take me a while, but you'll be able to see me from the windows in the living room when I start on the scooping," he explained. "I'll pile it into a huge mound for you to see all the snow, southern girl."

"Can I help?"

"Help me scoop out the drive?" He looked surprised.

She nodded. It sounded fun!

"You want to sit in the tractor with me while I shovel the snow?" he clarified.

She nodded enthusiastically. "I mean, when is the next time I am going to see this much snow?"

He looked wounded for some reason. She couldn't figure out what his deal was but then he said, "You're going to have to leave here. I get that. But you are welcome here whenever, however. Always."

His strong words surprised her. By the looks of it, they maybe even surprised him.

"I'm sorry. I didn't mean it like that," she apologized. "We have at least this week, right? I'm starting to realize how much I'm going to miss this place. I just wanted to play some more in the snow, okay?"

He nodded. "Okay. We'll get this figured out, Jordyn. I don't want this to be over in a week." He looked like he was going to kiss her again, but then he put his gloves on instead. "Chores will take me an hour, and then I'll swing by and pick you up in my chariot."

She smiled. "It's a date?"

He smirked at that. "With you, they've all been dates."

****

Well, this was new. A woman in his tractor with him. Lord, if the tabloids could see him now. He was pretty sure there were super cliché country songs about this very thing. Still, he had to admit he liked it. More than liked it. She was so attentive and wanted him to explain to her how everything worked. Which he was more than happy to do. Sometimes he was so used to tractors and animals that he had to take a minute and remind himself that it wasn't the way everyone made a living. He had known how to drive a pickup and tractor by the time he was — what — twelve?

He tried to get her to drive the tractor, though she refused. Somehow, he convinced her to run the levers for the loader. She was almost on his lap. That idea definitely paid off.

And the look on her face as she was pushing snow with a tractor was pure joy. She was a kid in a candy shop. Who would have thought that a grown woman would find so much entertainment in something so ordinary and simple? Maybe it was because she was from the South. Maybe it was because she had had a crappy childhood. Or maybe a combination of the two. He didn't care. She was different. Good different. His favorite flavor of different.

When they finished, they hopped in his pickup to make the short drive to check if the highway was clear. And it was. Having the green light for a trip to town, they headed back to the house for him to shower up so they could go into town to get lunch. He was excited. Aunt Rose was going to have a cow when he waltzed in there with Jordyn. He had texted her last weekend that he had someone from AgGroSo snowed in with him. He didn't tell her it was a woman.

And Aunt Rose . . . He should probably prepare Jordyn for her. But there wasn't really any preparing for a woman like Rose. Come to think of it, they'd probably be thick as thieves in about five minutes.

****

This small town was *cuuuuuute*. Shops, already decorated for Christmas despite the storm, lined either side of the road. There wasn't a single stoplight in town. A four-way stop was about as crazy as traffic got. It was lovely really. Compared to Houston and all the big interstates and beltways, it felt quaint. She adored this town, but she didn't want to fall for it.

Sure, she had this thing going with Beckett, but she didn't want to fall for his town too. She knew all too well that people in small towns could be pretty unforgiving. And once they all found out she'd been snowed in with Beckett, she was sure people would talk—even more so if he told them why she'd really been sent there. This lunch in town was just a casual thing, but it also packed a punch.

So though the town was adorable, she was sure to go into this with the right mindset. This was his town, not hers. Expecting them to welcome her with open arms was unrealistic. She was a visitor here—someone just passing through. They would be kind enough, to her face anyway, and she would be kind back.

When they pulled up in front of the café, she couldn't help but smile. There was a chalkboard sign in the window with the day's special: roast beef sandwiches with mashed potatoes, gravy, green beans, and a piece of apple pie for dessert to top it all off. The café itself looked like the lone busy store today, but it was the stuff small towns were made of. She was just sure little old ladies met for coffee here. And there was probably a steady stream of regulars that came every day. This small little café probably held all the town's secrets. And here she was. About to dive right in.

"Ready to meet Aunt Rose?" he asked.

Oh, yeah. His aunt owned the place too. "Sure." She smiled what she hoped was nicely. *Ready or not, here we come!*

As soon as she was in the door, because of all the stares and whispers they were getting, it became apparent that Beckett hadn't told anyone she was snowed in with him. And it was equally apparent that he hadn't exaggerated his celebrity status. She was surprised they kept their smartphones at bay and didn't snap any pictures. Then again, she spotted a good ol' boy in the corner still carrying a flip phone, so maybe not.

"Finally making it out to the land of the living, I see, my boy?" A little old woman came over and hugged Beckett. Since she was wearing a black server apron, it was safe to assume she was his aunt.

Aunt Rose was her size, probably only five and a half feet tall. Her gray hair was neatly piled on top of her head in a bun, which drew attention to the purple glasses on a sparkly string around her neck. The purple glasses just happened to match her purple tennis shoes. And they weren't old-people tennis shoes; they were trendy. She just looked like she could go toe to toe with anyone. And knew it. Before Jordyn had time to introduce herself or even say a word, his aunt hugged her. If she was surprised to see her with him, she didn't show it.

She pulled back and gave Jordyn's hand a firm squeeze while she introduced herself. "I'm Aunt Rose. Lovely to meet you, dear. And now I know why my nephew was in no hurry to get back to town."

Jordyn blushed. Wow. This lady didn't mess around. "Rose, I'm Jordyn. I'm—"

Aunt Rose interrupted with a knowing look. "You're his girl. And please just call me Aunt Rose. Everyone except my children call me that. It's either Momma or Aunt Rose."

She felt the need to clarify. People were watching. They were trying to act like they weren't, but they were. "I—"

Aunt Rose interrupted again, leading the way to a table. "Well, Beckett, is she, or is she not?" She turned to her nephew with a look that meant business.

He was grinning ear to ear, loving every single second of Jordyn's discomfort. "She is." And to seal the deal, he reached over to give her a kiss on the forehead.

Aunt Rose gave Jordyn an *I told you so* look, and then someone called her name. She held up a finger and turned away to holler something.

Jordyn smiled and whispered, "How did she know?"

Aunt Rose began walking away to help a customer in the back, but she turned back around, hands on her hips. "Sugar, I know everything in this town. And it would take a blind man not to see that you two have feelings for one another." With that, she put her glasses on her nose and stared at them both from over the top rims.

What the heck?! They had been here like thirty seconds.

Despite feeling uncomfortable, Jordyn smiled at Aunt Rose, then looked at Beckett. "Apparently your extreme perceptiveness was not hereditary."

Aunt Rose tipped her head back and laughed hard. "I like you already, darlin'."

****

Aunt Rose, as owner of the café and not a usual waitress, took it upon herself to be their waitress. Beckett wasn't surprised. It was the first time he had brought a woman in here, so of course Aunt Rose would be up to her snoopy ways. She did at least sit them in a corner booth, which was out of the way of traffic coming in and out—and Beckett's favorite spot to eat.

He jokingly had thought that Jordyn and Aunt Rose would be thick as thieves in five minutes, but in reality it took even less than five minutes. Jordyn ordered the daily special, earning her first brownie points with his aunt. (He ordered the special too, but did that matter to Aunt Rose? Nope.) Then she ordered an iced tea, and when Aunt Rose gave her the tea options, Jordyn was impressed. Apparently, they were kindred tea drinkers.

Yuck. Not his cup of tea. Literally. The only way he liked tea was if it had a good dose of sugar in it. Then again, that was the only way he liked his coffee. What could he say? He liked the sweeter things in life.

And along that topic, Jordyn had Aunt Rose totally under her spell. When Beckett explained that Jordyn worked for AgGroSo, Jordyn butted in and told the whole story. She even explained the real reason her boss sent her. Beckett wasn't expecting her to do that, but one thing about Jordyn that he appreciated was she didn't like to beat around the bush. Though coming clean with him about why Walt had sent her had pissed him off, he still respected that she did it so soon. Things could have taken a turn for the worse if she would've tried to keep that from him while their feelings for one another progressed.

Rose had pursed her lips at that part in the story but listened intently while Jordyn finished explaining. Then, when Jordyn was done, she simply looked at Beckett and asked, "So are you going to do the damn commercial and finally do something about your tarnished reputation, then?"

Beckett laughed. "Aren't you mad they sent someone attractive to try to seduce me?"

Aunt Rose rolled her eyes. "Please. Like it takes much to seduce you. You should be glad they sent someone as attractive as Jordyn."

Jordyn had almost spit out her tea at that, and Beckett looked at her and shook his head in amusement.

"Good point. If they let me do it the way Jordyn wants them to, then yes, I'll do it," Beckett explained.

"Good. It's about damn time," Aunt Rose said pointedly, giving him a scolding look.

"Rosalie, why do I get the feeling you're speaking in double meanings here?" he asked with a chuckle. He took a sip of his coffee.

Jordyn butted in. "Oh, look. Maybe I was wrong about the perceptiveness. Maybe it is hereditary after all."

He squinted at her while Aunt Rose tipped her head back and burst out laughing again. "Oh, you two. You bring me such joy. I always told Beckett his woman was going to have to have fire in her veins to deal with him on a daily basis." She winked at Jordyn and then sped off to get their food.

As soon as she was gone, Jordyn whispered, "I like your aunt."

Aunt Rose hollered back, "Likewise, honey."

Jordyn looked at him, probably confused how Rose could hear her, and Beckett shrugged. "I swear it's why she owns this café. She can hear *ev-er-y-thing*."

Jordyn laughed.

Their food soon arrived, and surprisingly, Rose let them eat in peace. They talked about the small town, and Beckett explained a couple of the regulars and what they did. By the time their dessert arrived, Jordyn seemed like she was having a great time. When she took a bite of her apple pie and made a small sound of approval, Beckett suddenly felt jealous of the pie.

Jealous of the pie? What the hell was happening to him?

When Aunt Rose came back, Jordyn asked her if it was cinnamon ice cream with the pie. Which it was. Which then launched a discussion about Rose's secret recipe for homemade cinnamon ice cream. Jordyn was listening to every word. Beckett was still feeling jealous of the pie.

By the time they left, all the other people there for lunch had already left. Beckett paid the bill and was helping Jordyn into her coat when Rose came back to say goodbye.

"It was so nice to meet you, Aunt Rose," Jordyn said as the woman hugged her. Again.

"Likewise, doll." Aunt Rose then turned to him, gave him a huge hug, and whispered loudly, "Never let that woman out of your sight."

Beckett grinned and shook his head. Aunt Rose approved. And now the whole town would know too. Oddly enough, he was glad. There were enough single men around Picketts that he didn't want Jordyn anywhere near them. As far as he was concerned, she was locked down.

Like Rose said, she was *his girl*. It definitely had a nice ring to it.

CHAPTER 13

His girl. Those were Aunt Rose's words, and she just could not stop smiling the whole way home.

Home. His place felt like home. And if she weren't so giddy from lunch, it would make her feel overwhelmed and helpless. But she just couldn't bring herself to spend this last week with Beckett depressed and sad. He had claimed her. In public. He had kissed her on the forehead and called her *his girl* in public. And then she had gone and immediately fallen for his aunt. She loved that woman. She had warned herself not to fall in love with Beckett's small town, but Aunt Rose was a hard woman not to love.

What did this mean?

It meant she was destined for heartbreak. But at least this time around, she knew exactly when her heart was going to break—the day she left. She knew it was coming. So maybe that would make it less painful?

She could only hope.

Just as they hit the driveway, Beckett's phone started ringing. He pulled up, looked at the screen, and immediately broke into a grin. "She doesn't waste time."

"Who?" she asked, confused.

"Aunt Rose. This would be my sister." He rolled his eyes before answering the phone. "Sis."

She could hear squealing on the other side. High-pitched yelling. She knew she was right about that because even Beckett held the phone away from his ear for a moment. He was getting an earful.

"Yes, I am actually seeing someone," he said when his sister had finally calmed down. "Why is that so hard to believe?"

More talking that she couldn't quite make out, followed with him saying, "Good point."

Another question was being asked. She was about to sneak inside to give him a minute to talk to his sister when Beckett said, "Hold on, B. She's right here. I'll just put her on speakerphone."

He hit a button as Beckett's sister said, "Good. I can't believe I missed out on lunch. Stupid finals."

"Hi," Jordyn said in a hesitant voice after she knew she could be heard. "I'm Jordyn."

"Hiiiiii," his sister said excitedly. "I'm Blakely. Beckett's sister. Please tell me he told you he has a sister?"

She laughed. "Yes, he did."

"Well, that's surprising. He doesn't tell people about me," she teased.

"You're my best kept secret," Beckett defended. "As in it's best for you to stay away from all the football players that wanted to date you just because you are my sister."

"Still holding a grudge because I'm the more attractive sibling, eh?" she asked playfully.

It again took all of two seconds for Jordyn to decide she adored his sister. She had a liveliness about her that was apparent from her first words to her. And for some reason, hearing his sister's voice helped her find the missing piece to who Beckett was. He had such a hard time with his parents' deaths. He had every reason to be hard and, well, checked out. But he wasn't. From the start, he was goading her and saying things just to be playful or make her mad. Beckett was always just so . . . *alive*. Now she got it. He didn't have the rest of his family, but he did have his sister. They had gotten each other through because they were the only thing they had left. And he was used to pushing women's buttons because he had a sister. It all made better sense now.

It made her want a sibling, to be honest. Sam's kids were a lot like siblings, the closest thing she'd get anyway, but she wondered what it would have been like to grow up with one. Would it have been easier when her mom bailed if she had a sibling to talk to? Maybe.

"Rose said you finally got him to do a commercial, huh?" she asked. You could tell by the way she asked it that she was smiling.

"I did. I think anyway." She shrugged and smiled at Beckett, still expecting him to change his mind any minute now.

"I'm mostly doing it to keep Jordyn around," he said honestly. "You know I could care less about my image."

"Huh. How about that?" Blakely laughed again. "If I had to bet on whether you would fix your image first or want a woman to stick around . . . I'm not sure which I would have bet on. Killing two birds with one stone, eh, B?"

"You know me." Beckett laughed and snuck her a wink.

"Gah!" Blakely said in dismay. "This makes me want to come home for the filming of the commercial. This is so, so stupid. Am I graduated yet?"

"Not quite," Beckett said. "But almost, sis. Almost."

"Yeah, yeah," Blakely muttered.

"Did Beckett tell you when we first met I twisted my ankle really bad? I could have used your physical therapy skills around here. I mean, he did great, but he also wasn't the most . . . *comforting*?"

Blakely busted out laughing at that.

"Yeah. She told me off and then walked away. Not two seconds later she slipped and went down," Beckett said with a chuckle, making Blakely laugh harder.

"Oh, this is great. And she told you off when she first met you? Gosh, I like this woman already." She stopped to giggle for a bit before adding politely, "Is the ankle okay now?"

"Yes," Jordyn said. "Still sore, especially if I move it side to side, but I can at least walk better now."

"Good. You might want to keep your activity on it to a minimum. It can take six to eight weeks for some sprains to heal. So don't be surprised if it takes a good while."

"Yeah," Beckett said to her pointedly. "No more snowball fights in the yard for you."

"You guys had a snowball fight?" Blakely was back to squealing.

"We did." Jordyn laughed. "I'm from Houston, and I hadn't ever really gotten to play in the snow."

The line went quiet.

"B?" Beckett asked. "You still there?"

"I'm still here. I don't even know what to say though. I don't have words. My brother, my dearest brother, was having a snowball fight with his new girlfriend in the snow. It's like a romance novel!" She was almost high-pitched again by the end but somehow dialed back her excitement just a touch.

Beckett rolled his eyes.

"I take it you don't meet or talk to many of Beckett's girlfriends?" Jordyn asked, laughing.

"Other than high school? No. Nope. Never," Blakely said seriously.

"Okay, okay, B. Before you start telling her embarrassing things about me, we need to go inside. We are sitting in the yard in the pickup. We didn't even get back home before you called. I'm sure Jordyn needs a moment to process all of this. Rose was typical Rose today."

Blakely laughed. "Which means she was probably harder on you than her. Ha. All right, you two, have fun. It was so good to meet you, Jordyn!"

"You too!"

"Love you, B," Blakely said.

"Love you too, little B," Beckett said back like it was their routine.

They nicknamed each other "B"? How stinking adorable was that?! And his words to his sister came so freely. For someone who didn't want to love someone, or had shut out the possibility of love in his dating life, he sure didn't hold back with his sister. Again, she supposed that was because they were the only immediate family each of them had left. Sure, they did have their Aunt Rose, but Rose had her own family too.

Thinking like this made her heart hurt. When she went back to Houston and this thing with Beckett officially ended, she didn't have a twin or great aunt to lean on. She had no one.

Just like always, she was *alone.*

****

Back inside, Jordyn was quiet. Too quiet. He knew Aunt Rose could be a lot. As could Blakely. Blakely was a pistol. And Jordyn could be too, but nothing about Blakely was relaxed or at ease. Jordyn could go with the flow, something she'd probably had to learn to do her entire life because of her crappy mom. That was not Blakely at all. Blakely didn't go with the flow; she made her own flow. Even if there was a perfectly fine flow that was much easier to follow. That was just his sister.

Jordyn was curled up on the couch with her Kindle on her lap while Beckett watched some college football, but he noticed she wasn't turning the pages. Which meant she had to be in her head big time.

He turned down the volume on the game and turned to face her, hand on her shoulder, massaging it. "What's wrong, Jordyn?"

She looked guilty, unable to deny there wasn't anything wrong. "I just . . ." She paused, then shrugged dejectedly. "I feel lonely. You have Aunt Rose and Blakely, and they are super incredible women . . . . "

"As are you," he insisted in her hesitation.

She smiled and looked him in the eyes. "I just had a thought right after we talked to Blakely that once I finally do have to go back to Houston, you'll have Blakely. She will be here over Christmas break. She will help you not miss me. And I . . . well, I don't even have a cat. So it's going to take some . . . getting used to?" She sighed in defeat. "No. I won't sugarcoat it . . . . It's going to suck."

He loved her honesty, but her words were like a punch to the gut. She thought he wouldn't miss her? The hell?

"If anything, Blakely being home for Christmas will only make me miss you more. But why do I have to miss you? Why don't you come back for Christmas? I'll even buy you a plane ticket so you don't have to drive." He was kind of thinking out loud, but after he said it, he thought it might be the best damn idea he'd ever had.

"What?!"

"You said you spend New Year's with Sam, so I assume you don't have Christmas plans," he explained. "It's just Blakely and me. We have lunch at Rose's café on Christmas Eve, go to church, and then we do our own thing here. Always have. Why don't you come back and spend Christmas with us?"

Her mouth opened. And shut. And opened. And shut.

"What?" he asked, grinning. He loved it when he did something to impress her, and it flustered her.

"I just . . . it's . . . you want to *date me*, date me, even after I have to leave?" she asked point-blank.

"When have I ever led you to believe otherwise?" he asked confused. Good Lord, he did not know how to do this dating thing. He didn't date. Maybe that was the problem. He didn't even know how. He thought his interest in her was made clear, but apparently not if she still didn't understand he was serious about dating her.

"Well, sometimes when you said we'd figure it out, I thought you meant we'd have to figure out how to move on from one another," she explained with a shrug.

Move on!? Excuse the hell out of him. No. Nope. The very thought of her near any other man made him want to tackle something. Yeah. Not happening.

He took a deep breath before he spoke to calm down. "Sweetheart, I don't want to move on. And I don't want you to move on. I can't ask you to move here. And I can't leave the farm right now. So we are at an impasse. Long-distance dating is all we've got. The other alternative isn't one I'm willing to consider."

She looked stunned. "So not only am I your girl, but we are also going to seriously try this thing?"

He nodded. He was sure. And he had no idea when he became so sure, but he was. Her moving on? Over his dead body. That was part of the reason they went to Rose's café today. He wanted the message sent loud and clear that they were together. He wanted it official.

She grabbed him by the shirt and kissed the dimple on his cheek. "Beckett Harper, you are so unexpected."

He laughed. "Right back at you."

And then he kissed her in such a way that he hoped she knew there was going to be no moving on. For either of them.

CHAPTER 14

Monday morning, they settled back into their routines, with Jordyn working remotely from Picketts and Beckett returning to the chores he couldn't do during the storm. It was like they were still in the middle of the storm of the century—but with a few added responsibilities. When Jordyn wasn't baking something, she talked on the phone with marketing, answered emails, and got things rolling with Walt for the commercial.

Everyone in Houston was freaking the heck out that she got Beckett to do the dang thing. As for the idea of not using his face in the commercial, the marketing team thought it was smart. Why even try to compete with all the other funny Super Bowl commercials? Instead, they could do something special, sentimental. It would be a way for them to honor their customer base in pointing out how important farms are to our economy. Instead of being a funny ad, it would be a feel-good commercial.

Marketing was coming up with a few different voice-over options for Beckett to read. Jordyn got the final say on the script. She came up with the idea that the crew would basically follow Beckett around for a few days with cameras. They would have hours and hours of footage, and then from that, they could piece together the most powerful parts of a farmer's day. They would need some aerial shots via drone too, and between those two things, they should have more than enough for their commercial. If they did it right, they would have a ton of fresh customers for the new year.

Her coworkers were so happy they were kissing her butt. Big time. As they should be because she saved their rears—and was doing their jobs for them. The AgGroSo commercial team was planning to arrive in Picketts the following Monday. One week from tomorrow morning would be their first shoot for the commercial. She had asked what they wanted her to do around the farm before they arrived, but after seeing the pictures she'd emailed from her phone, they told her not to do a thing. They wanted it authentic. And how much more authentic could you get than following a farmer around for a few days? The supposed "shadowing" Walt sent her here for was now going to be a real-life scenario.

"Hey, good lookin'," Beckett sang from the laundry room where he dumped his overalls off. "Whatcha got cookin'?"

She couldn't help but grin over the top of her laptop sitting on the kitchen table. "At least I now know you won't be leaving the farm to go on tour any time soon."

"Rude! Is that how you speak to your man?" He sounded angry, but that one dimple was showing . . . so he wasn't.

And "her man"?

She shrugged. "Yeah, pretty much."

He laughed. "Ha! I wouldn't expect anything less. But you could at least pretend to like my singing."

She looked at him and shook her head. "You know I don't like lying to you."

"Good point." He grinned. "But really, what is that amazing smell I am sniffing?"

"Homemade pizza. I wanted to make Stromboli instead, but marketing had me on the phone for hours this morning," she explained with an annoyed wave of her hand.

"Pizza? Heck yeah!" He pumped a fist in the air and then came over to give her a kiss on the cheek. "What do you say we go into town for a date tonight?"

"A date?" she asked intrigued.

"Not a *date* date since we are in Picketts here, but I would at least like to take you to Rose's for supper. I mean, I know you do actually have to work this week." He sighed. "A lot probably, since I am doing the dumb commercial, so let me at least buy you supper. You know I did cook all my meals before this, right? I can cook." He paused to smile. "So I'll either cook here or we can go into town. Eventually, when the dust settles, I would like a *date* date though. A real one."

She thought about that and couldn't help but reach to rub Beckett's face where his facial hair was scruffy. She secretly adored it. "I'd love to. And can we go to the grocery store too? I need to get some ingredients for stuff I want to make this week."

He raised his eyebrows. "You trying to fatten me up?"

She rolled her eyes. "Like I could. No. I'm just enjoying baking and cooking for someone other than myself. It's more fun when there is more than one person."

He looked oddly serious after that.

"What?!"

He shook his head. "When you say things like that, I really want to ask you to stay, quit your job, and never go back. I know you are independent. I know you love your job and are damn good at it . . . . But I *hate* that you are alone."

****

Grocery shopping with a woman? How far he had come in just a little over a week. He had done the chores early and showered up to go into town with Jordyn. What woman wanted to go grocery shopping while on a date anyway? Jordyn. Jordyn did.

Jordyn wasn't at all high maintenance. She was so down to earth it just made him like her even more. And the fact that everyone in her life had let her down made him even more adamant about doing things right with her. He didn't ever want to let her down. He didn't want her to write him off like she'd had to do with almost everyone else in her life.

As he drove them the eight and a half miles into town for their date, they held hands like it was something they did every day. And that should probably scare him, but it didn't. Just like her leaving soon should probably relieve him, but it didn't. He felt many, many things about her leaving, but relief was not on that list. What was happening to him?

He quickly glanced over at her and checked her out for the third time in five miles. For their date into town, she wore skinny jeans and a nice blouse thing with a cardigan sweater over it. Granted, she probably hadn't packed date clothes, but he loved that she didn't go over the top to impress him. Hell, he was already impressed; she didn't need to do anything. She did put on makeup and let her hair down but that was as glammed up as she got. She looked amazing. Amazing and comfortable. He was used to miniskirts, push-up bras, heels, makeup on thick with red lipstick, and perfume that made him want to gag.

Jordyn always smelled freaking amazing though. A nice sweet smell without overpowering. And her hair looked soft. None of that nasty hair-spray stuff. *Her hair.* He would like to see her hair down in a variety of different ways, none of which were appropriate to be thinking about right now.

He looked at her feet and saw that she had chosen a tall pair of flat boots over her skinny jeans. "No heels, Houston?" he asked, smiling.

She rolled her eyes and turned toward him. "Can I tell you a secret?"

He bounced his eyebrows. "Please do."

She grinned. "Though I do wear heels to work every day at the office, I actually hate them. Passionately. I only wore heels when we met because I knew Walt sent me to woo you over. Though I didn't want to play the part, I was at least trying to look it."

He laughed. "That's great. For the record, I don't like heels either."

"Wear them often, do you?" she asked.

He laughed again. He couldn't ever remember a woman who made him laugh as much as she did. Blakely was obnoxious; Jordyn was just witty. "Clever. No, I meant women wearing heels really aren't my thing. They are just so loud on the floor, and then sometimes they can't even walk right. I just don't get the appeal. It seems fake. Like what's the point in altering your natural height?"

She thought about that for a second. "I can see how you'd feel that way. I wear them for work because it helps me stay focused and professional. But I always take them off under my desk."

"You rebel." He smiled, imagining her doing exactly that.

"But maybe I should wear them around you. You're like a whole foot taller than me," she said.

He shrugged. "I don't mind. Most people are shorter than me. I'm used to it." He didn't add that he liked the way her small frame could curl into his, such as when they'd slept on the couch those few nights. He had zero problems with her size. Thinking of her body shape was distracting. He needed to get it together today.

"Is Blakely tall like you are?" she asked, snapping him out of those sorts of daydreams.

He snorted. "Yeah. And she hates it. She's right at six foot. So not as tall as me, but tall enough that her prom dates were intimidated that they had to look up to her."

"So you're both tall. Were your parents tall?" she asked.

He shrugged. "My grandpa was. My dad was six two. And my mom was barely five foot."

"That's funny, and yet you and Blakely are both tall?"

"Yeah." He shrugged again, then said, "Irish twinsies."

"Do you have similar personalities too?"

"Hell no." He laughed. "We look similar but still different—her hair and skin are a shade darker than mine. And we are both stubborn and driven personalitywise, but the similarities end there. I'm sure you noticed—she does not do laid-back or go with the flow very well."

She smiled. "I can about imagine."

"She's already texting me about having you back for Christmas, so for the record, she wants you here too. Have you thought on that anymore? She doesn't have a boyfriend or anything, so it'd just be the two of us. You wouldn't be imposing." Every time he asked her about it, she said she'd think about it and then changed the subject.

She sighed.

"Out with it," he commanded.

"I want to. It's just a big step. Meeting your family, spending the holidays together. It's just happening so fast." She squeezed his hand in his, resting on his knee.

He laughed and moved to kiss her on the cheek while they were at a stop sign, whispering, "Sweetheart, I ran a four-four-one forty time for the Combine. I don't do things slow."

She laughed pretty hard at that. "True. We are eating at Rose's, right?"

Beckett smiled. "Of course. Food and then groceries or groceries and food?"

"You can't grocery shop on an empty stomach. Or else I get stuck in the cookie aisle a while," she said with a laugh.

"Food it is."

****

"Back so soon?" Rose asked as she whisked them to Beckett's favorite booth.

"It was the beef," Beckett said jokingly.

Rose swatted at him with a menu. "Don't talk about your aunt like that." Then she moved to give Jordyn a hug. "You look cute, darlin'."

"Thank you," Jordyn said with a smile. She really did adore this woman. She barely knew her, but she seemed like such a sweetheart.

Aunt Rose gave Jordyn a wink before she went to go get them some drinks.

Seeing an entrance, a few guys Beckett knew came over and asked about the football game Friday and what he thought. They introduced themselves as two guys Beckett had played with in high school—and now they owned a construction business in town. After a few exchanged pleasantries, it was back to football. Their beloved team was going to a crappy bowl game, for the third year in a row. These people were not okay with mediocre bowl games apparently.

She thought at first they were being snoopy and trying to see who Beckett brought with him. But it turned out they were just really wanting his thoughts on the game. Or to impress him with how much they knew about the game. Probably more so the latter. She listened but was perfectly content to drink her iced tea in peace. Beckett was nice to them, but a couple of times she caught him looking at her like he wished they'd just go away. They were supposed to be on a date after all.

One must have felt rude because he turned to her and asked, "Are you a Husker fan, Jordyn?"

She shook her head. "I'm from Houston, so I follow the pros more so than college."

They both looked at Beckett as if they didn't approve.

He simply shrugged and then pierced Jordyn with an affectionate gaze. "I'll have her wearing red and singing the songs before long, boys. She knows football too. So it's only a matter of time. She'll come around."

One guy squinted at her, not believing Beckett.

"No really. She got frustrated the other night because Houston was running the ball on second and twenty-two. She said the words 'a slant route to the running back would be a better option,' " he said, staring her down with a heated gaze.

And here she thought he hadn't really been paying attention to her football talk. She didn't think he really cared too much. Judging by the way he was looking at her now, he must enjoy that she understood the game. She liked football — all the numbers, and the way certain plays worked better depending on what down it was. She even loved the statistics — the probability that if you went for it on fourth down more often, it'd totally pay off. That's what the numbers said, but that's not how too many teams played right now.

The guy who squinted at her looked impressed. "Darlin', can I have your number?" He reached his hand in to shake her hand.

Beckett playfully smacked it away. "Nope. She's mine. Find your own."

They briefly talked about their ten-year high school reunion coming up in the spring and a few other trivial things that Jordyn didn't care about, and then Beckett told them their food should almost be there. Finally, they went on their way.

"Well, honey, I hope you're ready," Rose said as she sat down their food shortly after.

"For what?" Jordyn asked.

"Tweedledee and Tweedledum over there are nothing but town gossips. You're goin' to be talked about around town even more than you already were," Rose explained.

Beckett just laughed and shrugged. "Let them talk, Rosalie. I don't care."

Rose gave him a sharp look. "Did you prepare her for what happens when the tabloids get word?"

Beckett stopped smiling at that. His grin vanished so quick it was like she made it up. "I was hoping to avoid that for a while."

Rose rolled her eyes and snorted. "Right. Everyone in town already knows. And you know most people here love and support you, but there are a few that are out for themselves. You know that."

He nodded and sighed. "Crap. Aunt Rose, why do you have to go and ruin my date like this?"

She reached in and gave Jordyn a quick hug before leaving. "Just making sure you're taking care of our girl."

After she left, Jordyn felt a bit freaked. Okay, a lot freaked. The tabloids?! This thing between Beckett and her could show up in the tabloids. She was going to be in the tabloids? Her? Why hadn't she realized this before now?

Oh my gosh. What if they researched her background? Found out her sob story. Could she do this? Was she doing this? Was she going to be okay with being scrutinized? It'd be high school all over again.

For the first time possibly ever, Jordyn understood she wasn't just dating Beckett Harper. She was also dating Heartbreak Harper. She was stupid to think she could date one and not the other. Of course the word would get out. If not here in Picketts, then in Houston. She wouldn't even put it past marketing to leak it to get some more coverage for the Super Bowl commercial.

Why hadn't she thought of this before? *Stupid, stupid, stupid.* Dating Beckett Harper was not going to be something she could do quietly.

She wished it would just snow again so they could go back to being in their own little world.

****

"Jordyn," Beckett said firmly.

She snapped her eyes up to his. At the word *tabloids*, she almost went full-panic mode, and he recognized it immediately. Of course he was interested in the only girl ever who preferred not to be in the tabloids. Of course. It was like the universe's way for getting back at him for his past. He wished he could hear what she was thinking about right now. Or maybe not, because it didn't look good for him.

"Stop worrying," he insisted. "We'll deal with it if and when it happens."

"You don't care if we are in the tabloids?" she asked.

He shook his head. "No. At least this time I'd actually be dating who they said I was."

"What if they" — she dropped her voice to a whisper — "find out things about me."

He clenched his fist under the table at that. She had a point there. He knew they'd want to know who she was, but to have her dirty laundry aired like that, have the story told about her mom . . . that just wasn't going to work. And if the thing with Thomas was ever brought to light, he'd have to kill someone. Probably Thomas. "Look, let's talk more about this later. I doubt anyone will care much who I'm dating anymore. The good news is that you aren't some high-profile name like some of my . . . *acquaintances* . . . were in the past."

As soon as the words were out of his mouth, he knew those were not the words he should have said. Wow, he sounded like a total ass. She was ticked. And the heat in her face was lovely, but the way she was looking at him was not. There was playful and flustered Jordyn, and there was angry Jordyn. This was not the type of angry he was looking for.

"'Conquests' is a better term."

"*Jordyn*," he hissed.

"What?" she snapped back, looking around to make sure no one was eavesdropping. "That's what they were."

He knew she probably would've said more, but she was trying not to make a scene. He ran a hand through his hair. Why was she so difficult? "Yeah, they were, but *you* are not. I didn't mean to make you feel like you were inadequate. That's not at all what I meant. You are anything but ordinary. I just meant that you aren't famous, and I'm washed up and obviously not going to play anymore. I doubt anyone cares."

His career was over. So maybe it would be okay. Heartbreak Harper had disappeared from the tabloids for almost two years now. And he preferred it that way.

"I'm just a bit scared," she said in a shaky voice. "It's intimidating to even think about or consider."

He reached across and grabbed her hand to give it a quick kiss on the knuckles. "I've got you."

She sighed, dropping it for now.

"This is the worst date. I hate this date. Let's eat and get out of here. Someday I'll take you on a real date," he promised.

They needed to get out of here. Before someone else came over and interrupted—and before Rose said something else that made Jordyn nervous. Sometimes he felt like their relationship was dangling by a thread. If it wasn't her having to go back to Houston, it was his reputation. They'd been nothing but doomed from the start.

CHAPTER 15

The rest of the evening went well. Rose, sensing her discomfort, came over and told a few embarrassing stories about Beckett. It gave Jordyn hope. Beckett was not what the tabloids thought he was, and she needed to remind herself daily. She couldn't date Beckett Harper without also dating his reputation no matter how badly she wanted to. She had been naïve enough, or still just shocked they were actually dating, that she never thought it would really be an issue. And he didn't seem to care that they'd be officially together like that in the tabloids. It was one thing for him to tell someone she was his girl; it was a whole other thing to be plastered in the tabloids with her. Regardless, if he was the celebrity here and didn't care, why should she?

"Divide and conquer in the store since it's getting late?" Beckett asked as he parked his truck at the grocery store. "I kind of wanted to cuddle up and watch a movie when we got home, especially since part one of our date went so terribly."

"You want to cuddle?" she asked, surprised.

"Well, yeah. Mable doesn't cuddle quite like you do." He shrugged with a grin. His one dimple when he joked around like this was going to be etched into her memory forever.

They split up the list, and she went to the produce while he went to the other end of the store; they'd work their way and meet up in the middle. But before he left to do his part, he was sure to leave her with a kiss on the cheek.

See? Beckett Harper was a gentleman. Heartbreak Harper would never be seen with a woman in a grocery store, much less kiss a woman on the cheek.

She was picking out some apples for an apple crisp she wanted to make when someone approached her. Honestly, she just wanted to get in and out of the grocery store as quickly as possible. What was with these small-town people?

"Hi, you must be Jordyn," the intruder said with a smile and reached her hand out to her.

Uh-oh. Was this one of Beckett's many admirers? She'd seen some of the looks women sent her at Rose's. It was either pity or jealousy most of the time. Since her mom left her at sixteen, she was used to the pity looks, so it didn't bother her too much. The jealousy looks were a bit weird, but since Beckett was a handsome bachelor, she got it.

"Hi," she said, shaking the intruder's hand.

"I'm Grace. I went to high school with Beckett. How are you liking it here?" she asked.

"It's cold?" Jordyn replied honestly. What was with these people from high school tonight? They were everywhere. Better his high school than hers though, she supposed.

Grace laughed. "I agree. I went to college in Florida just to get away from the winters here."

She seemed nice enough. And of course, exactly when Jordyn thought that, Grace had to go and butt in with "Beckett dated my sister in high school."

"Oh, okay. Small world," Jordyn said stupidly. She'd love to face-palm herself right now. Small world? Small town, so duh. She wanted to walk farther down to the bags of carrots, but that would seem rude given what Grace just said.

Grace smiled nicely. No animosity or jealousy that she could tell. *Hmm?*

"Just be careful with that one. He takes a while to get over," she said then panicked, eyes wide, like she said something wrong. She added, "But then again, my sister was young and that was a lifetime ago. He seems different with you. Sorry."

How would she know Beckett was different with her? She'd never even seen this person before. "Well, he doesn't seem like how I expected Heartbreak Harper to be, but thanks for the warning." She nodded curtly. This conversation was so weird. When did it get to end? Now, hopefully. Where were those carrots?

"He's not really how they make him out to be," said Grace. As soon as the words were out of her mouth, Grace looked startled. "I'm sorry, that's weird, and I'm being awkward. I'm married. Happily married. So is my sister. I didn't mean it like that. We all just grew up together, you know? I was more so trying to protect you. Sorry!"

If he wasn't how they made him out to be, what exactly did she need protection from?

But then she understood what Grace was getting at. She just knew. Getting over Beckett Harper was going to be a hell of a lot harder than it would've been to get over Heartbreak Harper. Heartbreak Harper was a one-night stand type of man; Beckett Harper was a gentleman. When Thomas broke her heart, it sucked, but the relationship was fairly easy to get over because he was such a dang jerk. Beckett had never been a jerk to her.

Yep. This type of heartbreak was going to be completely different and annihilating. It would cut deep, forging a chasm in her poor heart.

Fortunately, her conversation with Grace got to end because Beckett came over with a cart full of groceries. He looked at the two of them, confused, but kept his sights on Jordyn until he reached them.

"Grace." He nodded toward her before giving Jordyn a kiss on the cheek again. "You ready, Jordyn?"

Thank goodness. Saved by Beckett. She nodded. "Yep, let's go home. Nice to meet you, Grace."

As they walked away, checked out, and loaded the truck, Beckett could not stop smiling. When they were headed back out to the farm, she finally asked, "Is your ex-girlfriend's sister talking to me in the store so dang amusing?"

He shook his head, confused for a moment. "Whoa! Grace? No, not at all. That wasn't what I was smiling about. Why, what'd she say?"

Jordyn joined him in confusion. "I'm not really sure, but I think she was preparing me for the mother of all heartbreaks with you."

That seemed to make him mad. "Just because I dumped her sister doesn't mean I'm going to dump you."

Interesting choice of words. Then again, they were adults, and her breakup with Beckett would probably be mutual—no dumping in the traditional high school sense. Shoot, this wasn't even dating in the traditional sense. Maybe that's what Beckett meant. "I'm not sure that's what she meant. She was actually very nice. It was awkward but nice. She said she was happily married and so was your ex. So I have that going for me. I'm not sure I could compete with your high school love."

He scoffed at that. "It was not love. We were both young and stupid. And you could compete with the best of them, honey."

She laughed at his praise. "So why the heck were you smiling like a fool for the last five minutes, then?"

He slowly grinned. "When I asked if you were ready, you told me 'let's go home.' You said 'home.'"

She wanted to stop smiling as she realized her mistake. *Uh-oh.* Yes, Beckett's house was feeling more and more like home. She shouldn't have slipped up like that, but he was so happy, so darn pleased she'd said it, that she found she didn't regret it. "I guess I did."

****

What a night. First Rose and the tabloid nonsense, then Grace at the store. Sometimes he wanted to move far, far away and never come back. Most of the people here meant well though; Rose was right. He could think of at least ten people who, if he ever needed anything, would come running the second he'd mention it. Living in a town the size of Picketts was both a curse and blessing. But it was home.

The night did get better when they got to relax by the fire and watch a movie. Jordyn fell asleep about thirty minutes in, but he didn't mind.

Getting snowed in had offered him the solitude with this woman to develop some very real feelings for her, very fast. If they hadn't been snowed in together, would she have ever gotten over his being a football player? Would he have ever seen the girl who had been through hell and still made a name for herself — or would he have been stuck on the fact that she was from the city? She would have left that night, and he would've never seen her again.

Yeah. Getting snowed in with Jordyn was a miracle. Neither of them probably would have given each other a chance or even another passing thought if they weren't forced to live together for a week. And he had nine days left with her. Who was counting though, right? Nine days to prove to her . . . hell, he didn't know what he needed to prove to her. He just didn't want her to leave. But he couldn't be that clingy guy and ask her to stay. He had no idea how he got to be this guy anyway, but here he was. He should probably check on his manhood, but knowing the number of cold showers he'd been taking this last week, he knew everything was all still there and working properly. *All systems go.*

His phone buzzed in his pocket, but he was in no hurry to move. It was probably Blakely since they went to Rose's again. Then two more buzzes came, followed by text messages. He thought it would wake up Jordyn, so he moved to grab his cell phone.

Harper!

Hey you.

Heard you were doing a commercial, baby.

Who the hell was this and why were they calling him *baby*? Weird. He felt a prickling sensation on the back of his neck.

He responded with *Who is this?*

A response arrived almost immediately. *Please. You know. You can't forget me that easily, Harper.*

He clenched his jaw. Yep. It had to be Ariana. The supermodel. The supermodel who ruined women for him. The one girl he never wanted to see again. The one who told him he was a nobody and that he couldn't possibly support her. That same one he had deleted from his phone and wanted to delete from his memory for forever. He was still mad he fell for that crap and actually thought at one point she was a good person. He took a deep breath before responding back.

Ariana, I can forget you that easily. I meant what I said the last time we spoke. It's over. And the only reason you are texting me now is because you think you can get in on the commercial. Not happening.

And in true Ariana fashion, she responded with a simple *We'll see, Harper.*

Talk about a mood killer. This right here — Jordyn curled into him with her head on his chest while he ran his fingers through her soft hair — was a good thing he had going. No, it wasn't that physical yet. But it could be. It *would* be eventually. Considering the chemistry they had just kissing, he knew the rest was going to be pretty spectacular whenever they got around to it. Emotionally he was on a nine-day time crunch, but in not rushing the physical part of their relationship, he was hoping to show her that Heartbreak Harper was a thing of the past.

And then Ariana just had to come back snooping into his business after two years of radio silence. He guaranteed it was because she got wind of the Super Bowl commercial. If she could somehow get in on it, she would book her calendar for the rest of the year. Typical. She was a user. And all about herself. Ariana wasn't even her real name. It was her model name. Yeah. She was a trip.

He carried Jordyn down the hallway and into the guest bedroom, vowing not to let some two-faced toxic psycho ruin what he had with Jordyn. This was different. She was different. And he only had nine days to prove to her how much he cared.

Burnt Porkchops

CHAPTER 16

Laundry. She needed to do some serious laundry. Had Jordyn known she was going to be staying so long, she would've packed more outfits. And more leggings. And more hoodies. Hoodies were her weakness. She knew they were unflattering and bulky, but since she was always cold, they were her go-to. Even in Houston. Houston was weird in that in January and February it could get really cold. Not negative temperatures, thank the Lord, but the ever-present humidity made it feel colder than it was. Like a damp, chill-your-bones type of cold. So hoodies were a must. Just not in August or September when it was so hot your sweat had sweat.

She realized her mistake after the first load of laundry finished washing. She washed all her cardigans and hoodies together, thus didn't have one. And she was starting to feel cold. She had just decided to sit by the fire to finish her work emails when she opened the dryer to switch the clothes and found a load of Beckett's stuff.

There was one of his red Nebraska hooded sweatshirts. His alma mater. The team he played for.

Yep. That was hers now. *Finders keepers.*

She even went a little wild and crazy and gave the dryer a five-minute warm-up so she could put on Beckett's *warm* hoodie.

As she put it on she may have embarrassingly enough let out an "ahhh" type of noise. It was a huge hoodie, going way past her butt. Like she was fairly certain she could wear just his hoodie as a dress. Which led to other not-so-appropriate thoughts about wearing a T-shirt of Beckett's to bed every night, and possibly even a ring on her finger. Okay, she needed to stop.

Yeah. All that from a warm Beckett hoodie. She needed to get a grip. She rolled up the sleeves and tucked the back part into the back of her leggings, and then she was set to go. *And warm.*

Not long after, the doorbell rang. She jumped before she remembered that Beckett had told her the veterinarian was coming over to check on the hurt heifer, who Jordyn had affectionately nicknamed Bess.

She swung open the door, forgetting she was wearing Beckett's hoodie — and the fact that she probably looked super gangster with it on.

"Holy crap," the voice said.

She looked at the man and thought, *ditto.* This could not be the vet, could it? She was expecting some gray-haired, balding, pudgy old guy. With glasses. Possibly gout. Not this guy. He looked just as in shape as Beckett did! Did they do that CrossFit stuff together or something? Neither one of them had obviously skipped leg day in a while. Or arm day. Or neck day. *Allllll* the days.

"Hi," she finally sputtered, looking around him for someone else. Surely this was not the vet?!

"Hi." He smiled, one hand in his front pocket, the other holding his veterinary kit. "Beckett told me you were from Texas. So when I rang the doorbell and saw you in his Nebraska hoodie, I was taken by surprise for a second." He shook his head, a half smile tugging at one side of his mouth. "He's got you in red already. We were taking bets on it in town. Not even kidding."

She smiled. This town and their red wearing and Husker cheering. They were nothing but loyal, she'd give them that. "I'm Jordyn. And that's just fine. I was taken aback too. I was expecting someone . . . "

"Older?" he offered. "I get that a lot."

She smiled. "I'm sure you do." She was *surrrre* he did.

The man was attractive, like a hard-to-look-away type of attractive. He was obviously intelligent too if he was a doctor. He had on a work coat and jeans but still looked fit. And where Beckett was blond-haired, blue-eyed, and solid muscle, this guy had green eyes and brown hair—the same shade as hers—with a leaner frame.

She stepped aside, realizing she was just standing there gawking like an idiot. "Can I get you some coffee? I'll text Beckett, and he'll be right in from wherever he's at. That way you don't have to go chase him down."

He laughed. "I'm Mason, by the way. No coffee for me, but thanks, that'd be great." He left his work kit on the porch and then came in the house.

"Tea instead or just water?" she offered.

"Tea if he has it." He nodded.

She texted Beckett that the vet arrived and went to get them some warm teas.

They sat there chitchatting, and a few minutes later Beckett came in the house in a hurry. He turned the corner from the laundry room and stopped in his tracks. "The hell?!"

"What?" Jordyn asked. "Why does everyone keep saying stuff like that?"

He looked at his hoodie she was wearing, raising his eyebrows in surprise.

She rolled her eyes. "Mine are all in the wash, so I stole yours for a bit." Lies. She was never giving it back, but he didn't need to know that. She knew what he was getting paid for the commercial; he could buy another one if he even missed it. And she knew he had multiple red ones, gray ones, and black ones. He had enough Husker gear from when he was playing to wear a different Husker shirt every day of the week for a month. Maybe more.

He looked at her for so long, and with such heat in his gaze, that she finally asked, "Would you like me to take it off?"

"Yes!" he said too quickly, which made Mason chuckle. "But no."

"Do I need to give you guys a minute?" Mason asked playfully.

"Mase, I swear. You think you know a woman. Then she puts on your college hoodie and just gets that much hotter." If Beckett smiled any bigger, his face might bust.

"I was shocked you had her in red already. Thought for sure you'd need another week," Mason fired back. "We had bets going in town, dammit. I thought for sure this Texas girl would fight it. So how'd you do it? Play old highlight reels? Take out the high school championship footage?"

Mason didn't hesitate to give Beckett crap. She liked him already.

Beckett kept talking like she wasn't in the room. "With this one, Mason, I have no idea what I did or didn't do. None of the usual rules apply."

Mason laughed again. "Dude, the rumors are actually true for once. You're gone already."

She wasn't sure she knew what that meant, but it sounded in the realm of good. And it seemed like with men there was some unsaid man code that as long as they said "dude" in front of a statement, they could say something as emotional to one another as they wanted.

"Do y'all want some cookies, or are you just going to talk about me some more like I'm not in the room?" she asked as she sat a plate on the table.

Mason grabbed a cookie, took a bite, and let out a moan. "She bakes and y'alls?"

Beckett looked at Jordyn, staring her down. "Yep."

Mason chuckled again, taking another bite. "Totally a goner."

Becket snorted out a laugh. "I know. And I'm not even mad."

****

"So you met Mason," Beckett said.

Jordyn didn't hesitate to smile. "You could have told me he wasn't some fat old guy. I about had a heart attack!"

Beckett stepped away from the porkchops he was cooking to where she was at the table with her computer. He got eye level, just to be annoying. "Why? You interested in my vet, sweetheart?"

She rolled her eyes. "No. I initially wondered what kind of workouts you two do together. I mean, yes, he's attractive . . ."

He just stared her down. He wasn't really jealous. Well, not really. Of course, he did kind of want to know what she thought. Girls came from all over in pursuit of either Mason or Beckett. He was man enough to admit that Mason was probably more attractive than he was—prettier anyway. Beckett had played the sport this state worshipped, whereas Mason had been a pitcher for Kansas City. He was still a hometown hero, but hadn't quite reached the crazy-groupie level that Beckett was on. If Mason had played football instead of baseball though, Mason would win the contest, hands down.

She moved her computer and scooted closer to Beckett, who now had his arms on either side of her chair. *That was more like it. Bring it on in.*

"I think he's an attractive man, but I am not attracted to him. There. How's that?" she offered innocently. She was smooth, this one.

"Hmm. Acceptable answer, I suppose," he murmured, moving in closer to her so they were right in each other's faces. "Seriously, though, this hoodie. It's doing it for me."

She gave him a quick kiss on the dimple and laughed. "Seriously, Beckett? I have zero curves in this thing, I'm drowning in it. It's super unflattering on all five feet five of me."

He moved to whisper in her ear. "Yeah, but it's mine."

She whispered back, "And you're never getting it back either."

To which he groaned and said, "Good," before they were crashing into one another.

They ended up eating burnt porkchop because they'd been too distracted to keep an eye on supper, but Beckett wasn't complaining any. Zero complaints. Best damn burnt porkchop he'd ever had.

****

Wednesday had turned into such a surprise. Beckett had told her to have all her work done by two in the afternoon so they could go on a real date. So she did just that. She wore her skinny jeans and flat boots and a cute sweater she had packed along. She didn't have many options, but she was sure to do her hair and makeup to make a bigger impact. Beckett had somehow convinced Mason to come over and do the evening chores so they could drive into the nearest city without having to worry about rushing home.

It was an hour and a half to that city, so they had a bit of a road trip. Jordyn, though a self-declared small-town hater, thought it was adorable Beckett was an hour and a half from a Target. She wasn't sure how he survived, but then again, she could sit in traffic for an hour and a half if there was a bad accident or something. So it was oddly nice to drive and be able to see snow-covered field after field—and actually get somewhere when they were driving. It seemed like in Houston there was a ton of travel time but not that many miles driven.

They ate at a little restaurant with a rear party room that Beckett had rented—so they could eat without Beckett's celebrity status ruining their alone time. The waiter did ask for an autograph, but who could blame the poor kid, right?

After a nice, quiet meal, Beckett surprised her by stopping at a gas station. She figured he just wanted snacks, since he was always snacking, but he instead got them each a cup of hot chocolate.

"Gas-station hot chocolate?" she asked. "My favorite." It kind of was. That and those cappuccino things that were terrible for you. She didn't like coffee, but those were more like dessert in a cup. She loved it though. She wasn't above gas-station goodies. You didn't need all that fancy coffee; a seventy-five-cent hot cocoa would do perfectly fine most days.

He shook his head. "I guess I should have expected that, but I didn't."

She bounced her eyebrows. "So you don't get all of your conquests gas-station hot cocoa, then?" When he glared at her, she appeased him by changing the subject. "Are we heading home now?"

He went from annoyed to grinning in record speed. "There it was again — that H word. And no, not yet."

"Well, where are we going?"

He looked at her as he stopped at a stoplight. "We are going on a Harper family tradition. Hot cocoa and Christmas-lights looking. They have a little drive-through lights display area. I'm sure you've seen better in the big city, but it's not too bad. And no, I have never taken any woman other than Blakely on this tradition."

He was taking her Christmas-lights looking? Was this real life . . . ?!

"You do like Christmas lights, right?" he asked in her hesitation.

She nodded eagerly, taking in a huge breath of air, because all of a sudden she was feeling winded. "Of course I do. What sane woman wouldn't? I'm just touched you would share a family tradition like that with me. And do something so . . ."

"Mundane?"

She nodded.

He shrugged. "That's my life here. Or it was, until you came strolling — or *falling* — in."

As she tentatively took a sip of her hot cocoa, she thanked her lucky stars her heel gave out when it did back on that fateful day.

CHAPTER 17

His phone would not stop buzzing. He was a bit tired. Last night Jordyn had made him drive through the lights not once, not twice, but a record-setting three times. They had laughed and told stories and had the most amazing official first date. He was now in the shop trying to get some work done on his tractor with a bad radiator, but his phone just would not shut up. Which was fine — his heart wasn't in it anyway.

Jordyn was slammed with work, but he just wanted to hang out with her. He was trying to clean up the shop and work on the tractor to keep himself from doing something with her. He didn't care what they did; he just wanted to spend time with her. But he also knew she had to work this week. Over lunch she had barely even had time to say a word to him because she was so busy — probably because of the commercial. Hopefully it was all set up soon so they could get back to enjoying the few days together they had left.

Another phone call. At this rate, his phone was going to buzz right off the workbench and shatter. He finally gave up, washed his hands, and looked at the screen of his phone. He saw he missed two calls from his old agent, a call from Rose, and three calls from Blakely. This couldn't be good.

Well, if he was going to get bad news, he'd prefer it be from his sister. With all they'd been through, she knew him best, so he dialed her first.

She didn't even say hello. "You and Jordyn are in the tabloids," she blurted out.

He sighed. "Hello. Okay, which ones and what's going on?"

She rattled off two or three names. "You must have gone on a date in Hill Creek? In the picture, you are out on a date and holding hands. You are leaning in, whispering something, and she's laughing. There's no way you guys don't look like an item."

Well, it could've been worse. It could've been of them making out while they waited in line for the Christmas lights. Because that definitely happened. *Twice.*

"I just wanted to make sure you knew and that Jordyn was prepared," she explained.

He sighed again. "She's not. She had a crappy childhood. Her mom is a deadbeat, and she never even knew her dad. The last thing she wants is people digging into her past."

Blakely was quiet a moment. "Maybe they'll just focus on the commercial and AgGroSo so they stay away from all that."

"That's a good idea, B. I'll see what AgGroSo's PR team can do. Maybe they can help get the attention off her and onto the commercial. Hype it up a bit." He nodded his agreement, though his sister couldn't see it.

"Beckett Harper," Blakely said quietly. His full name. This wasn't going to be good.

"Yeah?"

"What happens when the commercial is over, and she has to go back?" she asked. His sister was never this serious with him, so she must be pretty concerned.

He sighed again. "I don't honestly know, B. I just know I don't want it to be over. Do I love her? I don't know. It's definitely stronger than 'like.' It's strong enough that I want to take it slow and do things right. But that many miles between us is going to be rough. Especially if the tabloids know."

"I just can't believe you actually really feel like this," she said. "For a while there, I thought you were going to be a bachelor for life."

"Me too, sis. She's just different. Way different than any woman I ever cared to get to know." He paused, thinking of her. "Sometimes in the little things she does—always getting me a cup of coffee the way I like it, or making cookies just because—she reminds me a lot of mom and her thoughtful ways. And Jordyn has been alone most of her life. It's just naturally who she is. Then the next second she calls me out on my crap."

Blakely sighed. "I think if you like it, then you should put a ring on it."

He laughed. "Ha. Good Lord, B. Slow down. It hasn't even been two weeks. I'm trying not to scare her off, no thanks to the tabloids. And I'm trying my damndest to be a man she deserves, not like Dad was to Mom. I also feel like trying to live down this Heartbreak Harper crap is going to be tough. I stayed out of the public eye for two years, and that still wasn't enough apparently."

Blakely was quiet a moment. "You won't be like Dad. You have too much of Mom in there too. And besides, I know you hated how he treated her, but they did love one another in their own way. You just have to learn from their relationship to know in what ways you want something different."

Well, when it came down to the way his dad was with his mom, he wanted to be *way* different.

"Now get off the phone with me and go tell Jordyn if she doesn't already know," Blakely commanded.

"Annnd there's my bossy little sister," he said with a laugh.

She tried not to laugh. He could hear it in her voice. "I'll see you in less than two weeks when I get back. I so can't wait for Christmas this year."

For once, neither could he. "Me too. See you, B."

"Love you, Big B," she said before she hung up.

"Love you too."

Great. So the word was out.

He got on his smartphone and googled his name. He supposed by this point he should have alerts for his name, but for the most part, he just didn't care. And back in his wild days, he really didn't care to see what anyone had to say. This was different though. Not that he cared what they said about him, but he cared what they said about *her*.

The picture taken had to have been from the waiter at supper last night. He had even autographed a piece of paper for the kid. He was angry. He was nothing but kind, even leaving him a huge tip, and this is how he went and repaid him?

He had to take a steadying breath. This was just a high school kid. There was no sense in getting him fired or something. If he was in high school and working there on a school night, he was obviously there for the money. He probably sold the picture to make a little more. The kid had no idea Jordyn had a past he didn't want them to dig into. So it really wasn't his fault.

The headline over the picture read, "Heartbreak Harper at It Again, Finally Making It to the Super Bowl."

A bit of a low blow. Freaking ouch.

He quickly skimmed the articles. Other than linking Jordyn to AgGroSo and Houston, nothing more was really said. Good. He'd like to keep it that way.

Now knowing what he was dealing with, he texted his agent that he'd call him back in a bit, then went inside to break the news to Jordyn. He hated this. He hated his reputation and trying to overcome it. He and Jordyn were at a good place right now. This was just another strain they didn't need on their relationship.

****

So she was in the tabloids. Super. Just super. Since Walt called this morning and told her, she'd done nothing but be on the phone with work. PR was working on running a press release telling the details of the commercial with Beckett, like a teaser for a commercial, if such a thing even existed. Then hopefully the articles would revolve around that and not who she was and how this ordinary nobody came to be dating Heartbreak Harper.

Hopefully?!

Beckett came in earlier in the afternoon than she expected, and with one look at his face, she understood that he also knew.

"You know?" he asked.

She nodded and said with an annoyed gesture, "I've been dealing with it all morning." He'd been in for lunch, but she was on the phone pretty much the whole time, so she hadn't even had a minute to tell him.

"You knew at lunch?" he asked.

She nodded.

"And you didn't tell me?" he asked. Judging by his crossed arms and tense neck, he was perhaps a little ticked off.

She sighed. "I was on the phone with Walt and then PR, trying to figure out what to do about it. And . . . and I guess I just didn't know what to do. We both knew it was a possibility." She stopped to shrug. "To be honest, it was bound to happen eventually. I just hope they don't go digging around for too much information on me. PR updated my personal file on our website so that only select vague information is given. I already double-checked my settings on my social media accounts, so that's the good news. Good thing Rose had it on my radar so I could do some of this before."

He looked at her a moment then looked away, jaw tight, that vein in his neck doing its thing.

"Are you mad?" she asked, knowing he was.

He looked out the windows a few seconds before responding, leaving her uneasy in the silence. "I'm more mad you didn't tell me you knew than at the stupid articles."

She thought about that a second. "Oh."

He pierced her with his gaze. "And not because I'm concerned with the tabloids or care if people know about the commercial. I'm not concerned about that. At all. What I am concerned about is *you*."

She felt the tears sting her eyes.

He closed the distance between them and wrapped her in his arms. "I'm sorry. I'm sorry dating me has to be this huge thing. I promise you I'm a normal person. I only played in the pros for two seasons, not even finishing the second one. The reason for all this whoopla is just my reputation. And believe me, I never thought that years later I would still be trying to live it down."

She smiled. "I know it isn't your fault. Well, I mean, it isn't Beckett Harper's fault. It may be Heartbreak Harper's fault, but I have yet to meet him."

"You won't," he said softly, running a hand through her hair. He must have a thing for her hair because he was always doing that.

"So now what?" she asked.

"Now I call my agent and do things on my end to smooth it over to keep them off your back. Then we shoot the most amazing commercial in the history of commercials."

She laughed and sniffed the rest of the tears away. "You really have come around to this idea of doing the commercial."

"Among other things," he offered slyly. "You didn't get in trouble with work, did you? For schmoozing the client?"

She rolled her eyes. "You mean by doing what Walt sent me to do? No. In fact, they were all excited. AgGroSo is trending on Twitter right now. Everyone wants to know what got Beckett Harper back into civilization."

He smirked. "Figures. I'm sorry I didn't know better. We should've just gone to Rose's again. I just wanted to do something different and special with you, but I should've considered the risks more."

She shrugged. "I loved our date. If this is a part of dating you, I need to learn to calm down and deal with it. It's just intimidating that we've only been dating such a short time and they've found out already. Today marks only a week left. I just feel like there are so many things trying to pull us apart."

He gave her a kiss on the cheek and whispered, "So don't let them."

She took a deep breath and nodded. "I'm going to take a long shower and relax after this morning. Then I'm going to turn off my phone and bake some brownies. How about you do the chores early, and then we can fire up those old college games you and Mason were talking about?"

He looked shocked. "Seriously? You want to see me play?"

Heck yes she wanted to see him play. She'd already looked up a video—or seven—of him already. "*Yes,*" she said strongly.

He grinned slowly, that single dimple taking its time torturing her. "You have been the best surprise."

His words melted her. And she knew exactly how he felt. He wasn't what she expected either. She kissed him on the cheek and turned to go shower, trying to shake off the questions and emotions that were rolling through her. What was she really doing here? Were they really going to try to date long-distance? Did she really want to come back for Christmas? And what did someone whose love life graced the tabloids see in a regular person like her?

She hoped her doubts and insecurities would drown in the shower, but she had a sneaking suspicion they'd stick around for a while.

****

"Ohhhhh, he got burned!" Jordyn clapped as Beckett scored a touchdown. She then punched him on the arm and said, "You totally smoked that guy. And how did you even catch that ball?! It was like all fingertips. Didn't bobble at all. And you stuck the two-foot landing so he couldn't push you out. Freaking wow!"

He had to admit, watching himself play was a little weird. Seemed a little self-serving and egotistical. But seeing his girl get all sorts of excited about it was a major turn-on. *Major.*

Then she started clapping along to his alma mater's school song, and he busted out laughing.

"You've really come a long way in the last couple of weeks, Houston," he said with a laugh.

"You too, *Harper*," she laughed back.

He told some stories and gave her insider information as they watched the game: what the play calls were, what the quarterback saw and didn't like so he called an audible to switch the play, the dirty things the defense was doing on the bottom of the pile—stuff like that. And she acted like this was the most fun she'd had in forever. She even paused it a few times to have him explain a few things, playwise, and how they were going to pan out.

They took a break only to make hot dogs and popcorn. "Game food," she had simply explained to him as she camped out to eat in the living room.

And it was at that moment—seeing Jordyn cheer for him, even when she already knew the outcome of the game—that he missed playing the most. What he wouldn't give to still be able to play. To have Jordyn sitting in the stands, watching and cheering for him. To have that extra motivation to do well.

It was also at that moment that he knew he needed her. Yeah, he wanted her too. Definitely that too. But he needed her to cheer for him.

When they got to the play where his career ended, he paused and explained everything to her before it happened. A fast route to the corner of the endzone. He was double teamed. The ball was thrown exactly where it should have been too; it was no one's fault—just bad timing.

Feeling her tense up beside him as the footage replayed the play in slow motion, he grabbed her hand and intertwined his fingers with hers.

"Just remember that I'm okay today, and that's more than some people can say," he said, watching the tears fill her eyes.

"What hurt worse, knee or back?" she asked quietly, breath quivering.

He nodded twice. "Yes. All of it. I was in a ton of pain. I wanted to get up but couldn't. I was trying and failing to not be a sissy about it. I knew my knee was messed up, but as I lay there, I knew it was way worse than just that. The medical team and trainers came running out and yelling at me to not move. I can distinctly remember lying as still as possible but still wiggling my toes. In that exact moment, I just wanted to be sure I could walk again someday."

He stopped to swallow hard. "But I could move my toes and that gave me a small amount of hope. This," —he paused as he knew they were about to put the neck brace around him on the TV— "was a terrifying moment. I can still smell that neck brace. Smelled like it had been in a hospital for all of eternity. I have never felt more vulnerable in my life than this moment right here. I still wish I would've been knocked out for this part."

She caught her breath so he looked at her.

"Oh my gosh, Beckett, you still have the ball," she snorted through her tears. She stared at the screen as the medical team took the ball before they put on the neck brace.

He smiled at her. "Told you I caught it."

She shook her head and then looked back to the TV.

He knew without even looking they were getting ready to place him on a stretcher while his team looked on.

With searching eyes, she looked back at him.

"What?"

She squeezed his hand. "I'm so sorry that happened. And how terrifying that was." A tear spilled out of her eye and rolled down her cheek. "And I also want you to know how proud I am of the person you are today."

Now it was his turn to fight down emotion. He wiped her tear away with a kiss and then kissed her hard.

Yep. He needed Jordyn. She was part of his team now. And she was filling a huge, gaping hole he hadn't really realized was there from when his parents died. He'd date her for years with them living in two different cities if he had to; he just couldn't let her go.

CHAPTER 18

Watching Beckett's college tapes that night had been amazing. He was freakishly talented. Remembering how fast he snagged that dropped Christmas ball while tree decorating, she knew he still was. His injury stole his love of football away from him though. Snatched it all right out of his hands. And she knew, other than watching games from the comfort of his couch, it still hurt four years later to do much else with the sport. He couldn't be on the field and not want to reach up and grab the ball himself.

It was a weird sensation being able to watch the exact moment someone's heart broke. Because in the few seconds it took for Beckett to reach for the ball and land, he lost the love of his life. He lost the opportunity to play football. It was all over in the blink of an eye. He had gone up for balls like that time and time again. He snagged the ball in one hand like a beast and twisted to make sure his feet were in. A wrong hit and getting mixed up in another guy's limbs were all it took. Just like that, Beckett's promising football career was over.

And she knew a few months later he buried his mom. No wonder he was a mess after that. No wonder he went a little crazy afterward. His whole world was off-kilter. Nothing probably made sense. How he got from Heartbreak Harper back to the man he was today was beyond her. He lost almost everything he cared about in the span of six months. He'd had to deal with the pain and surgeries, grieve the loss of his football career, *and* mourn for his mom at the same time. Knowing how far he'd evolved from that shell of a man, how hard he'd worked to make a successful living off his grandfather's land . . . well, it made her never want to leave.

Yep. As Mason had said, she was a goner.

She was pathetic really. She hated small towns. She hated football players.

But one blizzard and two weeks later, she was falling for both.

****

They were cuddled up on the couch in their usual spot after watching the football tapes. They had been talking some more on what the tabloid rumors meant for them and what they needed to do about it. Jordyn logically had lots of "what if" scenarios running through her pretty mind, and he fielded her questions. She was being brutally honest, per her usual way.

He supposed part of it had to be because she'd seen the statement he and his agent threw together. It stated he was in fact "smitten" with the AgGroSo representative who was helping with the commercial and she was a big part of the reason he'd decided to do an endorsement when he had refused in the past. It went on to sing Jordyn's praises, without actually saying her name of course, and then explained the feel of the commercial he'd be doing. It would effectively confirm they were dating, despite his usual refusal to state he was dating anyone, and simultaneously take the heat off her and put it on AgGroSo. It was an admission of their dating, but a bit of a tease for the commercial. Everyone would hopefully be more concerned about what he was up to with AgGroSo and less about where she came from.

After answering her slew of questions, he decided to take his sweet time kissing her, as if that could help alleviate her doubts.

She moved to put her hands under his shirt. Her cool hands on his skin were affecting him for sure, trailing what felt like fire across his skin where her fingers touched. He wanted more. So damn much more.

Despite struggling to breathe or think or do anything other than feel, he had a quick, rational thought that she was only touching him like this because of his statement confirming they were dating. That wasn't why he did it. And he didn't want her to do anything she would regret. He'd known from the start she was not the type of woman to sleep around. He respected her for that. And he also knew for a fact that once the clothes started coming off, stopping it became impossible. He was stuck between a rock and a hard place. No pun intended.

He forced himself to stop her hands, look her in the eyes, and whisper, "You aren't this type of woman. We don't have to do this."

He turned her down. The one woman he probably wanted more than any before. He was going to regret it later. He was absolutely certain of it.

That seemed to snap her out of her haze. "What?"

She looked so good like this. All disoriented and well kissed. He'd love nothing more than to get tangled up with her in the sheets for a decade or so.

Beckett smiled and leaned in to kiss her cheek, putting her hands on his chest, on top of his shirt. "Believe me, I want you." He stopped to take a still-shaky breath. "So freaking bad, Jordyn. Just not yet. I don't want you to do anything that you would hate yourself for in the morning."

"So you're stopping me?" she frowned. "I mean, I don't think I would've let it go *that* far anyway."

He nodded. "That may be, but I'm going to stop you before either one of us even puts it on the table. Even though stopping you is killing me, Jordyn. *Kill-ing. Me.*"

She thought about that for a long moment before asking at a whisper, "Okay, but aren't you worried that I won't measure up?"

No. What?! Hell no. Though they were still stuck on first base, he was already completely convinced the rest of it was going to be a great time. Fantastic. It was going to be fan-freaking-tastic.

"Definitely not. I'm more worried you'll ruin me," he said honestly with a laugh.

****

On Friday morning, she woke up a kind of a celebrity now too. AgGroSo coworkers she didn't know so well were being super nice to her in her work emails. Social media friends she hadn't talked to in forever were *coincidentally* reaching out. And in all the extra attention, the only people she cared to talk with were Sam and Walt. Sure, Walt was her boss, but he had also been a fatherlike figure for her in Houston. And when Walt called her to discuss work things, he always, always just checked on her first.

Walt was the reason why she stuck with AgGroSo. She didn't want to work for an agriculture-type company. That wasn't her big dream out of college, but he offered her a fair wage. And then he earned her trust and her loyalty. She could do much worse jobwise. After living with her mom for so long, her unpredictability and horrible ways with finances, she wanted to work hard and earn an honest living. So she did. She had a 401k and a savings account, things her mother probably still didn't have. She was smart with her money, she invested, and she never, ever needed a man to provide for her. Granted, she wasn't as well off as Beckett, but she wasn't doing terrible either. She was making it. Completely on her own.

As far as bosses go, Walt was a man of integrity, and she loved the way he carried himself and handled his business. She was not just an employee to him. None of his employees were. And that's why she hadn't left once she started. AgGroSo was home. It was a small company that had gradually expanded in the last few years, but recently they were making a killing. Obviously. They were doing well enough to buy the Super Bowl commercial slot, and those things were not cheap. She appreciated how

Walt had grown his business from the ground up. And though his success was mounting, he never let it go to his head. He could afford to drive whatever yuppy car he wanted, but he preferred a Chevy truck.

He had checked on her a ton in the last twenty-four hours. He was running interference for her, and she appreciated it. Yes, he had sent her here because she was a pretty face to present to Heartbreak Harper, but she highly doubted he ever thought she would end up dating the man. So he felt a little responsible. He knew Jordyn. He knew she didn't like the spotlight or to be the center of attention. And he had his own personal PR team working around the clock to make sure certain stories from her past were not dug up. She wasn't sure how it was possible, but nothing about her background had come out yet, so she supposed they were good at their jobs. Walt was probably paying extra for that, but hey, he got his fancy commercial, so he could deal with the ramifications.

Walt was even flying in himself on Wednesday for the wrap-up of the commercial filming. It was unusual for him to get out of his office, so she knew how excited he was about this. The entire company was. Everyone had an extra spring in their step, according to Walt. The following year was going to be their year.

"Hey honey, you need some more hot tea in there?" Beckett asked from the kitchen. He had spent part of the morning in the shop sprucing up and power washing the main tractor that was going to be used in the commercial. He had apparently worked up a very large appetite because he was in the kitchen cooking up a storm for brunch.

"I already have some, thanks!" she hollered back. She was curled up in her new favorite work spot—the couch in front of the tree they had decorated together. Mable always camped out with her in the living room and kept her company too.

"You sure you aren't empty yet? I've seen how much of that stuff you consume," he yelled back.

"Ha, ha," she responded, smiling. "Says the man who drinks his sugar with coffee and no fewer than four cups a day."

"What can I say? I appreciate the sweet things in life," he said.

"Good thing I can bake," she said back. "And speaking of that, check that coffee cake in the oven for me, will ya?"

He opened the oven and let out a moan. "So that's the amazing smell. Hell yes, darlin'. Hell to the yes."

She finished her email and pet Mable while her computer shut down. Beckett continued puttering and clanging in the kitchen, mumbling about bacon and how bacon goes with everything.

Then she kind of had a moment of panic. That entire conversation—everything they had just said to one another—didn't sound like a couple making a run at trying to date. It sounded like a married couple. A couple that enjoyed being in one another's presence and giving one another crap. A couple that *knew* one another.

The blizzard had afforded her the opportunity to date this man at a rapid pace. She already understood that much. Maybe her going back to Houston in a week would put the brakes on some of these feelings. This right here was the exact reason she had told herself she'd never live with a man she didn't marry, quite unlike her mother. She didn't want a trial run on marriage, or a pretend go at it. She just wanted a permanent, never-give-up type of commitment. Her mother was currently on marriage number four, and while Jordyn grew up, she probably lived with four or five more men her mother had never married. She wanted to be as far opposite of that as possible.

And Beckett. Beckett had been nothing but a gentleman with her, even stopping her last night.

Who the heck was this man?

Yep. That was just what she needed. Air. Going to Houston would be a nice slowdown. Because things were moving extremely fast, and if she wasn't careful, she'd start planning out the rest of their lives together. And if life had taught Jordyn anything, it was that "happily ever afters" weren't meant to happen to her.

The Repeat Offender
CHAPTER 19

Friday had been the best day. Had been. Past tense, for sure.

They went into town that afternoon to run a few errands and then to Rose's for an early supper, and since it was Friday, there were still a whole passel of people there despite it being earlier. Since the entire world knew they were dating now, it didn't really bother either of them. Aunt Rose was Aunt Rose, and they all had a splendid time. It was looking like it would end up a good day.

They planned to watch some of his, and her, favorite football movies later that night after he finished up the chores. He already owned most of them, and she got to pick the order. They were going to pig out on the popcorn and candy they'd bought in town for this very reason, and stay up late for their football movie marathon.

Yeah, she wasn't just a woman he wanted to date, but their dates were actually fun. For both of them. And at this point, it wasn't like they were being over the top trying to impress one another either. It turned out, if you lived under the same roof with a woman, for however short amount of time, you learned who the real person was pretty fast. That was probably the reason why he refused to even stay over at any other woman's place before. It didn't take long for all the false pretenses to fade away when you were spending day in and day out with one another. Things could get pretty ugly pretty fast.

Just not with Jordyn. He loved that she had been the one to suggest the football movie marathon night. They had been having an argument about whether *The Replacements* or *The Blind Side* was better, and she asked if they could watch them to find out. He wanted to kiss her senseless for suggesting it. Because who does that?

But he did at least try to make it more of a date. He wore jeans and a nice T-shirt. He also set up some candles in the living room to make it a little more romantic. He knew girls were supposed to like fluffy stuff like that. Or that's what Blakely told him anyway. Shoot, he even got some flowers for her while they were in town. She didn't seem like the flowers type of woman, but he was just trying to show her, any way he could, that he wanted them to figure this thing out.

They weren't very far into *The Blind Side* when there was a knock on his door. He was mad before he even got up. They were having a great evening. They were laughing and giving each other crap, and at supper Jordyn had finally admitted to him that she wanted to come for Christmas.

"Hi, baby," said a super fake, seductive voice as cracked open the door.

Yep. His whole entire day just went to hell. Completely shot. Ka-put. And as he looked at Ariana—all fake lips, fake eyelashes, and fake other parts that were falling out of her shirt right now—he just didn't recall what he ever saw in her. Yeah, she was a looker all right, but underneath all that, she had disappointed him. When he first met her, she had been charming and kind, something he thought was different from the women he had been seeing. Now that he really knew her, he knew she was manipulative and selfish. He had never been more wrong about a person in his entire life. And this was the one woman he had even considered dating. To say it backfired was an understatement. He was so glad he didn't date her long. She was an exhausting creature. However long their semblance of a relationship had lasted was more than long enough for him.

Yet here she was. In the flesh. This was *so* not good. Fortunately, Jordyn had gone to the restroom when they paused the movie because of the knock at the door, so maybe he could hurry up and get Ariana out of here before she ruined more than just his mood for the evening.

"I'm not your baby, Ariana. I don't know why you came here, but please leave."

She rolled her eyes and pushed open the door a little farther. "Is she here?"

"Ariana, get out." He seriously hated this chick. Who the heck did she think she was? And her wanting to see Jordyn?? No. *Helllll no.*

"Is everything okay?" Jordyn asked from behind him.

Dammit. "Yes, darlin'. Just taking out the trash." He tried to send Jordyn a look that told her how much he cared about her.

Ariana rolled her eyes. "I'll tell you what's *not* trash. This little farmhouse. Why were you holding out on me? I didn't know you inherited this place. It's got to be worth a pretty penny."

He groaned. "Which you would have wanted me to sell. Not happening. Ever."

Ariana actually pouted. Or she tried to. The extra collagen in her lips made it look weird though. Like duck-face-meets-horror-movie type of wrong. Did people actually find all that fakeness attractive? Well, he guessed he did at some point in time, but now it was almost comical.

"Ariana. Leave. *Now.*"

Jordyn, sensing his anger, came up and wrapped her arm around his waist, tucking her small body inside the frame of his. And he loved her for it. She didn't know what was happening, or who Ariana was, but she was automatically loyal and trusting of him. Her natural urge was to comfort and help him.

"Did you tell her who *I* am?" Ariana asked and then proceeded to introduce herself to Jordyn.

Jordyn tried to introduce herself back, but Ariana cut her off. "I already know who *you* are. And that is someone terribly normal. Way too normal for our Beckett. Now, about this commercial. I only have your best interests at hand, and I have a few ideas. Your first endorsement needs to be impacting or it'll be hard to do anything else."

The hell? Like he wanted to do anything else? Excuse the hell out of him.

It was Jordyn's turn to lose her temper apparently. "This commercial has nothing to do with you and will have nothing to do with you. Beckett will not even be seen in the commercial, as it is about farm life. So unless you want to grab a shovel and scoop some cow dung, you won't be in it, nor will your ideas. Correction. No living person is in it. There are no actors. Just Beckett's voice and shots of the farm. So, no matter how you think you'll manipulate yourself into it, you won't be a part of this."

Holy freaking hell. He didn't know if he wanted to high-five her, kiss her, or just ask her to marry him right there on the spot.

Ariana opened her mouth to say something more, but Jordyn cut back in. "I will say though that the company shooting the commercial is big name. And that's probably why you're here. I've been working with them personally, as has my boss. If you stay out of production's way, I'll allow you to return the last day of filming to schmooze the production team. Though my company wouldn't want you *at all*, you could at least put yourself out there for other opportunities. But only if you stay out of the way and off this farm until Wednesday. If you don't, I'll make sure your name is blacklisted as far as commercials go. If you don't believe me, you're welcome to try it and see what happens." Jordyn ended her verbal lashing by placing her hands on her hips, daring Ariana to test her.

Ariana's mouth opened, and then shut. A few seconds later, she said, "I underestimated you."

Jordyn didn't hesitate. "Most people do. It's fun for me, not for them. See you Wednesday." And then she shut the door right in Ariana's face.

****

"Dang it. Nothing like a gold digger to ruin a good Thanksgiving moment on *The Blind Side*," Jordyn teased and went back over to the couch.

That was something. Emotionally draining. And good Lord, she couldn't believe that woman's appearance. She was all long raven-black hair, puffy lips, size zero, tall, and with heels even taller. Like how did she think she could even compete with all that? Jordyn was a size four on a good day. Wow. Just wow. That woman looked like a real Barbie, but with black hair instead of blond. Never in a million years did she think that she'd have to deal with one of Beckett's exes so soon. And she just knew this was that one woman he had more than one night with. Which means he must have seen something in her at some point in time.

But what exactly did he see? Because she was night-and-day different to that woman. If he found *that* attractive, if *that* was what he was looking for, then this was going to be over faster than his pro career. She was not like that woman at all.

Swallowing down her insecurities, she was about to push *play* on the remote when she realized Beckett still hadn't moved from the door.

"Waiting to make sure she leaves?" She turned back around to check on him. "Think she'll stay in town or leave and come back?"

He wasn't looking out the door though; he was staring at her with the weirdest look on his face. "I could care less about her. And I doubt she stays here longer than she has to. She probably can't survive any place without a spa."

"What're you doing, then?" she asked.

He ran a hand over his facial hair on the side of his cheek. "I have never been more impressed in my life. That woman tends to squeeze the life out of everyone she meets, but you outwitted her in less than two minutes of meeting her." He never took his eyes off hers and moved toward her.

"I take it that was the repeat offender?" she asked with a smile.

Beckett laughed, a real laugh, but was not deterred by her funny word choice. "Yes. And trust me, that's over. Has been for two years. There will be no more repeating."

She nodded. "Okay."

"That's it? Okay?" he asked.

She shrugged. "You obviously didn't know she was coming. And she was obviously trying to use you for the commercial. I wasn't about to let that happen."

He shook his head. "I just didn't know you had that in you."

She smiled. "What can I say? I'm loyal to a fault."

Still shaking his head, he added, "Jordyn Mack, you are going to ruin me."

Two-Week Anniversary
CHAPTER 20

Saturday, Beckett let himself sleep in. The night before had been draining, so he got a couple extra hours. It was only 8:00 a.m. when he rolled out of bed, but Jordyn was already ahead of him. She had a fresh batch of waffles made but was flying around the kitchen doing other things.

"Big plans today, darlin'?" he asked, confused. Was today something special? He guessed it was like their two-weeks-of-knowing-one-another anniversary. Females liked to track crap like that, right? But that was hopefully not what she was doing. Yes, it was probably his longest relationship in like six years, but she didn't need to shove that in his face, did she?

"Game food!" she hollered, putting her hands in the air with two potholders in the signal of a touchdown.

He almost spit out his orange juice, which he only ever drank with waffles or pancakes, and somehow Jordyn already knew that about him. He should be scared really. "Game food?"

She nodded. "Conference championships are today. They start this afternoon, so I have to have all my game snackies and work emails done before then so I can veg for all the games. Plus the food for church tomorrow morning too. You game for all that? You and me and a bunch of unhealthy food?"

He didn't give this woman credit enough. Here he was freaking out because he thought she'd be wanting to celebrate their two-week anniversary. As it turned out, she just wanted to watch college football with a bunch of game food. And him.

He really should just marry this girl . . . like tomorrow.

"What? Why are you looking at me like that?" she asked like he was crazy. "You have plans with the guys already or something? It's no big deal if you do."

He wasn't about to tell her the truth of what he was really thinking about. "Not at all. I've just never seen a woman so jazzed up about game food," he said honestly.

She shrugged, potholders still in her hands. "I like football. I like game food."

And he *definitely* liked her. "Well, what's on the menu for said game food? You doing the pigs-in-a-blanket kind of little smokies? They're my favorite."

She laughed. "They are? I didn't see you as a pig-in-a-blanket type of guy. And yes, of course. I am doing those and the bacon-wrapped smokies as well. I'm surprised those aren't your favorite since they're sprinkled in brown sugar. I know how you like bacon. And I know how you like your sweets."

"That's a thing?!" he asked excitedly. She had just described heaven for him. Bacon and sugar. And her. Yep, yep, and yep. Sign him up.

She nodded and asked incredulously, "You've never had them??"

He shook his head no.

"They'll probably change your life." She laughed. "I think I like the salty-and-sweet combination most."

He couldn't have stopped the smile creeping across his face even if he'd wanted to. "Salty and sweet. I've never heard a more accurate description for you."

She shrugged and simply said, "Guilty as charged." She proceeded with telling him her menu and the tons of food she was making, both for today and for tomorrow for church, but he was a bit zoned out. He couldn't help but think that the bacon smokies weren't the only thing changing his life.

****

"Come *onnnnn,*" she yelled at the screen. At first she tried to play it cool watching football around Beckett. But he let her know he got a kick out of her liking football, so she wasn't holding back as much now. Poor Mable even knew she enjoyed football, and it was the only time the cat kept her distance.

Beckett was also into the game, which was quickly becoming a nail-biter. It wasn't teams he cared about, but he liked to cheer for the underdog. She supposed it was because he spent a lot of his college career as an underdog since Nebraska didn't have the best record in the years he played there.

"You cheering for Georgia because I am, or because you just don't seem to like Bama?" he asked at one point early in the first quarter.

She was mildly offended. Like she would choose a team just because he did? *Yeah, nope.* Did he not know her at all? "No, I'm cheering for Georgia because they are the better team. They've had the tougher schedule. And though I can't say a bad thing about Alabama and their dominance in recent years, I do know that their strength of schedule has been going down. They've found a way to work the system. I just think they need to play more conference games if they want to go around calling themselves the greatest team in college football."

He looked surprised. "I thought you didn't follow college football."

She shook her head. "No, I just said I preferred pro. I used to live about thirty minutes from College Station. I'd have to have been an idiot to not know anything about college football."

His eyebrows shot up. "Aggies?"

She nodded. "I wasn't a big fan or anything. Always rooted for the Texas teams in the area—Houston, UT, A&M, Baylor, TCU."

He playfully tugged on her shirt, one of the many Nebraska items he'd gotten in her size and had shipped to him. "Just be sure to remember what hue of red looks best on you, honey."

She laughed. "Let me guess. Good ol' Nebraska U?"

He nodded and brought her in close. "And don't you ever forget it."

After a distraction of the best kind, Beckett kissing her senseless, they soon got back into the game. Beckett would give some input on what plays he did and didn't like. She would ask him what he would have run instead. Watching football live, she realized that his knowledge for football was a lot more than she even thought it was. It was more than just knowing the routes he had to run. He knew the quarterback position well, which had probably only helped him as a receiver. And he had these amazing instincts; he knew when something was going to go bad two beats before it actually did. She had no idea why he didn't coach, but she finally had to ask.

"Beckett," she started.

He ran a hand through her hair. "I sense a serious question coming on. What's up, honey?"

He knew her too dang well. "Why don't you coach?" she blurted out. "I don't mean to open any sore wounds. I just think you're brilliant, and you would make an excellent coach."

He shrugged before he started explaining. "I only played two seasons. I'm not interested in coaching at the college level because of all the job hopping you have to do to make a name for yourself. And I don't want to recruit a bunch of spoiled brats . . . . " He trailed off, but she gave him plenty of time to think and finish while she listened. "Maybe high school someday. The high school coach here in Picketts is getting older, and I've thought about it a bit. I just wasn't sure I was ready to give my life back over to football."

"I can understand that." She paused to give him a kiss on his dimple. "But for what it's worth, I think you'd be excellent. There has to be a way to have it all — both the farm and football." *And her,* she added mentally.

He nodded. "Thanks, Jord. Means more to me than you know."

He just called her "Jord." He gave her a nickname. Lord have mercy, things were moving fast! And though she had hated it when her mom used to call her that, it sounded completely different on Beckett's lips. She was absolutely okay with it. More than okay.

"No problem, Becks," she said with a laugh. If they were doing nicknames, she wasn't scared.

He looked to the big screen and back to the game. "Uh-oh. Fourth and one and Bama is going for it. What should Georgia run, defense girl?"

She looked at him, a bit insulted. *Please. An easier question could not be asked.* "Blitz. Duh. Bring the dang house. Send 'em all."

He laughed. "I love that you know your stuff. I just wish you were an offense girl instead."

She leaned in to whisper, "Well, offense is starting to grow on me."

He caught her hand and brought her closer into his chest. "That's what I like to hear."

They finished that game, though the team they were rooting for lost— but it was a heck of a game so they couldn't even be mad. They watched all of the next game too. They were so comfortable and it felt so normal, even though they hadn't known each other very long. Jordyn was absolutely certain that game food wasn't nearly as fun when it was just her. She was going to remember this day for a long time.

CHAPTER 21

Sunday, Beckett took her to church. No, not to marry her, though the thought was growing on him. He used to wonder how you knew that one person was it for you—for the rest of your life. How you decided or how you "knew." But now that he knew Jordyn, when he thought about what life would be like without her, he felt like the days would all be cloudy without her brightness. She shined so bright he didn't even remember what the cloudy days were like.

The fact that he actually thought crap like that scared him. He was not romantic. He hadn't probably ever felt emotionally attached to a woman who wasn't his mom or his sister or his aunt. But for some reason, Jordyn was different. He could feel it. And man, he didn't want her to go. Watching football with her all day yesterday was a blast and felt like a new tradition starting. He wanted her there every Saturday. In fact, he wanted her there all the time, and not just for her cooking either.

So he took her to church in Picketts Sunday morning. He would be the first to tell you he wasn't always the best Christian man, but despite his past decisions, he did believe, and so did Jordyn. So church seemed like common ground, a normal thing to do. He went most Sundays, half because he wanted to and half because, if he didn't, Rose would come find him and drag him there.

Aunt Rose had even asked on Friday, making sure Beckett was bringing her. They had skipped the previous week, since Beckett had been unsure if Jordyn was really ready for all that. But today's visit would be Jordyn's last step in becoming acclimated to Picketts. And, of course, Rose knew that when she asked. After Jordyn came with him to church, she was as good as gold here. Practically a local. Rose was pushy.

His church wasn't perfect. There was a crew of little old women who called themselves the Pink Ladies, like off the movie *Grease*. They gave him the stink eye whenever he saw them—his reputation being well known after all. And since it was a small town, everyone knew a lot of one another's sins. If the preacher said something about addiction, eyes would automatically roam to Mr. Graver, one of the town drunks. So it was your typical church. A little bit of hypocrisy, but a big dose of love. You just couldn't let the town gossips ruin the message for ya. He'd learned that from experience. But if you thought about it, they were all works in progress, weren't they? So expecting everyone who walked in those church doors to be perfect would be ludicrous, but he wasn't going to be the one to tell the self-proclaimed Pink Ladies that. They scared the hell out of him.

This Sunday happened to be communion Sunday, so in addition to the usual communion, they all brought breakfast foods and had a little feast with their communion following the service. Much like the Last Supper scripture that was recited for the actual communion, they sat around long tables, did communion, and then ate a potluck of breakfast foods.

Jordyn had loved the idea, and they went a little crazy bringing food with them. It was times like these, when she got excited over something as silly as baking for other people or game snacks, he realized again how utterly alone she usually was. But she didn't feel sorry for herself or mope. Instead, she rocked the hell out of her independence. It was refreshing how she didn't let any obstacle get in her way. Even if that obstacle was his rude ex-girlfriend.

Following the church service, Jordyn made new friends with at least ten little old ladies who "hadn't had a cinnamon roll that good in a long time." Rose was feigning being mad at Jordyn for holding out on her about her real baking skills. And Jordyn had half of the Pink Ladies eating out of her hand.

While Jordyn finished up talking to probably her hundredth admirer, the guys, Mason, and some of the others gave him crap about the infamous college hoodie Jordyn had worn/stolen. And he fielded lots of questions about whether Jordyn was really living with him. He assured everyone she had her own room and that she would've been at a hotel, but she got hurt and then stuck at his place as the storm hit. Otherwise he'd be expecting a not-so-random visit from the Pink Ladies any day now. He'd like to avoid them at all costs.

He was terrified for their husbands honestly. Not only were these ladies vicious, but they could smell fear. It was like an extra police force in town. They took it upon themselves to make sure everyone was toeing the line—when they weren't grabbing coffee and gossiping about the town, that is. He wouldn't even put it past them to have a police scanner.

He also answered a ton of questions about the commercial. Everyone in town was excited. There was going to be a lot of traffic in Picketts with the camera crews and what not. Stuff like that just didn't happen here, so everyone had questions. Jordyn helped with taking a lot of those questions and explained the vision behind the commercial. If people didn't like her before, they definitely did after that.

Though they were a bit of a scandal for being in the tabloids, Picketts adored Jordyn. The cowboy-preacher man had given a sermon that morning on the theme of "choosing to love others anyway," and it got Beckett to thinking that choosing to love Jordyn wasn't going to be hard at all. It'd be the easiest decision of his life if only he'd let himself do it. His problem was that this five-foot-five fireball of a woman had all the power to bring him to his knees. Was he really ready to hand over that kind of power? Was he really ready for all *that*?

****

She sighed in the pickup on the way back to Beckett's house.

"Was that an 'I'm worrying and upset' sigh, or was that a happy sigh?" Beckett asked with a smirk.

She smiled. "A happy one. That was just so much fun. Before that first time you took me into Rose's, I swore to myself I would not fall for this town. Small towns have been nothing but heartache for me."

"And how's that going for you?" he asked. It sounded like he was joking around and trying to play it cool, but from the way he was looking at her, she also knew he really was interested in her answer.

She shook her head and reached over to give him a kiss on the cheek. "You are somehow managing to erase my hatred for both small towns and football players all in one go."

He grinned, that one dimple popping. He took her hand and gave it a kiss. "Honey, you know I play to win."

She laughed. "That you do, Beckett Harper. That you do."

And she thought that may be what scared her most . . . .

****

That afternoon they spent every minute together because he wanted to, Jordyn even going with him and riding along in the tractor to do chores. They both knew this was their last day alone. Everyone involved with the commercial showed up some time tomorrow, and they had only three busy and hectic days together left. Which majorly sucked. He just wanted to hang out with her, enjoying the time they had together left, but instead they were slammed with a huge to-do list.

She gave him the rundown on what the next three days were going to be like. He had contracts and paperwork to sign tomorrow afternoon once everyone arrived. The camera crews were going to do some walking around and checking angles/sunlight for the best shots. Beckett would also do the recordings for the voice-over, which should only take a couple of hours and would be done in a mini recording-studio van the camera team was bringing. Then Tuesday and Wednesday were going to be the long days. Tuesday, Beckett was going to do typical farm tasks; he'd just be followed by about three different cameras. Wednesday, they'd shadow him for morning chores and do some more sunrise shots of the farm, and then any other shots they needed to wrap up.

And then they'd all be out of his hair, Jordyn included. It would take them a while to go through and choose, out of hours and hours of footage, which shots and stills would be best for the thirty-second commercial. The company filming would give multiple options to AgGroSo, and AgGroSo, or Jordyn specifically, would have to sign off on which one they wanted, or which parts of which ones they wanted. AgGroSo and the filming company would go back and forth numerous times until they all settled on what they preferred. He was glad he got to stay out of that part . . . . It sounded monotonous. And boring as hell.

Meanwhile, he could tell Jordyn's work was piling up. She was doing a good job of keeping up, but with her having to do double duty, she couldn't do it all. She told him her boss, Walt, had told her to hire an assistant. So if one good thing were to come out of this stupid commercial, at least it was helping Jordyn's career. Even though he'd secretly love it if she just quit and moved to Picketts. He wasn't sure what a major in statistics could do in Picketts, but there had to be something, right?

After they got their schedule for the week figured out, they rode to Picketts to pick up pizza to go from Rose's. He didn't want Jordyn to have to cook him supper; he just wanted to spend every second with her. Besides, she had already made her special M&M and chocolate chip cookies. They were his favorite. She had made a triple batch and put the rest in the freezer so he would have some when she was gone.

And that thought sucked, but neither one of them was avoiding it or acting like it wasn't going to happen. They were both bummed. Clearly.

But they were going to make this work. They had to. Because any other alternative was out of the question.

"Jordyn?" he asked as they curled up in front of the TV later that night.

"Yeah?" she said sleepily as she played with the veins on his arm.

He spoke softly into her forehead. "Thank you for coming. Thank you for hurting your ankle and getting snowed in with me. And thank you for making me do this stupid commercial. You are fixing my bad reputation in more ways than one."

"Thank you for forcing me to stay safe that first night. And thank you for proving to me that not all small towns and football players are bad." She smiled up at him.

"I don't want you to leave, honey," he said honestly with a sigh. He repositioned their bodies on the couch to look her in the eyes, searching for a way out of this separation they were about to geographically experience.

She smiled but her breathing was unsteady, like she was fighting off tears. "And I don't want to leave. But it's less than a month before Christmas, and I think it'll be good for us. To see how we feel about one another when we aren't under the same roof."

Wow. What mature perspective she had. That must make him immature because he didn't think a month away from her was going to be "good" at all.

He smirked. "Storm of the century *indeed.*"

He wasn't talking about the damn snow either.

CHAPTER 22

Monday morning was the calm before the storm. She had done her best to mentally prepare Beckett for the craziness of the next few days. She knew what was about to go down, and she was feeling the stress. Not just because she was leaving Beckett soon, because that was definitely on the forefront of her mind, but also because she wanted this commercial to match up to the vision she had in her head. She wanted this commercial to be amazing. She wanted to make America cry and bask in a bathtub full of their tears. But the concept was her idea, so doubts about whether or not she could make her dream a reality plagued her. Honor the American farmer and fix Beckett's reputation . . . . There was a lot riding on her idea. Her brain.

She didn't go with Beckett out to do chores because she was busy organizing the arrival times for everyone on a big board she set up in the dining room. There was a team of twenty-five or so people who would all arrive between one and three o'clock in the afternoon. AgGroSo people would be the first to arrive, so they could take care of the contract and the paperwork involved in the commercial. Beckett's agent would also arrive and be there for that. And then after all the *i*'s were dotted and the *t*'s were crossed, it would be go time. The only curveball Jordyn could think of would be Ariana, but she already had a little plan to help that out, though she hopefully wouldn't have to deal with her until Wednesday anyway.

Ready or not, the commercial was about to happen. Heartbreak Harper was on his way to showing the world who Beckett Harper was. With any luck, the world would fall for Beckett just as hard and fast as she did and maybe, just maybe, Beckett could leave his reputation in the past. She'd like to think his days of heartbreaking were a thing of the past.

Or at least she hoped so.

****

He closed the front door and slid down it dramatically until his butt hit the cold floor. She had warned him, but short of a good ol' Catholic confessional, he felt like he just signed his soul over in paperwork. And then, after the paperwork, there was the voice-over that he was trying to get just right. For this first day only being a half day, he was already shot.

"I told you it's a lot to take in." Jordyn laughed.

"Are they all gone? Tell me they're really gone." He looked from right to left making sure all those scoundrels had truly left.

There was a lot that went into this commercial business. And Super Bowl commercials were the granddaddy of them all. He wasn't the only one beat; his agent had been too. There were lots of specifics and logistics about the commercial, but fortunately all the stupid part, the paperwork, was done. He hadn't signed so many papers since he signed with Denver. And that was for his career, not a thirty-second commercial. How could there be that much to it?

"Only two more days," she assured him. "And tomorrow is easier. You'll just have people with cameras breathing down your neck all day."

"I'm used to people breathing down my neck." He shrugged and moved to the couch, where he could be closer to her.

She laughed and plopped down next to him. "Yes, but the cameramen are not safeties or corners. You are actually going to have to allow them to get close to you," she teased.

"Hmm." *Was she flirting with him right now?*

"I know that'll be a new concept for you but just try your hardest," she said with a playful shrug.

"You sayin' I've got skills, honey?"

"Like you needed me to tell you that." She giggled as he kissed her.

A few moments later when he pulled back, he said, "It was fun seeing you in your element though—bossing everyone around, calling the shots. They all listen and respect you."

She looked down as if unsure how to take that compliment. "They've all seen me pull some long hours over the years. That respect was earned as I helped Walt grow the company."

Beckett had made it a point to be close to her, hold her hand, and brush up against her as often as he could this afternoon. She didn't seem like she minded. He thought she might try to pull away a bit once everyone arrived, but she didn't. He liked that. He guessed the tabloids figuring out they were dating had worked out in his favor just this once. They didn't have to pretend they weren't dating because everyone clearly already knew they were.

Not that Jordyn went easy on her job. If anything, she was even more fierce—explaining to the filming crew exactly what her vision was and what kind of shots she wanted. She had pulled tons of photos to show them—ones she had taken herself that he didn't even know about. Let's just say she didn't have to worry about any of them thinking less of her for dating Beckett. She made it clear from the get-go she knew exactly what she was doing. If he didn't know better, he'd think she had done this sort of thing in the past. But he did know better, and today was probably just as nerve-wracking for her as it was for him.

"Well, we survived the first day." He sighed into her hair. Damn, she smelled good.

"Two more to go."

"I have never wanted time to go so fast and at the same time so slow," he admitted.

She reached up to kiss him on the cheek. "I know exactly what you mean."

****

Beckett was not thrilled. Despite her warning, he seemed to have forgotten that the filming for the next day began at 5:00 a.m. She had a big to-go mug of coffee ready, and there was a lone camera man in the kitchen ready for every single shot of the day. Though Beckett's face wouldn't be in the commercial, shots of him drinking his coffee, driving a tractor, chipping ice, and the like were perfectly acceptable. And the filming crew didn't want to miss a second of Beckett's day from literally sun up to sun down.

He was irritated but still introduced himself to the camera guy. Jordyn was glad he wasn't going to try to ignore that they were there. If they wanted this commercial to be a success, they needed the most realistic footage possible. That involved Beckett feeling as comfortable as possible.

"Thanks, darlin'." He kissed her cheek as he grabbed the coffee and headed out the door. "See you at lunch?"

"You bet," she said with a grin. "Do try to have some fun today."

He snorted and turned back to her with a smile. "Are you doubting my acting skills, Houston?"

She laughed. "Well, you rarely *act* your age, so how am I supposed to know?"

He rolled his eyes. "I've got this, honey. We've been over this. I've got skills."

"Yes, you do," she said, shaking her head, then shutting the door. At least she'd leave him with a smile on his face to start the first day of filming.

She had a couple meetings with the marketing team this morning, and then she'd just be waiting on Beckett—and getting some last-minute quality time in with that double oven she was going to miss an unsettling amount.

She was going to be distracted all morning wondering what they were doing and what types of shots the cameramen were taking though. She needed to let go and trust the filming crew even if it was against her natural instincts. As much as she wanted to, she couldn't control this.

. . . Any part of this.

****

They had all known there was a chance of snow that afternoon, but when it started to snow big, huge snowflakes, the camera crew went nuts. They were giddy about all sorts of shots they could take with the fresh snow. They quickly got the drone in the air and went around finding the best spots to take footage.

Beckett didn't mind; it got the attention off him and onto the scenery. Granted, his face wasn't actually going to be in the commercial, but they were always right there with him. Literally right over his shoulder. He was afraid to even pee. He was ready to eat some of Jordyn's cookies and curl up on the couch with her in his arms. He just wanted peace and quiet. No TV, no radio, nothing. Just silence and his girl. Yep, that sounded pretty freaking good right about now.

As a beautiful pink-and-purple-hued Nebraska sunset began to set later that evening, the camera crews were getting some shots of the snow from the front yard, so he snuck up on Jordyn. She was off the side of the deck, past the remnants of her first snowman. She was hanging back from the cameras but walking slow so she could look at the snow around her. He caught her trying to catch a snowflake in her mouth and grinned. He loved how playful she could be. She was hardcore career woman one minute and then playful the next.

He quietly followed her until he was close enough to scoop her into his arms like he was going to tackle her. He didn't actually bring her down—but just made it seem like he was to scare her.

And he succeeded.

She let out a yelp as he lifted her. "Beckett William Harper, *put me down.*"

He put her feet back on the ground as requested but kept her close, glad for a moment alone with her. They were content to just look at each other, eyes to eyes. And seeing her gaze at him like she adored him—with big, fluffy snowflakes in her hair—made him want to live every day like this. *With her.*

She was breathtaking.

He finally cleared his throat and found his voice. "The last time you whipped out my middle name, I do believe we were making snow angels and snowmen."

She smiled and turned to walk toward some of the AgGroSo people heading to the barn. "I hope it snows at Christmas. I could use a repeat trial run at a snowman. Unfortunately, we are just too busy today. And it's getting dark on us."

He remembered the way her poor creature looked after her first snowman attempt. His eyes darted over to what was left of it, and he lifted his head back to laugh. "You do need the practice."

She playfully squinted at him. "Does that statement come with some sort of double meaning?"

"What?" What was she getting at?

She laughed and turned to say over her shoulder, "Because I'm not as experienced or practiced as, oh, say, Ms. Supermodel?"

Oh hell no. *Oh. Hell. No.*

He did the only rational thing he could think of; he grabbed her by the hand to spin her back into him, picked her up to get eye level, and kissed her. Which apparently shocked her because she let out a surprised gasp as he did it. But when their lips met, they knew what to do. And in a kiss, in the snow, he communicated exactly how much he cared. And exactly how glad he was that she wasn't that other woman whose name he couldn't even remember right now.

As he put her feet back on the ground, she was out of breath. *Good.*

"You do realize there are cameras, right?" she asked with a grin.

He nodded. "My face can't be used, remember? So who cares?"

And with that, they turned and walked hand in hand over to the people she needed to speak to, snow crunching under their boots as they went. He felt glad for a few minutes alone with her. He had thought of sneaking off to the barn with her, but for now, flirting in the snow and that kiss was all that was going to happen. Maybe tomorrow he could whisk her away to the barn and make sure she wouldn't forget him. Because tomorrow he'd also have to tell her goodbye.

Unfortunately, this bout of snow wasn't going to turn into a blizzard and force her to stay. This time she'd have to come to that conclusion on her own.

Goodbye

CHAPTER 23

Wednesday. This was it. Her last day. Tomorrow she left for Houston. Walt was even nice enough to buy her a plane ticket home and send the AgGroSo truck with someone else. Either he was being nice, or he was smart enough to know that if he made her drive, she'd never make all sixteen hours before she turned around and drove right back to Beckett.

Her last day. And then goodbye. At least for a while, until Christmas. Which really wasn't that far away, but a lot could happen in two weeks, right?

Yeah. A flipping lot could happen in two weeks. How she even got to this point, she had no idea. She wanted to mope. She wanted to wear Beckett's college hoodie and bake cookies and eat so many of them that she felt as miserable physically as she felt emotionally. But she didn't have time for that. She had to kick butt with this commercial for one last day.

She and Beckett were up at 5:00 a.m. again. The camera crews followed him around all morning, and by noon they were content with everything they had. She'd had Aunt Rose cater all their meals, and his aunt, being the saint she was, brought a feast out for lunch since it was everyone's last day in Picketts. They used the shop for laying out the food, but luckily, it wasn't nearly as cold as the day before; some of the snow from yesterday had already melted, so people were standing around in the yard between the shop and the house.

She was standing with Walt when the she-devil Ariana arrived. She had told her she could, so she wasn't surprised. But really, who had the audacity to do that? To schmooze a filming team that was there for a man she had rudely brushed off? It took guts. Or stupidity. Stupidity disguised by guts perhaps.

And just as planned, shortly after Ariana arrived, the Pink Ladies did too. Jordyn had explained to Aunt Rose that the woman was up to no good at church on Sunday. Before she had even said a word more, the Pink Ladies approached her and were asking for a time and a place to speak with this imposer. For as much as they pretended to dislike Beckett, they were also protective of him. The whole town was. He was *their* hometown hero.

And all be darned if every time Ariana tried to approach someone with the filming team, one of the Pink Ladies was asking her a question or interrupting the conversation. It was so comical Jordyn had to keep her back to Ariana or she would giggle the entire time. Ariana deserved it though. She was so dang insolent.

She took Walt, who arrived that morning happy as a lark, to speak with Beckett about finalizing everything for the commercial. As they headed the direction of the house from the shop, Ariana brushed past her shoulder and into the house to "use the ladies' room" or something like that. She probably just needed a break from the Pink Ladies. *Ha, ha, ha.* Jordyn felt zero remorse. Zero.

"That woman is no good," Walt stated casually. He had only briefly met Ariana and already didn't like her. That was Walt for you. A solid judge of character.

"She's a royal pain in the arse but at least only for today. I kept her out of the way the rest of the days by telling her she could only come here today — or else I would blacklist her with the filming company," Jordyn admitted.

Walt let out a loud chuckle. "That's my girl."

Without voicing what they were doing, they slowed their pace so hurricane Ariana would be out of the house by the time they got there. The last thing Beckett needed was more of Ariana's meddling into his endorsements.

"Remind me to never make you mad," Beckett whispered loudly in her ear, scaring her. They were almost to the front porch, and he had found them, wrapping an arm around Jordyn.

"Why?" she asked with a slow smile.

He moved to pierce her with his blue eyes. "You sicced the Pink Ladies on Ariana?" He busted out laughing. "That woman will rue the day she ever thought she could intimidate you."

She shrugged innocently. "They offered."

He looked at her, grinning ear to ear. "And?"

She gestured and batted her eyelashes. "And so I told them the time and the place. I can't turn down my elders!"

Both Walt and Beckett laughed hard at that. Fortunately for them, Ariana had just exited the house, hurrying back over to woo one of the camera guys. Jordyn didn't have to wait and watch for the Pink Ladies; she knew one of them was going to intercept.

She maybe loved small towns. Or maybe just this one.

Beckett and Walt finished up in short order and were talking so long about random topics that Jordyn went for a walk. She wanted everyone to leave. Now. She just wanted time with Beckett. Time to decompress after the last three insanely busy days. But a walk would clear her head and give her a chance to say goodbye to the farm at least.

It ended up being a wasted effort. She got maybe ten minutes of time to herself before Ariana came storming up to her, grabbed her by the arm a little rougher than necessary, and said, "I need to speak with you in the barn." Then she took off.

Ariana in a barn? Maybe hell really did freeze over.

She tried to tell her she wasn't going anywhere with her, but Ariana had already headed that way. The last thing she wanted was to have Ariana not shut a gate or let out Bess, who was still barn-ridden until her round of antibiotics was up.

[188]

She could be an adult. She could deal with whatever Ariana was going to spew at her, which she was sure was something about the Pink Ladies messing up her chances. Jordyn was the one dating Beckett. Not Ariana. So Ariana could just get used to this. She wasn't on their team. She was the opposing team.

As she opened the barn door, she saw Beckett too. He was tossing some hay over Bess's stall with a pitchfork, so he didn't turn their way. Ariana was heading right for him too, on a mission. She wondered if Ariana was going to tackle him or something, and she almost wanted to laugh. She'd probably bounce right off Beckett and land in a pile of long limbs, boobs, and hay. Hopefully on some cow crap too. That would just be the cherry on top.

But then as Ariana got close, Beckett's arm moved to grab her. Ariana turned toward him, letting him bring her into his body; at the same time, she looked right at Jordyn and smiled the evilest smile she had ever seen, and then she leaned in and kissed Beckett.

It all happened in three seconds or less. Beckett still had his back to her and didn't know she was there. The way he put an arm around Ariana and pulled her into him though. It was something he had done to Jordyn at least a dozen times. Which made this a thousand times worse because it meant he had wanted her there. *He* had wanted *her*. It wasn't that he didn't stop Ariana's advances quickly enough; it was *him* reaching for *her*.

This had to be some sort of twisted joke, right? Except that it wasn't. Her own two eyes had just seen it all transpire. And the immediate heartache she felt told her this was real. It wasn't some nightmare. The shockwaves of watching that moment were cutting too sharp to have been made up; like a shard of glass straight into her heart, they sliced deeper with each beat after. She had watched the moment Beckett's heart broke. Now she was living the moment hers did.

One moment. So much potential shot to hell. The loss of the love of your life.

She backed away, eyes stinging. Of course Ariana wasn't going to tackle him. Her weapon was much worse. She found a way to finally introduce Jordyn to none other than Heartbreak Harper.

"Go, dear," a woman said gently. One of the Pink Ladies. The ring leader. Glenda.

Another one said, "We came for backup. We'll handle this."

And without another thought, Jordyn ran.

CHAPTER 24

"ARIANA?!" He pulled away immediately. He could have sworn it was Jordyn. Sworn. Ariana was wearing her perfume or lotion or something. He had zero doubt it was Jordyn when he grabbed her by the waist. And then when he realized it was Ariana instead of Jordyn, it was too late.

Ariana kissed him in his surprised stupor. Then she laughed, that pompous glint in her eyes. "Hi."

"What the hell, Ariana?!" What was she doing in here? In a barn of all places. And why in the hell did she smell like Jordyn?

She shrugged. "Good luck getting your little girlfriend to forgive that." She pointed out the open barn door, where three Pink Ladies stood mad as hornets. Jordyn was already booking it toward the house. Almost there by the looks of it.

Dammit.

He was set up. He had to go tell Jordyn. Right this second. He moved for the door, but Ariana grabbed him by the shoulder and pulled him back around.

He wasn't in the mood for her games. "Woman, what do you want? You already ruined the best damn thing that ever happened to me so what more can I do for you today, Ariana?" He was breathing heavily, ticked the hell off. "Seriously, why are you such a life-suckingly cruel person? Find someone else to irritate to death."

Ariana had the audacity to look surprised with his level of anger.

"What?!" he snapped, stepping toward the door.

She shrugged and looked a little confused. "I thought I was doing you a favor. I thought you'd probably want to dump her as soon as you got the commercial done."

If he could kill her with a look, he would. "You thought wrong. And why the hell do you smell like her anyway?!"

Ariana tilted her face to the side a little. "Oh, hun. Didn't realize you'd fallen into the love pit. You poor thing." She paused a moment, thoughtful. "Her lotion was on the counter in the bathroom, and my hands are all dried out because of this God-forsaken cold. It's just cheap lotion, so I didn't think she'd mind if I borrowed some."

And he wouldn't have put it past Ariana to purposefully use Jordyn's lotion as part of her plan. "Ariana. Get off my property before I press charges and get a restraining order against you. I never want to see your face again. Got it?"

Ariana looked hurt—so hurt for a moment he almost felt bad for his harsh words. But then, as she reassumed her model poise and mask, she headed for the door. Right before she exited, she turned, whipping back her long black hair in the process. "Well, if I can't have you, at least she can't either now."

He let out a frustrated sigh that turned into a yell, which scared Bess, making him feel even worse.

He had to make this right. He had to fix this. *Had to.*

As he slid the barn door shut, he came face to face with the Pink Ladies. He didn't have time for this crap. Jordyn was probably leaving right this minute, and he needed to find her. Did no one understand what the hell had just happened back there? Ariana was trying to ruin his relationship with Jordyn.

When he moved to leave, he got cut off by one of the little old ladies. So he started explaining in short sentences. "Ladies. I assume you heard all that. I thought Ariana was Jordyn. She had Jordyn's lotion on, so I thought it was her."

"You sure about that, sonny?" Letty asked.

"You weren't just trying to have a side piece, were ya?" the vicious one, Glenda, said as she actually poked him in the arm. "You are Heartbreak Harper after all."

A side piece? "No. God no. Now please, let me go after her." He was about to just run away. Who gave a damn about respecting your elders when Jordyn thought he had disrespected her? He could carry all three of these women on his back if he had to, so why again was he still standing here getting bossed around by little old ladies?

"But how serious are you about this girl?" the third Pink Lady, Beth, asked.

"Pretty serious," he said. There. Could he go now?

"How serious?" Glenda asked loudly. She wasn't here to play games evidently. "I don't want you to kiss and make up with her unless you are in it for the long haul. You may not have a side piece, but I don't see you making any serious commitments either. Don't go crawling back to her if you are just going to break up with her later. No more random hook ups, sonny. No more Netflix and chill."

Frustrated was not an accurate enough word for how Beckett felt right now. And if Jordyn wasn't about to flee from his farm, he may have even thought how much the Pink Ladies loved Jordyn was endearing. Right now, it was annoying. He was soooo frustrated. He grabbed at his hair and pulled. "I want to marry that girl, okay? Is that what you are looking for? It's been three weeks and I know that sounds ridiculous, but I was doing it right this time, okay?" By the end he was almost yelling, and then felt bad about yelling at little old women whose only real offense was loving Jordyn.

Man, when he messed up, he just committed to it. Mess-up piled on top of mess-up.

"Well, what are you waiting for, then? Go get her!" Glenda gave him a clap on the back as he shot toward the house.

Finally. He was free to go after Jordyn.

But by the time he reached the house, everyone was already gone. Everyone had cleared out in five minutes or less. And though he once thought having the house back to himself would be freeing, he felt nothing but misery instead.

Misery. Misery, he'd soon find, was his friend. His good friend. His good friend that was never going to leave. And he wasn't sure he wanted him to.

For the next two days, Beckett was hopeless. She wasn't answering his phone calls. Or texts. Or emails. He had tried to call Walt even, but he got an earful there. Walt wanted to cancel the entire commercial for how he had treated Jordyn.

Beckett was going to hop the earliest plane to Houston and go pound on Jordyn's door, but Walt had warned the commercial would be off if he stepped a foot in Houston before the meeting for the final commercial viewing. Jordyn didn't want to see him, and Walt was only trying to protect her.

And he couldn't say he blamed Walt for that. He knew what it looked like.

But by the afternoon of the second day, he had calmed down enough to let a plan form. He was due in Houston for the final-commercial choosing and showing on Friday of next week, in exactly one week. Walt had wanted him there and he eagerly agreed. He hadn't told Jordyn because he wanted to surprise her. He was still planning on doing just that. He would make her understand somehow. He had to. He just hoped she would start talking to him before then. Start to figure out what had really happened.

When his doorbell rang later that afternoon, he hightailed it for the door, wondering if Jordyn had come back. Maybe she had figured it out, or someone had told her the truth behind what happened.

He was beyond disappointed to find not only the Pink Ladies, but also Aunt Rose.

The firing squad. Great. He opened the door only because they saw him through the glass; there was no ignoring them now.

"You look like crap," Aunt Rose said bluntly.

"Yeah, when's the last time you showered?" Glenda asked.

He took a deep breath and shut his eyes to avoid rolling them. "I'm not in the mood today, ladies." He began to shut the door.

Rose stopped him with a hand on the door.

"What do you want from me?" he asked defeated.

Rose came on in and patted him on the shoulder. "Go take a shower. We have some planning to do."

Glenda stepped in, without invitation, looked around disapprovingly, and gestured to her posse as they all invited themselves in as well. "And we'll start the dishes since it looks like hogs would've been cleaner these last few days."

He still stood there with the door open, shaking his head. "Excuse me? Planning?"

Aunt Rose smiled. "You do have a plan for getting her back, right?"

He nodded. "Working on it, yeah."

Rose grinned. "Well, that's why we're here, sugar. We're going to help you make sure that plan is foolproof. We want your girl back almost as bad as you do." She stopped and looked oddly like she was going to cry, but that was crazy because Aunt Rose was tough as nails. "Jordyn belongs in Picketts, and we all knew it the minute we met her."

He took a deep breath and swallowed down the ache he felt having heard that. He thought Jordyn belonged here too. "I wasn't aware I needed help with my plan." Then he looked at Glenda accusingly. "And when I was trying to run after Jordyn to stop her from leaving, you weren't exactly so helpful with *that* plan."

Glenda gave him the stink eye and gestured wildly. "Nonsense! Jordyn was going to need a minute to calm down after what she saw.

From our angle, it looked really bad. That's why when you go to get her back, you better make sure it'll work. Are you absolutely sure this plan of yours will work, boy?"

He absolutely hated that this seventy-year-old spice of a woman had a point. He shook his head no. "I know how devastated she must feel because I feel the same. So no, I don't know for sure if it'll work. I don't know if she'll even hear me out."

Glenda nodded in understanding and touched her permed hair as if pleased she was right.

Rose clapped her hands together once. "Well, that's why we're here. We'll work our magic on your plan, and it will be foolproof."

He was 99.9 percent sure they were just being nosy asses.

A car door slammed, turning all their attention since the front door was still open where Beckett held it. Blakely was lugging her suitcase out of her jeep.

"Am I late to the intervention or did I make it in time?" she hollered.

"Right on time, dear!" Rose called back.

Beckett rolled his eyes. The women in his life were going to be the death of him. All of them.

And this was either going to be the best idea ever—or the worst idea ever.

CHAPTER 25

She wanted to just lie around and eat cookies all day. Correction. Not cookies. Cookies reminded her of Beckett's favorite cookie, and so then she'd just cry. She was done crying, so no cookies. Maybe brownies. Brownies with ice cream. Yep, that would do. Instead, here she was, sitting in meeting after meeting at AgGroSo.

Walt had taken her personally to the airport, gotten them earlier tickets to Houston, and flown back with her, allowing her to cry on his shoulder. He told her she could have the next week off if she wanted to and apologized at least a hundred times. Needless to say, he was feeling guilty for what went down in Nebraska.

But she wasn't about to be made a spectacle of or gossiped about at the office. And though the tabloids hadn't gotten word yet, they would. And she was *not* going to be moping and heartbroken when they found her. She was going to be kicking butt at work because that was what she did best. So, she did the only thing worse than not going back to work: she went back to work. Right away Thursday morning. And Friday.

She stayed strong. She managed to somehow sit in marketing meetings and talk about the commercial. Sure, there were whispers and stares everywhere she went, but when she looked marketing in the eye and told them nothing about the remaining plans had changed, they all had gotten back to work.

Walt was proud of her for staying strong, but he was worried. Probably because he was the only one she allowed herself to break down in front of. Everyone else she stared down and brushed off until they knew she was okay.

It was a big, fat facade. She was so not okay. Nothing was okay. Nothing was the same. And it felt like nothing would ever be the same again. Twice now, she had fallen for a football player. And twice now, reality had slapped her in the face. She hadn't even known she had developed feelings so deep for Beckett. She had known him less than a month! But the moment it was all yanked out from under her, she knew she only hurt as bad as she did because she really loved him. And this time, it wasn't young love. She couldn't even blame it on being naive.

She probably should have known better. She had fallen for Beckett, and he had stomped on her heart. And that was that.

Fortunately, Jordyn knew what it was like to be brokenhearted. She knew what it felt like to have your heart put through the paper shredder. And twice now she knew what it felt like to find out she wasn't the only woman in her man's life. Just like last time, she would pick herself up and put herself back together. One day at a time. Because if she didn't, if she allowed herself to mope, then Heartbreak Harper won the day. And she was not going to allow Heartbreak Harper to have that power over her. Nope.

She would admit she missed Picketts. She missed Rose, the café, the kind people at church, and even the Pink Ladies. But she would *not* miss Harper. No way. After what he did to her, she realized how silly it all was to imagine anything serious with him. And of course he had said that he wanted to date her long-distance. He had probably wanted Jordyn to leave so he could bounce between her and Ariana more.

And that thought made her want to projectile vomit.

Yep. Beckett Harper was dead to her now. Sure, her heart may still be hurting, but her mind was determined to write him off.

****

"Let's go to Rose's," Blakely suggested. "It's Saturday, and we always go to Rose's on Saturdays when I'm home."

"No!" Beckett said strongly, annoyed with his little sister.

Blakely grabbed his cup of coffee out of his hand, took a sip, and almost spit it out. "Yuck! Why are you drinking your coffee black? And you do realize you can't hide from everyone forever?"

He nodded. "Yes, but I'd like to avoid them as much as possible for the next week."

She thought about that. "But with Rose and the Pink Ladies on your side, everyone here in Picketts knows the true story. No one will probably even have the guts to say anything. Well, besides Aunt Rose."

He rolled his eyes and ran a hand down his face. "I don't care what they think. There's only one person's thoughts I care about, and she currently won't even speak to me. Not that I blame her." He sounded a little like a junior higher in that moment, but he didn't even care.

Blakely put a hand on his shoulder. "She will, B. Give it time. The plan will work." After a second she added, "Why the black coffee though? You hate it black."

He shrugged. "Jordyn always made my coffee exactly right. I can't get the mix right now, so I'm drinking it plain." He shrugged again. "Why bother."

Blakely gave him a look.

"What?!" he asked. Having Blakely home after her completed semester of college was a double-edged sword. It was nice to have her around. Those first two days without Jordyn the house was so . . . *empty*. But with Blakely here, she didn't let him mope around or feel sorry for himself. She kept trying to pull him out of his misery, and he wasn't sure he needed saving from that just yet.

"You're punishing yourself," she said knowingly. "Coffee purgatory."

He sighed and ran a hand through his hair. "Yeah, I guess I am. A little."

Blakely shook her head. "She just doesn't know the truth, B. Once she does, it'll all fall into place. I just know it."

"Do you know how many times I have called, texted, emailed? I'm trying to tell her the truth. She won't even talk to me." He sighed.

Blakely clapped her hands together, probably to make sure he was looking at her and not at his coffee. "Hey, that's exactly why we aren't giving her the opportunity to *not* talk to you." She paused a moment. "You hear back from Walt?"

He nodded.

"He believes you?"

He nodded again. "He does now. Apparently, the Pink Ladies had already put in multiple calls to his secretary. He had to finally talk to Glenda or else they weren't going to stop calling."

Blakely had a good laugh at that. He would someday, but not until Jordyn knew the truth. He thought of every person who had ever let Jordyn down. In her mind, he was just another one of those people. In her mind, he was probably worse. Hell, he was probably just another Thomas George to her. That thought gutted him. He was nothing like that sorry excuse of a jerk.

Getting her to trust him again, even talk to him again, was going to take nothing short of a miracle. Unfortunately for him, he seemed to be fresh out of those.

He just missed her like hell. Until she left, he never realized the reason why his Heartbreak Harper days were so unfulfilling was because he was only filling one need. He hadn't understood all the many ways she completed and complimented his life. She filled needs he didn't even know he had. And he had to go and mess it all up, creating this huge, glaring void.

"Grab your jacket," Blakely insisted.

"Blakely, I don't want to go to Rose's," he grumbled. He loved his sister, but sometimes he just wanted to strangle her.

She scrunched up her nose. "Oh, so you're going to continue moping around and punishing yourself for something out of your control? My brother, the football hero who kept going even when his pro career didn't, is now going to feel sorry for himself?" She glared at him and he didn't say a word, so she just kept going, really letting him have it. "You have your plan; you have your flight to Houston. You just have to wait it out. If you ask me, you should stop trying to talk to her. Let Walt tell her what really went down. Let him plant that seed and then let her sit on it a while. And in the meantime, you can carry yourself like a man who isn't guilty of something." She paused and gave him a squint. "Because if you really aren't guilty, then you should stop acting like it."

Damn. She had him there. He wasn't guilty. And Jordyn would find out the truth if it was the last thing he did.

****

Walt called her into his office Monday morning right away. The weekend had sucked. She ended up getting a ton of stuff done that she'd been meaning to get caught up on because when she was working, she couldn't think about how sad she was. So she had worked, and worked, and then worked some more. So, he was either going to chastise her for all the work-related emails over the weekend, or he was going to check and see if she was okay. Both of which annoyed her. She was fine. Why didn't people get that? And the more they asked, the more she wasn't fine. She wished they'd just leave her alone. It was hard enough trying to put herself together without someone reminding her of the pain she felt.

She put on her heels from under her desk and headed toward his office. "What can I do for you this morning, Walt? Please tell me not another field trip."

He looked up at her and smirked. "Nope. I learned my lesson with those. But about that . . ." He moved to take off his glasses.

She put up her hand to stop him. "Walt, I don't want to hear it."

He furrowed his brow. "Okay, then. But do you know a Glenda Harrington? Leader of that pack of she-wolves in Picketts perhaps?"

She nodded and swallowed hard, feeling tears prick the backs of her eyes. Of course she knew Glenda. She must be pretty pathetic if she even missed Glenda. She'd known her like a week, but she still loved the old snoop.

"Well, she's blowing up my email and calling me daily. She wants to speak with you directly and said that you have been ignoring her emails," he explained.

"I don't want to speak with anyone from Picketts," she said stiffly.

He sighed, rubbing his bald head. "I get that, dear, I do. All I'm saying is that she is one persistent little bugger. I wouldn't put it past her to book a plane ticket and come here herself—or worse, talk to the tabloids if you keep ignoring her. And that is about the last thing we need while we finish up the commercial. So can you do me a favor and just call her back and tell her why you aren't going to be speaking with her any further?"

She groaned. *Small towns! Ugh.*

Walt added, "Look, I know you hate Beckett, but not everyone from Picketts is a jerk. She's a gossipy old hoot, but she means well. Just talk to her, would ya?"

She nodded in defeat. "Is that all?"

He nodded back.

She left but not before grumbling, "I'm so ready for this dang commercial to be over and done with."

CHAPTER 26

One week. The slowest week of his life. He had gone one week without Jordyn to talk to, watch football with, or just give crap to. And yeah, he could give Blakely crap. Hell, making her mad was probably even easier than it was Jordyn. But getting under Jordyn's skin was *wayyy* more fun. He missed the way her green eyes squinted at him like she saw right through him. He missed her laughing at something stupid one of them said. He missed the way she got into football games and always said, "Come *onnnn*." He missed her curled into his chest. And maybe his sap meter was maxed out right now, but he even missed playing with her hair. And kissing on her, but that was a given. Don't even get him started on *that*. It had been like their souls took a mutual sigh of relief every time their lips met.

He wondered how she was holding up. He hated more than anything he'd made her cry, been the reason for her tears. And worse than that, he hated that she wouldn't even hear him out. He knew she had every reason not to trust him, but he had done everything in his power to do everything right with her. They had taken it slow. He had tried to show her how much she meant to him. And he thought she knew that, but she must not have if she ran so damn fast.

Maybe he needed to do a better job of not just showing her how he felt, but actually telling her too. He wasn't the most poetic with words—he wasn't going to write her some verbose love letter—but he would tell her so she understood how he felt. He was going to make it abundantly clear to her.

In two days.

His flight to Houston left in two days.

His doorbell rang, and he couldn't help but still be hopeful. Every time that stupid thing rang in the last week, he was praying for it to be Jordyn. It wasn't though. Aunt Rose had brought out lunch for him and Blakely.

"Just can't stay away, can ya?" Beckett asked when he opened the door.

"I only have one niece and nephew, you know," she said with a wink as she came in and took her coat off. She then looked around as if checking to make sure the house was still in working order.

He rolled his eyes. "I've been doing my dishes, Rose. And everything is fine. I'm even showered. I don't need the Pink Ladies on my case again."

"Good," she said with a nod. "And only two more days and you're Houston-bound to get our girl."

Blakely hollered down from upstairs. "Is that Aunt Rose?"

"Get that booty down here if you want lunch," Rose yelled.

While they ate, Rose filled them in on the latest town news. The Pink Ladies were in full force in Picketts. Some young high school kids had gotten caught making out in the church parking lot after hours. No clothes were missing, but since it was the house of God and all, the town gossips were in all sorts of a tizzy about it. Rose said as upset as Glenda was about it, you would've thought the altercation happened on the pulpit itself.

Beckett found himself laughing and having a great time. It was a lot more fun talking about the Pink Ladies when you weren't the one on their radar. And since he knew he'd see Jordyn in just two days, he wasn't feeling as down. He didn't have long to wait anymore.

Blakely had gone to the freezer, gotten out some of Jordyn's cookies, and warmed them up on a plate in the microwave. "I swear to God I'm going to gain ten pounds this Christmas. This girl can make a cookie, I'll give her that."

Rose nodded. "No joke." Then she snapped her attention to Beckett. "These are your favorite. Why aren't you having one?"

This woman didn't miss anything. He sometimes wondered if she had cat-like instincts, the way she saw and heard everything. Nine lives maybe? And she could sniff out weaknesses too. She probably should've played football actually.

"Are you punishing yourself again?" Blakely asked, frowning. "I thought we were past that."

He shook his head. "No. Not at all. I guess I was just pathetic enough to be waiting for a fresh one."

Rose patted his hand and had to clear her throat. "Only two days, my boy. Only two days. And I couldn't be prouder of the choice you've made."

He smirked. "You talk like I'm getting married in two days."

Rose winked. "You might as well be. Mark my words, you'll be married to that girl by next Christmas."

He rolled his eyes. *Women.*

****

A date. The last thing in the entire world Jordyn wanted to be doing right now was going on a date, but one of her friends from work had a nephew her age, and she assured her that this one was a "a *good* man." She didn't miss the implication that Harper most definitely had not been. She had been a little insulted. That woman didn't know Beckett, and she didn't know her. So why was she judging her judgment?

But after she thought about it, the woman had meant well. Obviously, her judgment had been impaired if she had ever seen a future with

Beckett. And so maybe a date was what she needed. To prove to herself that she wasn't as broken as she felt. To prove to herself that she would find her someone, that she wouldn't just give up. And to prove to her coworkers at AgGroSo that she was doing just fine, whether she felt like it or not.

Because behind closed doors, she felt like she was going to be alone forever. It was shocking she didn't already own at least seven cats. In fact, she had thought about going and adopting a cat when she got home and realized how much she missed Mable, but she felt as if she would be cheating on Mable. And though Beckett *did* cheat on her, Mable didn't. Mable didn't deserve that.

Her only big reservation about this date was the tabloids getting wind. But fortunately for her, Ethan, her date, had suggested meeting at the movies. Which was perfect. She didn't even really have to talk much to the guy. She could eat an outrageous amount of buttery popcorn and then be on her way. Sure, he might ask to do something after, but if she wasn't feeling it, she had an out.

As she pulled into the movie theatre and parked, her heart nagged at her—so much so she had to take a minute and rest her forehead on her steering wheel. She didn't want to be here or doing this. It didn't help that she had talked to Glenda. She had told her "not everything was as it seemed" and that Jordyn should read her other emails from her. Jordyn hadn't. She hadn't wanted to reopen the wounds she was still struggling to close. She saw with her own eyes that Harper grabbed Ariana and kissed her. There wasn't a way she could twist it in which that wasn't what had played out.

And Harper—though at first relentless with his phone calls, emails, and texts—had now stopped trying to reach her. He had probably moved on to his next conquest, or back to Ariana. Or both. And that thought hurt her more than she cared to admit. But, tomorrow was the last showing of the commercial, and then it all should be finalized. Other than having to watch the stupid thing during the Super Bowl, she was finally done with all things Beckett Harper.

"Hi, I'm Ethan," her date said with a smile as he reached out his hand to shake hers. He had waited for her outside the front of the theatre.

"Jordyn," she said and tried to smile. Her first thought was that Ethan was so short compared to Beckett. And so . . . well, he didn't look anything like Beckett. Which was probably a good thing and should probably interest her more, but her stupid traitorous heart was still missing seeing Beckett. How messed up was that? Not that this man wasn't attractive. He was attractive enough, in a nerdy sort of way. He even wore glasses. He was cute.

They had met fifteen minutes before the movie so they could chat and get to know one another while they waited for the previews to start. It took less than five of those minutes for her to realize that Ethan was not going to be her forever. She made sure to keep her elbows in by her sides so he wouldn't try to hold her hand or anything.

Not that Ethan wasn't nice. He was. And again, he was an attractive enough man. He just . . .

Ethan didn't joke around. He was all about his career as an accountant. He was rational and analytical in the short conversations they had before the movie, but it seemed to annoy her. Ethan was too much like her. What she had appreciated in dating Beckett was how similar — and extremely unsimilar — they were. She liked that Beckett was playful and drew that out of her. She liked how they could joke around with one another and bond over football. They were opposites, but they provided one another with balance. They were very different, but still held some of the same hobbies, like food or football, to be able to relate to one another with. Different, but also the same.

And though she never wanted to date another football player *ever* again, she did know that she wanted to find someone different from her. Someone who could balance out her own analytical ways. A partner to cover up her weaknesses and spotlight her strengths.

So after their rom-com movie, when she was feeling more helpless than ever that she'd never find love and a happy ending, Jordyn declined Ethan's offer to go grab some drinks and talk afterward. She didn't even drink alcohol, but Ethan didn't need to know that. She was thinking of hiring him to do her taxes though, so she had that going for her. From what he explained to her, he really knew his stuff. So at least one good thing came from this stupid date.

And that was the extent of her love life. She had better luck finding a tax man than finding a decent boyfriend. What a sad, sad state of affairs it was.

"So would you like to go out another time, then, or are you just not interested?" Ethan asked.

Shoot. She didn't want to break the poor guy's heart, but she didn't want to lead him on either. "No," she said with a sigh. "I don't want to go out with you again. I just got out of a rough relationship, which I'm sure you knew. I wanted to be ready to date again, but the truth is . . . I'm not. I could use a friend, and I could use an accountant for my taxes this spring, but anything other than that, I'm afraid I just cannot do."

He smiled, taking it well. "Hey, I'm good with that. Thanks for giving it a shot even though it's probably too soon. And at least now we can both tell my aunt we tried but it didn't work out, so she can quit bothering each of us about the other."

She laughed for the first time that night, glad he was being a good sport. "No kidding. Thank you, Ethan. I enjoyed the movie, and it was nice to get out of the house, even if we aren't the right person for one another. I'm sure you'll find your person. She's out there somewhere."

He nodded. "You too."

And just like that, her first date post-Harper had ended. It was a flipping disaster. She made the drive home somehow keeping the tears at bay, though they were hardcore threatening her, then threw herself on her bed and cried once she got home. She hadn't cried the last three days but this called for some serious feeling sorry for herself.

No matter how hard she forced it, no matter how hard she wanted to hate Beckett, she was having a heck of a time getting over this. Why couldn't her heart get on board with her head? He had cheated on her. *Cheated.* So why was he this hard to get over?

Why couldn't she just forget Beckett and move on like she had with Thomas? Had she met Ethan before dating Beckett, she totally would have given him another date. But now? Now she just kept looking for Beckett. And that probably made her pathetic. Heartbreak Harper had broken her heart in two, yet she still missed Beckett Harper. Why, oh why, couldn't she convince herself they were the same person?

CHAPTER 27

Houston. Today was the day.

Blakely had decided to make the trip with him, most likely to distract him and help him not feel as nervous, but he didn't mind. If Blakely sitting by his side in that conference room helped Jordyn to have one little doubt about what she'd seen, he'd take it. Because if he really was guilty like she thought he was, why would Blakely be with him? She wouldn't be. And if things went south and Jordyn refused to talk to him or hear him out, he'd at least have Blakely there.

So he allowed it. They had to be up at an ungodly hour. He had arranged for someone else to do chores for a few days. Blakely and Beckett had stayed in a hotel the night before so they could fly directly from Omaha to Houston the next morning. Their flight was so early that they had to be up before he even normally was.

For once he didn't mind an early morning flight though. The tires of that plane could not touch down in Houston soon enough for Beckett.

Walt had someone from AgGroSo waiting to pick them up.

"Walt informed you I have a stop I need to make first, right?" Beckett asked the driver.

The driver nodded, so Beckett handed over the address he had written on a piece of paper in his suit jacket. He had no idea where the place he needed was, but he was counting on GPS and the driver to get them there.

Blakely looked at him, eyebrows furrowed. "You have a stop to make? Please tell me it's for coffee."

Beckett smiled. "No. I have one more trick up my sleeve for making sure that Jordyn comes home."

"And what would that be?" Blakely asked, sitting up straight in her seat, finally looking among the living. "You calling an audible right now?! Do the Pink Ladies and Rose know about this?"

She had not enjoyed the early morning flight as much as he had. He was fairly certain she may be regretting her choice to come already. Maybe they needed another stop to get her some coffee. Surprisingly, he was doing okay, amped up just like he used to get before big games.

Beckett grinned. "No, you'll just have to wait and see. Let's just say I'm pulling out the trick plays."

Blakely looked intrigued. "So you're saying you're calling a flea-flicker?"

Beckett tipped his head back and laughed. If only his sister knew. "*Exactly*, B."

****

"We have final viewings for the commercial this afternoon," Walt reminded Jordyn Friday morning, the morning after her dreadful date.

It had been nine days. Nine days since she ran from Beckett's farm. And today they'd have to watch the final options from the filming company and decide on one. Jordyn had tried to get out of it, like she had with all the going back and forth between marketing and the film company, but this time Walt didn't let her. Since it was her vision that led the whole thing and this was the last step, she supposed he was probably right. But that didn't mean she had to like it.

"I remember." She let out a heavy sigh. "Let me go grab some lunch first. The meeting is at one, right?"

He nodded.

She took a steadying breath. Watching the commercial options were going to be driving the dagger in her chest in even deeper. She missed Beckett's farm. Immensely. Irrevocably. But she was going to get through this. She had to. And then, hopefully, everything Beckett-related in her life would finally be over.

CHAPTER 28

To say he was nervous was the understatement of the decade. And he hated that he was stuck wearing this suit and tie, but he was technically here for business after all. Walt had personally taken them to lunch, and he had been starving but could hardly eat at the same time. He was nervous, but he was also excited to lay eyes on his girl. *Finally.* He reached to adjust his tie for what had to be the hundredth time.

"Stop fidgeting," Blakely hissed from beside him. "I swear, I've never seen you fidget in my life. And I've seen you before some pretty big games."

He whisper-yelled back to her, "Well, nothing has ever been this important in my life."

Blakely grinned but rolled her eyes and whispered, "So dramatic. Stop putting so much pressure on yourself. If this doesn't work, we'll follow her home and then tie her to a chair until she listens. She's little and we aren't. We can easily overpower her. We've got this."

That made Beckett smirk. "You're insane."

Blakely nodded pointedly. "We're blood, so if I am, it's a pretty safe bet you are too."

Beckett groaned, not in the mood for these games with Blakely today.

They were in the stuffy conference room by themselves. Walt had shown them in, told them to get comfortable, and explained he would bring Jordyn in. Jordyn thought she was going to a meeting with marketing and a bunch of people, but really she was going to be cornered by Beckett.

And she was going to see the commercial options—that part wasn't a lie. One option, though not the one they would go with, had a bit of her and him in it. Beckett needed her to see it. He needed to remind her that what they had—*have*—is real. To remind her where her home was. With him.

They heard voices down the hall. This was it. This was go time. And if he could get through rival football games and away games and not choke, he wasn't about to start now.

"And how was your date last night, by the way?" Walt asked casually before he could even see them, probably thinking they couldn't hear.

Beckett was immediately standing, hands clenched into fists at his side. *She had a date? She went on a date?! WHAT. THE. HELL.*

Blakely put a hand on his wrist and squeezed, having heard it as well. She shook her head at him, and he knew she was telling him to stay calm without her having to actually say the words. Telling him to keep his cool was something she had done to him a ton growing up.

It usually worked, just not this time. He was so ticked off he didn't even hear Jordyn's answer until she rounded the corner and stopped dead in her tracks. Those green eyes he had been craving were finally looking into his, and he didn't even care that she didn't look pleased. He wasn't pleased either if she had gone on a freaking date.

But God, she was beautiful. She was wearing a black dress and matching heels with one of those sweaters she loved over the top. Probably because she was cold. She was always cold. Her hair was down his favorite way. Other than some dark circles under her eyes, she looked normal. Completely normal. Had she even felt as devastated as he did when she left? Apparently not if she was dating already!

She took one long blink to reset her facial features. He picked up on it right away. Maybe she was more affected than she made it look. But she *had* gone on a date.

He took two steps toward her. He asked—okay, more like demanded because he was hurt and being a brat, "You went on a date?!"

At the same time, she asked, "What are you doing here?"

He then added, "And what are you wearing?!" He didn't mean to sound like a prick. She just looked amazing. Too amazing if other guys were asking her out obviously. She looked so good it physically hurt him. He just missed the hell out of her. And now he was shooting himself in the foot. Big time.

"I'm sorry?" she asked, squinting at him. Now she was mad. And he was terrified. Terrified this master plan was not going to work. "It's called a dress, Harper. I believe *you* are more familiar with them than I am. Or maybe just taking them off."

He heard Blakely cough to hide a snicker. *Traitor.*

"So it's back to 'Harper' just like that?" he asked, taking a step closer. Trying to calm down. This was his shot. No more messing up.

He just wanted to kiss her senseless and get rid of all her hostilities. But Walt and Blakely were both in the room with them, and now was *not* the time for that. That would be a major prick move — another wrong move. Jordyn probably wouldn't even let him right now, and he didn't want to further hurt her by rushing things. This was not at all going as planned. He hadn't wanted to make her mad; he was just pissed she went on a date. Already. It had only been a little over a week!

Jordyn gave him a look that would absolutely gut him if he had any reason to feel guilty for what went down with Ariana. "Well, I finally met Heartbreak Harper with my own two eyes, so it seems fitting." She snapped to Walt, "Why did you bring me here for this? Where is marketing?"

Walt looked on with wide eyes at the two of them very obviously not making up.

"Was I that easy to get over?" he asked quietly. "That you would already be dating?"

She sighed, looked to the floor, and answered quietly, "I want you to be."

She wanted him to be that easy to get over? So that meant she wasn't over it, right? . . . *So she was saying there's a chance?*

Walt, hands in the air in surrender, piped in: "Marketing left our options to look over. You and Beckett get final approval. And he had his flight booked for this meeting before filming was over."

Jordyn sighed again. And in that sigh he heard everything he needed to hear. She was hurting. She looked fine, she was trying to act fine, but underneath her strong front, she was struggling. Which meant she cared. He just wanted to explain everything, shout that he wasn't guilty of doing what she thought he was, and then take her home.

"I'm Blakely." Blakely waved. "We spoke on the phone, but never in person."

They exchanged handshakes, and Jordyn moved to the seat across the table from where Blakely had been sitting. Beckett still stood in the corner where he had approached Jordyn. He wanted to block any and all exits Jordyn had in this room. He wanted her to stay until she knew the truth.

She gave him an annoyed look and gestured with her head to the chair beside Blakely. "Sit. Let's get this over with, shall we?"

He nodded and unbuttoned his suit jacket for something to do. "Yes, fine. But you need to listen to what I am about to say . . . . " She looked like she was about to say something, so he added, "Without interrupting. Then we will watch these videos, and I'll be out of your hair forever."

Like hell he would, but he thought if he said that, she'd calm down. And it did seem to work.

She nodded, in work mode. And she was amazing in work mode. He'd seen her boss everyone around back at the farm, so he knew she was good. But he didn't want to talk to that Jordyn; he wanted to talk to the woman who had been burned by everyone she loved. He wanted to talk to the woman who held a heifer's head in her lap while he stitched it up. The woman who yelled at the TV during football and loved to bake for people. The woman who tried to catch a snowflake in her mouth. But he'd take work Jordyn because that was all he could get right now. She accused him of having two different sides when she was the same exact way. He ventured to think that they all were that way really—the person we wanted the world to see versus the person we really were.

He now stood directly across from Jordyn with his hands resting on the conference table, his only barrier to her. He couldn't bring himself to sit down yet. "I thought it was you in the barn," he began, resisting the urge to walk over to her and wrap his arms around her. Or grovel on his hands and knees. He was not against begging if that's what it took.

"*I was there*, Beckett. I *saw* it." Her voice cracked but she kept going. "With my own two eyes. Are you really going to try to play *that* card right now?" She shook her head.

He cut her off. "No interrupting, remember? And it's the truth." He moved to put his hands on his hips so he wouldn't try to reach for her or hurdle the table to get to her. "I heard the barn door open, and I smelled you. I know that sounds crazy, maybe slightly creepy, but I love the way you smell. I could pick your lotion out of a lineup. And *she* smelled like *you*. Ariana even admitted to me that she used your lotion when she went inside to use the bathroom that day. So when I grabbed her by the waist, there was no doubt in my mind that it was you I was grabbing—not her. I had no idea Ariana would even step foot in a barn."

Jordyn's eyebrows furrowed in thought. She was still mad, but she was at least thinking about the words he was saying.

"By the time I did know it was her, she had already kissed me and it was too late. Then I had to deal with her. And then I got confronted by some Pink Ladies that were mad as hell." He almost smiled. "I went after you, but you were already gone. I called, I emailed, I texted. I was trying everything I could think of to just talk to you to explain . . . . " He felt something lodged in the back of his throat. He hadn't cried since his mom died. He had to get through this . . . . She *had* to know the truth.

"I thought it was you, Jordyn," he said, his voice now cracking. "Please think about what you know about Ariana and me. You know I don't like her anymore. You know I don't want anything to do with her.

What you and I had was real. I wouldn't have cheated on you like that. Even if there is zero future for us, I need you to know the truth."

Jordyn was now deep in thought, her eyes bouncing from Beckett to Blakely to Walt. No one said a word.

"Don't say anything yet. Just think about what I said and please watch the commercials. This was your vision, and they turned out pretty spectacular."

He nodded to Walt, and Walt hit play on the remote in his hand for the TV in the corner of the room. In a few short minutes, this commercial would either seal his fate with Jordyn or destroy it.

CHAPTER 29

Why was Beckett Harper here?! In Houston?

When she came face to face with him a few minutes ago, she thought she was dreaming. It was like she was trying to shove him out of her memory so hard that her subconscious had found a way to conjure him back up. And he was in a suit and tie. He looked professional. And handsome. Black suit, white dress shirt, skinny black tie. His hair was gelled. His facial hair was trimmed. He looked good. He never got closer than ten feet away, and she was glad. She didn't trust herself around him. Especially looking like *that.*

And he was not only here but trying to confuse her with this wild story of him not knowing it wasn't her. *That's what it was, right? Some wild story. There was no way what he was saying was actually true . . . right?*

But then she thought about Glenda reaching out to her. *Not everything is as it seemed.* There was no way the Pink Ladies would do anything but what was on the up and up. They would not feed into a story like that. She knew that.

Her heart ached. She wanted this version of the story to be real. She didn't want to hate Beckett. She didn't want to have this weight bearing down on her soul. But it seemed too easy, too good to be true.

Fortunately for her, she had a moment to regroup and watch the commercial options. She didn't know what to think about Beckett right now. Was it possible? Or was this just him trying to further manipulate her?

Beckett left the table and positioned himself leaning against the back wall behind her. Though it could be to see better, she wondered if it was because he wanted to be able to stop her if she tried to bail. She stayed where she was and mentally prepared for what she was about to see. She didn't want to see this at all, but it had been *her* idea, so she needed to see it through. She didn't want all that hard work and those three weeks to be a total waste.

The commercial began with the sound of an alarm going off, followed by Beckett leaving for the day, coffee in hand, while the sun wasn't even up yet. She had been the one to hand him that very coffee, but she tried to ignore that. Then there was the noise of the tractor starting up. Some calming music started playing with Beckett's voice-over on farm life. She remembered when he recorded it how silly he thought he sounded. He hated reading out loud, and though he loved the words of the script, he thought he was going to sound silly reading them.

But he didn't. He *reallllly* didn't.

The camera angles followed Beckett as the sun rose around them, showing him feeding the heifers, chopping some ice, throwing some hay to the bulls—and to Bess in the barn. The beam of sunlight shining in the barn when he first opened the door was perhaps her favorite part. She tried her best not to cry and to keep it together. Though she was super ticked off at Beckett right now, she did love that farm: the barn, the house, the shop, the land. All of it. And so far, the commercial was *exactly* how she envisioned it. You knew it was Beckett you were looking at; you just didn't see his actual face. And it was beautiful. It was raw farm life— exactly what they had been going for.

When they got to the aerial footage from the drones and the footage of the fresh snow, she literally had to bite down on her bottom lip to keep from crying. Beckett's voice-over finished, quoting, "So to those of you who work sun up to sun down providing food for our tables . . . thank you."

The commercial ended with an aerial view of the farm fading to black. She had to sniffle. Lord have mercy, she was trying so hard not to lose it and she was not doing a good enough job of it. She remembered Beckett had had to go over that last line at least a dozen times because he wanted it just right. And it was perfect. And the view of his farm, freshly covered in puffy snow? It was . . . *exquisite.*

Walt looked to her and smiled. "What do you think?"

She nodded. "I think it was perfect. Loved the snow shots. That's the one."

"Well, let's give the second version a fair shot, shall we?" he asked with a smile.

She shrugged. "Doesn't matter. That's the one. This version is what I've been hounding the team for."

Beckett huffed behind her. Had he already seen them and liked the second option better or something?

Walt looked at her. "But you have to see the other one to know for sure. So let's make sure we do this right. You do know what I spent on this commercial, right?"

She laughed nervously. "Yes, I know. You haven't let any of us forget it. Let's see it, then. But I'm telling you right now, the first one is going to be it."

Walt squinted at her, pretending to be mad. "I'm telling you right now, you need to see both options, which I thought you'd be all for, Miss Statistics Degree."

She rolled her eyes. "Yeah, yeah, Walt. Let's see it, then."

The second option started out exactly the same. Same voice-over, same shots. The only thing that was different in the first few seconds was when Beckett grabbed his coffee, you could see him giving someone a kiss on the cheek, though the faces were blurred.

She was in the commercial? Considering it was only her hand as she handed off the coffee and then her cheek, she didn't mind. It did add an element to the commercial that farm life is rarely done solo. Hmm. She wasn't mad, she supposed. Sucked to remember those happy days with Beckett, but it'd be okay. She imagined there were worse cheeks to be on television.

It wasn't until the final five seconds, after the voice-over, that everything went to hell. They had somehow captured a shot of Beckett scooping her up in the snow that day. Though again, you couldn't see who Jordyn really was, but what you could see was how *happy* Beckett was. She must have said something to make him laugh, because he was smiling ear to ear. She was sure if the camera had been close enough to capture it, his one dimple would've been obvious. And then the shot stayed on them while they walked hand in hand across the freshly fallen snow toward the barn, footprints trailing behind them. In the distance, the setting sun blushed pink in the sky, and bits of ice and snow on the roof of the barn sparkled and blinked like Christmas lights.

She had so many different questions. Had Beckett changed his mind about the commercial and not having his face in it? Why was she in there? How had the filming crew got that footage without them knowing? She knew at the time they had thought they were alone.

The television was back on a blue screen before she could process it all. But what she did notice was the traitorous tear that had accidentally leaked out of her eye and forged a trail of sorrow down her cheek.

Seeing *that* version of the commercial . . . well, it wrecked her. It absolutely wrecked her.

****

Seeing Jordyn cry was the worst feeling in the world. He supposed it was a good thing though because it meant she truly cared. But knowing how much she was hurting — all because of him and the stupid stunt Ariana pulled — made him want to do nothing more than make it up to her the rest of her life. He was not going to be just another person in her life who let her down. He refused.

Never again.

Before she could get up and flee, he went to where she was sitting in her chair. He put his hands on her armrests to force her to stay put, then leaned down so he could look her in the eyes. It was something he'd done more than once with her back at the farm, so he'd done so intentionally.

"Jordyn, listen to me, please. I thought it was you in that barn. I had no doubt in my mind. I wanted it to be you." He took a deep breath and tried not to lose his composure. "And if I could go back and fix it, I would. You left before you got to hear me rip out Ariana. And I tried to run after you. I tried to text, call, email, everything. I'm here now. For you. I had the filming crew put together a special version of the commercial *for you*. To remind you what we have. To remind you where home is." He was feeling brave, so he took her cheek in his hand to add, "With me."

He didn't tell her how much this version of the commercial had cost him out of his endorsement check, and he wasn't going to either.

She was looking at him now with less hatred. Like she was considering his words. She hadn't flinched with his touch. She wasn't ready to melt into him yet, but he wasn't done either. Her softened body language was enough motivation to keep speaking, to keep explaining.

"My life was a blur before you came along. I didn't even know it, but everything was a haze. All the days were the same, and it was . . . just . . . *blurry*. When you came into my life, everything came into focus. And not just because you are attractive." He stopped to grin. "It's so much more than that. You are so stubborn sometimes I want to shake you." She dropped her chin to glare at him, but he ignored it and kept going. "You are playful and funny, intelligent and logical, and hell, I even love that you love football as much as me. You are kind, and you are always thinking of others, even when others have done nothing but let you down. I know *I* let you down. I can't promise you I won't again, but I can promise you that I want to be the person who lets you down the least."

He stopped to steady himself. "I'm no poet. I'm not wordsy. But that blizzard was the best damn thing that ever happened to me because it gave me you. And though I've only known you a few weeks, I know, without a doubt, that you are it for me. I love you, Jordyn Mack. I want nothing more than to be snowed in with you every day for the rest of my life."

She went to open her mouth, but he stopped her.

He nodded at Blakely, who got up to go get what he needed.

"There's more?" she asked quietly, swallowing hard while he brushed away a few tears from her eyes.

He nodded, and in a few short seconds later, Blakely arrived with the puppy from their stop they made upon landing. The pet adoption center. The little guy was squirming in Blakely's arms. This was his "flea-flicker" move. Pun intended.

Beckett backed away just for a moment so Blakely could gently place the dog, a black lab mix puppy, in her lap.

More tears spilled out of Jordyn's eyes and down her cheeks, though she tried to bat them away. "You got a dog?"

He shook his head, leaning back in. "No, sweetheart, I got *you* a dog."

She took the animal, hugged it, and smiled through her tears. "You got *me* a dog?"

Was he using her love for animals to lure her back to Picketts? Damn right he was. He was playing dirty. But he was playing to win. The trick play.

He took a deep breath, nodding. "Now. I know you have a life here. I know your work is important and that you totally kick butt here at it. I know you have every reason not to trust me, and it may take a while to earn your trust back. I'm ready to put in the work if you are. Jordyn . . . *come home.* Come home, please? If that video showed you anything, it showed you where home is. Don't let Ariana win. Don't throw away what we had because of some huge misunderstanding. We can fix this. Just come home."

She wiped at her nose and with the puppy still in her arms simply said, "I thought you'd never ask."

He hadn't technically asked. He'd just phrased his suggestion to sound like a question because he'd been too afraid she'd say no.

He couldn't stop the grin from spreading across his face. He'd won. She would come home.

She reached down to gently put the dog on the floor before she launched herself at him.

It was the best damn catch he'd ever made.

****

When the dust settled, and she had her puppy and her man, it took her all of five seconds to realize she was moving to Picketts. Not back in with Beckett — no, she'd get an apartment or little house somewhere. Somewhere to have her own space while they figured stuff out. Though she believed Beckett, it was still a good idea to take things slow. Their whole relationship was just a whirlwind. Literally, a whirlwind of snow had started it all.

She turned to Walt, puppy back in her arms. "I can't work for you anymore. I have no idea what I'll do in Picketts, but I have to go. I can either continue to work for you from there, or I will help you find my replacement."

Walt grinned, took off his glasses, and stood to rock back on his heels. "Funny you mention it. We happen to be doing this big Super Bowl commercial you may have heard about . . . . I was thinking of opening a midwest office since over half of our customers are based there. Think you'd be interested in managing it? You'd get to hire a few field techs and salesmen, and you could continue working with data development if you wanted to."

What? He would do that for her? She couldn't even form words. She wanted to kiss his bald head.

He shrugged. "You're one of my most talented hires, and you've helped me build this company. Do you really think I'd let some other company take you from me now?"

"But—how . . . " She couldn't even form a coherent thought. "You knew I was going back, didn't you? This isn't just something you are throwing out there—you have all your ducks in a row. You don't do these things unless you've done your research."

He nodded. "After that first phone call from Glenda, I knew you were going back. As soon as you'd get out of your stubborn head enough to hear the truth."

She looked at Walt, then to Beckett, then back to Walt. "I don't even know what to say, Walt."

He scratched by his ear, his nervous tick. "Say you'll take the job."

She nodded so aggressively she almost scared the pup. "I'll take the job."

He smiled. "Good. Now that extra vacation I promised you if you got Beckett to do the commercial starts immediately. After the first of the year, I'll fly up, and we will find a location for the new AgGroSo office. You are officially on vacation until then." He grinned and put his glasses back on. "So get the hell out of here."

Blakely apparently could not keep quiet another moment. "I do love a happy ending!"

Jordyn had to admit she was right. She got the dog, she got the job, and she got the man. Life surprised the heck out of her. It had given her a snowstorm, and somehow, she found her happy ending in it.

The Super Bowl

EPILOGUE

"Zeus, stop pestering Mable. She may be smaller, but she will still kick your butt." Jordyn laughed from the couch, watching the two animals torment one another in mutual annoyance.

"Maybe we should've gotten two puppies," Beckett said. "He just wants someone to play with."

She looked at him and squinted. "You're just jealous because he stays at my place with me."

Beckett grinned because she was totally right and reached to put his arm around her. "That's true. I get stuck with crabby old Mable who doesn't even like me and you get the puppy. Rude."

She rolled her eyes. "Well, he was *my* Christmas gift." She paused. "Okay, I have to get up and go check on our game food. Will you make sure these two don't burn down the house while I'm in the kitchen?"

He nodded. "Sure thing, honey. I don't know why you made so much dang food for the two of us."

She shrugged. "I'm mourning the loss of another football season by comfort eating."

"God, I love you," he laughed as she headed to the kitchen.

When she was halfway, he added, "Hey, Jord."

She spun back around. "What?"

"Nice hoodie." He grinned.

She rolled her eyes again and mumbled something about crazy Husker fans, then got to work in the kitchen. He knew for a fact she now had a plethora of his alma mater's T-shirts and hoodies. The fact that she still chose to wear one of his college hoodies made him grin. She looked ridiculous. It almost came down to her knees. But he wasn't complaining one bit. He loved every second of it.

The day of the Super Bowl was finally here. Beckett was relieved. All that work surrounding the commercial was finally winding down. He was fixing his reputation. He was proving to Jordyn that they were worth it, and he finally was at a point in his life when he felt . . . *happy*. More than happy really. He wasn't just getting by anymore; he was living in full color.

There was just one thing left to do.

****

She knew the commercial would play during the break between the first quarter and the second. And she was beyond nervous. Of course, the actual commercial they would be showing was the version without Beckett and Jordyn in it. They had wanted to keep the other for themselves. From the second version, Jordyn had taken a still shot of Beckett grinning after their kiss in the snow, then made it into a canvas she gave to Beckett as a Christmas gift. It was currently on the wall next to the mantle.

So much had happened in the last two months — or three really. That afternoon back in December, she and Beckett left right for her townhouse, which she immediately packed up to move. Blakely flew back to Nebraska while Beckett and Jordyn rented a moving van and got her stuff. Walt had included a relocation package that would help get her townhouse sold. It was so easy saying goodbye to the city life. She left Houston and honestly never looked back.

She had found a little run-down house in Picketts that she and Beckett began remodeling. She felt much safer here in Picketts than she ever did in Houston. And she had Zeus to protect her too. Not that he was much help, but at least she wasn't ever alone, for the first time in her life. Almost every evening either she came out to Beckett's or he came the eight miles into town to her place. And at least one day a week, someone random dropped by too, whether it was Aunt Rose or one of the Pink Ladies. It was a new feeling that sometimes took a little getting used to, but she honestly loved her life.

The AgGroSo office in the neighboring town of Homesteel was opening next month. She was insanely busy but excited about everything they would be able to accomplish from a location that was much closer to a vast portion of their customer base. And sure, she had to drive the seventeen miles there and back every day, but she spent at least seventeen minutes in traffic in Houston every day. And in Houston she didn't get anywhere. This commute was much more beautiful. She got to see the clouds and the open fields as she went to work.

So it turned out she didn't hate small towns so much. The one she was from had sucked and had burned her, but Picketts, though still far from perfect, had won her over. She loved this place. It may be in the middle of nowhere, but there was nowhere she'd rather be.

And as it turned out, she didn't really hate football players either. Beckett was *not* her type, and that's probably the reason why he was exactly what she hadn't been looking for but needed.

They put down their plates of game food at almost the same time, knowing the commercial was coming up. Beckett had known she was nervous for it, which was probably why he insisted on them skipping the big Super Bowl Bash at Rose's and doing their own thing. She was surprised but secretly pleased. She liked spending time with just Beckett. It reminded her of those first few days they were snowed in together when they went from strangers to tolerant of one another . . . to so much more.

She knew there was really nothing to be nervous about with the commercial. It was a done deal. The film crew did great. Marketing was happy. Walt was happy. Beckett was happy. It really was a great commercial that would honor the American farmer. And it was her first and last commercial. Or at least she hoped.

When the commercial started, she stood, just like it was an important part in the game. She listened to every word and tried to look at it with fresh eyes, like the average American at home would. What did they think when they saw this commercial?

She barely listened to Beckett's voice-over — though his voice did sound good on television, she had to admit. And then, before she had time to really fret over what the impression of the commercial would be, the thirty seconds were up, and the commercial was over.

Thank goodness she worked in data and not marketing. She was ready to be done with this commercial business. Well, everything but Beckett anyway.

Thinking of him, she realized he was super quiet for his big commercial debut.

"Did you —" The words caught in her throat as she spun around to talk to him.

There he was. On the living room floor by the couch they'd spent so much time on while snowed in together. And he was on one knee. With a little box.

No flipping way. If there were earrings in that box, she was going to deck him.

"Jordyn, I love you," he said, piercing her with his gaze. "I know it's only been three months since we met, but I'm tired of two separate houses. I'm tired of you spending a minute of your day somewhere other than work or here. When we got snowed in together, I got a small glimpse of what life with you as a wife could be like, and it was freaking spectacular." He stopped to grin, his dimple sweetening the deal. "My heartbreaking days are over. I just want to wake up every morning next to you. I want to give you my last name and start a family with you. Please say you'll be my wife. Please marry me. Please get snowed in with me every year, for forever."

She didn't have words, only tears. And he didn't even ask (again), but he did say please.

"We're a team, Houston. Don't let me down now," he said, noticing her lack of words.

She sniffed loudly and took a deep breath, feeling her chin quiver. "Of course I'll marry you, you idiot! Now get over here and kiss me."

The End

Acknowledgments

Thank you, God. With you I can achieve infinitely more than I thought possible. My hustle, your pace. Therefore you definitely deserve every speck of the glory. I was in the middle of a move across the country with three children five and under when you put it on my heart to get this book ready. I didn't know if it would even be possible. Or if I wanted it to be. Yet here we are. You eat impossible odds for breakfast. And you keep my head above water. Always. Maybe I should take the time to listen more often, eh?

A huge thank you to my husband and boys. I am surrounded by handsome men and can't imagine life any other way! Thanks for believing in me even when I don't, babe. Boys, you are the *best* things I've ever done. I used to dream of what my family would be like someday. Reality is so much sweeter. Being your Mommy is the greatest honor and privilege of my life! Thank you for teaching me what unconditional love is supposed to look like. I love you all! Thank you for supporting me and loving me even when I have crazy dreams and aspirations.

My writing assistant Bubba Gump, the English Bulldog. I don't even know how to work without your snoring as background noise. Thanks, Bubbers. Just work on the gas though, k?

My betas and writer nerds. You heard me complain a ton these last few months about a new genre and the doubts threatening to drown me. Thanks for helping me through it. Thanks for being there to listen. And for not telling me I'm being absurd even when I am! Melissa, you specifically saved my arse big time with this book. Thank you for always being honest and always having ears to hear. Your old, sensitive soul has made me a better writer and a better person. Sam, thanks for always being in my corner and having my back, whether it's if I'm having a bad mom day, or being my promoter, or making me bomb teasers. You are thee best. Looking forward to that writing retreat, y'all. On Sundays, we wear blue!

My editor. Andrea, you are the MVP this time. Oh my gosh. All my fears about finding an editor and if he/she would be a good fit or not went right out the window with the sample chapter you edited for me. Thank you for helping me polish this story into something more enjoyable. Your hard work is appreciated! You are a sweet tea in a sea of editorial lemonades. :)

The cover designer. Thanks, Jessica. You took my vision and made it a beautiful reality. I'm in love! I was so nervous, and even the first draft had so very little wrong with it!

All of our extended family and friends who pose as my marketing team. Your love is felt and appreciated. Thank you! And a special shout-out to my Grandma Patti. Glenda was not hard to write at all since I grew up with someone an awful lot like her!

MY READERS. You. You reading this right now. Thank you for fueling my dreams. My readers are some of the kindest, smartest people on the planet and I will never tire of bragging about y'all. Thanks for sticking with me through the risk of trying out something different. I promise we will be back to huge novels like you're used to soon. I have lots planned for y'all. *Squints off in distance looking for another cliff to take you off of . . .*

Author's Bio

Tricia Wentworth began writing at a young age but didn't realize it was her jam until after college. Truth be told, she's more of a reader than a writer. She currently resides in Nebraska with her husband, three sons, and English bulldog. When not reading, writing, or momming, she can be found squeezing in a run or feeding her sugar addiction by baking something ridiculously delicious.

She is currently working on the spinoff to her YA trilogy as well as the next book in this series, which will follow Blakely, Beckett's sister.

Be sure to follow the author for release updates and teasers. Her Facebook page is where she is most active.

Website: triciawentworth.com
Facebook Page: facebook.com/triciawentworthauthor

Don't forget to check out her YA series, *The Culling*, on Amazon!

Made in the USA
San Bernardino, CA
11 February 2020